DIAMOND IN THE ROUGH

DIAMOND IN THE ROUGH

MOONLIGHT DETECTIVE AGENCY™ BOOK TWO

ISOBELLA CROWLEY ELL LEIGH CLARKE
MICHAEL ANDERLE

This book is a work of fiction. All of the characters, organizations, and events portrayed in this novel are either products of the author's imagination or are used fictitiously. Sometimes both.

This book is a Michael Anderle Production

LMBPN Publishing
PMB 196, 2540 South Maryland Pkwy
Las Vegas, NV 89109

First US edition, October 2019
eBook ISBN: 978-1-64202-487-6
Print ISBN: 978-1-64202-488-3

THE DIAMOND IN THE ROUGH TEAM

Thanks to our Beta Readers:
Diane L. Smith, Suellen Wiseman, Sara Keyes, Jackey Hankard-Brodie

Thanks to the JIT Readers

Dave Hicks
Micky Cocker
Peter Manis
Deb Mader
Nicole Emens
Jeff Eaton
Kelly O'Donnell
Jackey Hankard-Brodie
John Ashmore
Larry Omans
Dorothy Lloyd

If I've missed anyone, please let me know!

Editor
The Skyhunter Editing Team

To Family, Friends and
Those Who Love
to Read.
May We All Enjoy Grace
to Live the Life We Are
Called.

PROLOGUE

Temple Ruins, South of Dimona, Israel

Alexander Thomas grinned. He almost shivered with delight, too, but managed to stop himself—professional dignity and all that. Besides, he was the only Australian on the team and had to make his home country look good.

He and the others stood in rows slightly within the temple's entrance. The hot and blinding sunlight of the Negev Desert stopped only a few centimeters behind their heels. Being in there, in the shade, somehow made them all feel safe.

Dr Eitan Feldman, the eminent archaeologist and historian, moved slowly toward a position facing the group and deeper into the gloom. The clacking noises of his cane echoed on the stone and drowned out his soft footsteps.

Feldman turned and his gaze roved over the faces of his team. "Thank you," he said in his dry old voice, "for helping me bring this new discovery to light." He was fluent in English but still spoke with a thick Israeli accent.

Everyone nodded. Alex made sure to do so but tapped

his foot constantly with impatience. The sub-basement was right over there, beyond where the old man now stood. He didn't want to wait. They had to open it and see what was down there.

Oblivious to his sentiments, Feldman continued. "To quickly review for those of you who have only now arrived… This temple was discovered five years ago by the local Bedouin. We are certain it was built by the Nabataeans in approximately CE 100. Six months ago, operations here were almost closed when a junior archaeologist discovered the hidden basement."

Alex had arrived about three weeks ago, so he already knew all this. Of course, a few of the other junior researchers had only disembarked from the plane in Beersheba within the last forty-eight hours, and no one knew how much briefing they'd had.

"What is extraordinary," the old man continued, "is that the crude seal over the sub-basement's entrance dates to between 1700 and 1820, and the markings are Bedouin good-luck symbols and passages from the Quran. We believe the nomads discovered this site at that time but reacted with superstitious dread to a pagan temple and tried to…" He paused and frowned as he seemed to search for the right words. "Tried to seal it away from the human world."

Alex's eyes flitted to the left. A large, black, blood-sucking tick crawled up the shoulder of the attractive American sheila who stood beside him. He reached out and plucked the insect off.

The girl looked sharply at him before her gaze fell to

the tick that writhed between his thumb and forefinger. "Oh." She gasped. "Thanks."

He smiled. "Think nothing of it, love. We get far worse than this out in the bush back home." He flicked the bug out into the desert. In fact, he came from a rather nice suburban corner of Melbourne but he wasn't above trading in Aussie stereotypes when they stood to benefit him.

Dr Feldman cleared his throat. "Please, no more interruptions," he stated. "Now, we are ready to open this lower crypt. We must exercise the utmost caution when we explore it. The atmosphere has already been tested after drilling a hole, and it should not be hazardous. However, we do not know what may be within. Look and survey, but touch nothing. The materials may be delicate and require special care. There may even be...traps."

He paused, then smiled. "For once, archaeology is like the movies."

A few of the team chuckled, mainly the Americans.

Alex took a deep breath again to calm himself as the two hardware guys moved toward the engraved stone slab covering the sub-basement's entrance. Both wore hazmat suits and welders' masks and were armed with laser cutters, which they'd use to cut carefully through the stone. This would reduce the risk of damaging anything, not to mention collapsing the temple on their heads.

As the men worked, he looked around. The temple's interior was less impressive than he'd hoped. Still, its sheer age filled him with excitement. The façade, although not large, was incredible and in the same almost Romanesque style as the more famous ruins of Petra to the east in Jordan.

Behind him lay the Negev Desert. Although hot and desolate, it had a kind of austere beauty. Even his one brief excursion into the Outback could not match its status as a true wasteland. Undulating brown waves of denuded rock and forgotten dust stretched to the horizon, where the sapphire-hued sky turned bruise-purple with dusk's approach.

Alex had come all this way for opportunity. Most archaeologists spent their careers hunting pottery fragments. He, on the other hand—not long out of grad school—was already involved in the kind of find that made headlines around the world. He'd always wanted to go to the so-called Holy Land. People paid more attention when a discovery could be tied in with the Abrahamic religions. He'd even begun to learn Hebrew to be safe.

This was his big break.

And yet, he hadn't done much since he'd arrived. Feldman would get most of the credit, of course. Alex had even fobbed off the worst of the menial labor onto the other junior crew. But with the sub-basement about to be opened, anything was possible.

Hissing air escaped the vault as the workers' laser saws drew black lines across the stone. It sounded almost like an enraged animal. The sheila to the left jumped in place and Alex almost mirrored her.

It wasn't only the sound that had unsettled him. There was also the smell. The odor was old beyond the human conception of time and unclean beyond human tolerance.

He snorted when the tension dissipated. "They could have tidied up before they sealed the place instead of simply leaving the mess for us to deal with."

One or two people snickered but most had focused on the doorway.

The workmen carefully removed the slab and set it against the adjacent wall. Beyond, they could see only the beginning of a ramp leading down into total darkness.

Everyone hesitated and the temple's gallery was silent.

Alex stepped forward. "I volunteer to go first," he proclaimed and raised a hand.

Dr Feldman nodded. "I would, but I cannot walk fast. Someone else will have to help me, and I will be in the back. Take care, Dr Thomas."

He allowed one of the hazmat-suited workmen to accompany him at the front and the two men walked side by side into the gloom. Their flashlights carved visible order out of the dark nothingness. The other members of the team followed with slow, trudging steps.

The passage was rudely cut into the sandstone and unadorned. Unsurprisingly, the temperature dropped rapidly as they descended. The ramp finally leveled off and his light beam probed ahead into some larger space beyond an opening. His heart thumped against his ribcage.

They emerged into the cavern and he gasped.

"My God..." He forgot to close his jaw.

The chamber around them was completely covered with hieroglyphics, ancient and primitive. The young archaeologist's first thought was that they could only be Egyptian, but this was a long way from the Nile. Could it be, he wondered, some offshoot or forebears of the Sumerians? Or perhaps some other, even older people yet unknown to modern science and who predated both cultures?

Behind him, the team shuffled in and similar gasps filled the heavy, musty air.

"Remember!" Feldman's voice rose warningly. "Touch nothing."

They fanned out to explore the perimeter of the sunken vault while the second hardware guy began to set a lamp up attached to a long extension cord.

"Incredible." The old man virtually breathed the words. "These hieroglyphics appear to be very early Egyptian."

Alex smirked. It wasn't only him, then. The old expert had confirmed his suspicions. But that only further reminded him that this was Feldman's grand discovery, first and foremost.

So far.

The lamp blazed to life. Its illumination was soft and indirect since some materials could be damaged by too much direct light. Still, they could see far better now.

The sub-basement was about the same size as the temple gallery above it—not large but certainly big enough to accommodate the entire team. The ceiling was lower and everything was covered with pale brown dust. There were no signs of insects, spiders, scorpions, or bats—or any other thing that lived, for that matter.

The American girl whom Alex had rescued from the tick sidled up. "Do you think the Nabataeans built the temple on top of this place? Like, they found a really old Egyptian tomb and kind of appropriated it as their cellar?"

Inwardly, he cursed. Everyone else seemed to reach conclusions as rapidly as he did. His chance to suddenly prove himself a genius was slipping away.

"Aye, probably," he replied. "If it was the Egyptians—"

He broke off when something caught his eye over in the far corner. Ignoring the sheila, for now, he sauntered toward it and squinted to see better while his entire body seemed to prickle with anticipation.

Something lay on the floor. At first, it had merely looked like a fragment of rock, but as he drew closer, he realized it was much more. He recognized it as a pressure latch—a button of sorts, which could be triggered by stepping on it.

He examined the device, thankful that no one else had come to peer over his shoulder yet. The latch was too obvious to be a booby trap and it was surrounded by hieroglyphs on the floor—instructions, possibly, or perhaps the usual litany of curses directed at potential grave robbers.

Alex glanced up. Two subtle vertical lines ran through the stone wall in the rear corner—a doorway, obviously.

He put his hands in his pockets and hovered his foot over the latch. *If something bad happens, I can always claim I didn't see it and stepped on it by accident. And if it leads us to the real discovery, I can claim I was the one who found it and worked out how to open it.*

With a slow smile, he stepped on the button.

The tomb shook. Stone shrieked and growled. His team cried out in alarm while some of them wobbled precariously, and Dr Feldman almost toppled before one of the hardware guys caught him.

"Shit," Alex muttered through clenched teeth as he struggled to keep his balance.

The door swung inwards slowly to reveal a black space

beyond. A slight gold-tinted vapor escaped into the free air.

"What did you do?" someone snapped.

The two hazmat-suited guys rushed forward and motioned for everyone to fall back, but for a moment, it seemed the entire team stood frozen in half-terrified fascination.

Alex sensed immediately that he would have to go with the "This Was an Accident" storyline. They still had no idea what was in there but somehow, it didn't seem good.

"I'm sorry," he said. "I didn't see it. I was studying the markings on the ceiling, and—"

No one paid him any attention, at this point, and he didn't manage to finish his story, anyway.

Something streaked out of the void behind the newly opened door. He fell to one side, operating almost entirely on instinctive reflex, and a brown blur hurtled past him, through the sub-basement, and into the team members, who huddled in the middle of the space.

The American sheila screamed in pain and fear and for a second or less, the creature from the crypt hunched over her, enveloped her, and a few drops of her blood spattered the dusty floor. They appeared almost purplish in the odd glow of the lamp.

"What the hell?" someone yelled. "What—"

Like a scorpion on two legs, the being dashed forward again and this time, left both the hazmat-suited hardware men sprawled on the floor. They groaned and bled from deep gashes in their stomachs.

"Oh, my God!" Screams echoed around the crypt and chaos erupted as everyone tried to stumble up through the passage. Alex hung back and simply stared as whatever had been unleashed rushed after them. It was faster than they were and within moments, thuds followed as their bodies fell, one by one.

He waited and counted. Some would make it to the temple antechamber and the creature would be distracted while it finished them off. That would be his chance to escape.

The sounds moved up and away, into the higher chamber. By now, he was virtually hyperventilating while he stared at the corpse of Eitan Feldman. His hero lay sprawled against the far wall, his face and neck split open as if by a machete.

Now. He breathed deep and forced himself to focus. High on adrenaline, he fled.

His race up the ramp seemed to take forever. When at last he burst into the antechamber, the beast—what else could he call it?—was in the process of butchering the last two humans, both cornered and helpless.

Alex ignored the blood and the twitching bodies and urged himself toward the rectangle of reddish light and the freedom it represented.

He staggered out, gasping, into what little remained of the Negev's daylight. One of their trucks was only about fifty meters away. He could make it. He—

Instinct penetrated. He heard and sensed the abomination from the hidden tomb fill the doorway and realized a little hysterically that it actually displaced air by its presence. It intended to pounce on his back—any second now—and that would be the end of Alexander Thomas.

The archaeologist threw himself to the side, not sure if

the creature had launched itself yet, and rolled and stumbled alternately toward the deeply-shadowed recess beneath a low cliff. Some stupid and primitive urge compelled him to seek safety in darkness.

He had no way of knowing, at the time, that it was the worst thing he could have done.

For an instant, there was silence. His back heaved against the sandy rock behind him and his heart thumped like a fist against his ribs. When he dragged in a breath, he could smell the ancient dust all around.

In the next moment, it stood in front of him.

He clapped a hand over his mouth to keep from crying out. The gesture was entirely pointless but somehow, that was his first reaction. His eyes bulged and he simply stared while his vision assimilated the sight.

The creature was a woman. Or had originally been a woman.

She was relatively tall—about the height of an average-sized man—and lean, although with a noticeably curvy figure. Straight black hair had been cut above her shoulders and was held away from her face by a golden circlet around her brow. Her skin was odd, though. It should have been a deep chestnut-brown, but it looked as though the color had somehow been drained from beneath it—as though a translucent brown veil lay over a corpse gone ashen with pallor.

Her garb was both simple and elegant. It consisted of a strange, short dress, almost a tunic, which was much the same shade as the surrounding desert but trimmed with gold and set with lapis lazuli.

He looked at her eyes, and his brain ceased to function. All thoughts but the panicked desire to live were expelled.

"Don't kill me," he gasped. He raised his trembling hands, his fingers spread and palms outward in the universal human gesture of peace. For some reason, he laughed, but the sound gurgled and died in his throat. "I'll do anything. Literally anything you want. But please don't kill me. Let me live."

The woman's face had filled his whole world now. It was beautiful in a stern, somehow archaic way, long and sharp, with high, prominent cheekbones. The eyes were almond-shaped and deep pools of ebony, a brown that was not quite black.

The full, cracked lips parted and beneath them were fangs dripping with gore.

The woman said something—or hissed it, rather. Alex did not understand her. In the back of his mind, he snarked at himself for even considering that this primordial monster would speak modern English.

He prepared for the end but it did not come. Instead, the woman said something else, then spoke again. Each of the brief phrases she uttered sounded completely different and he realized she was switching between different languages.

A tiny spark of hope ignited near the bottom of his soul. She was trying to communicate with him.

Finally, she said something that did register, although it took a second. In heavily accented and barely comprehensible Hebrew, she asked, "What year is it?"

Alex blinked. "Uh..." he stuttered and wracked his brain for the appropriate Hebrew numbers. "2020. Two thousand and twenty years after Christ. If you...uh, care about that."

The woman leaned back, folded her hands across her breast, and closed her eyes.

Her voice was like sand rustled by the wind. "Almost three hundred years..."

He had never been the type to believe that, even on a dig like this, he would encounter a living mummy—or vampire, or ghoul, or whatever the hell she was. But now, faced with her reluctance to kill him outright, his brain rapidly re-adapted to the situation.

"You need me," he said quickly. "You have been away from everyone and everything for a long time. I could... help you learn. Help you deal with people again." His Hebrew was still mediocre at best and he only hoped he hadn't mangled what he had tried to say.

The dark eyes opened again and he froze before them.

"Yes," the woman agreed. She leaned forward and loomed over him. "But will you dedicate your life to my service?"

"I will, yes," he replied at once. It wasn't the kind of question with multiple correct answers. "Anything."

She smiled. Her left arm drifted up and out toward him, the talon-like nail at the end of her index finger pointed directly at his heart. "Then let it be done," she rasped.

Alex gasped in pain as something burned on his chest although it didn't kill him. Instead, it marked him and seared its way obscenely into the very essence of his being.

CHAPTER ONE

The Hidden Garden, Greenwich Village, Manhattan

David Remington adjusted his tie and put on his best, most confident, and most public-relations-friendly smile. Standing before the front doors almost felt like being back in business.

"Showtime," he remarked, mostly to himself.

The Hidden Garden had opened only six months before but already, it had gained a reputation as one of New York City's best and most exclusive restaurants. It was so exclusive that only high society was even aware of its existence, for the most part.

And yet, despite this narrow pool of potential clientele, they had an extensive waiting list. The prospective diner might not be permitted in for weeks after making the call. Walk-ins were not welcome.

A crisply-uniformed doorman opened the entrance and bowed as he waved David in. "Sir," he intoned. "Please present your identification at the front and they'll see to your reservation."

He nodded. "Much obliged, Jeeves." He had no idea what the doorman's name was but Jeeves seemed appropriate. He'd used it before, when in doubt, and always to good effect.

Without hesitation, he strode in, presented his ID at the desk, and found the establishment more brightly-lit than he'd anticipated given its dark exterior. He paused to look around.

The appellation of Garden was well-chosen. The whole interior was filled with plants and small trees, most of them growing in earth-filled marble embankments which ran the length and breadth of the space to serve in much the same capacity as walls to divide the dining areas into different sections.

There were also artificial streams crossed by short, broad bridges, and hanging chandeliers dressed with artificial flowers. The illumination was, at present, normal electric light, but amidst the fixtures, he recognized sun lamps for the benefit of the greenery. All the diners were, of course, dressed to the nines.

"Ah," he exhaled. "Now this is the kind of place where a Remington belongs."

It reminded him that, no matter how much certain members of his family might protest, he was still one of them. Even though they hadn't spoken to him in months, even though they'd cut him off from his inheritance and locked the door on the family fortune, and even though they'd given him a list of requirements that had to be fulfilled before he so much as considered showing his face before them.

He was still David fucking Remington, dammit. He'd

matured considerably lately. And slowly but surely, his bank account and cash flow moved in the right direction.

The maître 'd approached, a fat, older man although pleasant-looking and obviously a professional.

"Mr Remington," he stated with a slight bow. "I'm pleased to see you. Your table is ready, as promised."

Despite his age and girth, the maître 'd moved with impressive speed and grace along one of the little canals, and he directed him to a table near the back corner of the restaurant, which lay mostly in the shade of one of the larger trees, a black poplar.

David thanked the man and took a seat. He sighed, stretched his arms, cracked his knuckles with intertwined hands, and surveyed the premises.

He only recognized about half of the diners, but they were among the *crème de la crème* of New York society. One, a svelte Italian woman, noticed him briefly and smiled before she returned to her conversation. He knew her—in various senses of the term—and in fact, she might have had a hand in allowing his presence there tonight.

After his downward spiral, being cut off from his inheritance, and after he'd begun to "work" at a "job" in a desperate last-ditch effort... After all these things, he'd thought he'd perhaps spent the last of his influence.

As it turned out, this was not so. Some people still gave two shits about him. It had taken a fair amount of finagling, calling in of old favors, and vaguely worded promises, but he'd done it. He'd secured the privilege of supping with the very best once again.

He picked the menu up. The selections fit on one side of a single laminated sheet, but they were all sufficiently appealing to justify the lack of variety. David was finally learning to cook, but he still preferred to leave some things to the professionals when he could afford it.

More importantly, people would see him there. Tongues would wag. Rumor would get around that the youngest Remington was not beyond salvation.

A waiter approached and he ordered a bottle of Merlot older than himself and a plate of fettuccine alfredo with roast chicken and porcini mushrooms. The waiter seemed happy to put the order in and he even left a glass of ice water for good measure.

David leaned back and relaxed. He'd worked hard for the agency lately, and he deserved this little excursion.

While waiting for his dinner, he considered getting up to mingle and converse with some of the Beautiful People. Then he saw something—or, rather, someone.

Near the entrance, a woman had appeared. She was on the petite side, ivory and slender, with blue-black hair above and beside her fine features. Her eyes were dark and mesmerizing. She wore a black suit jacket and dress over black leggings. The only real color in her ensemble came from her nails, which were as red as fresh blood.

"Taylor." David sighed. "And here I was thinking this was my day off."

She was too far away for him to hear anything, but the staff had practically pounced on her only to grovel in obeisance. They seemed surprised so she must not have had a reservation, yet they bent over backward to accommodate her.

That particular truth rankled a little and David sipped his ice water and examined the poplar over his left shoulder. "It's a good thing I'm nice and shadowed over here," he muttered to himself. Then he remembered that certain species had much better night vision than humans did. *Crap*.

The woman, with her instant entourage hovering around her, walked toward the rear of the restaurant and the hurried conversation became audible.

"Ms Steele..." The maître 'd panted with both exertion and nervousness. "We were not prepared for your visit, welcome though it is. We can have a table cleared for you within a matter of minutes."

"No," she replied in her soft, melodious voice. "That's fine. I'm actually here to meet with someone I know."

David pretended to scratch an eyebrow as an excuse to cover his face, although he could already feel her gaze. At this point, failure was essentially the only option.

"Oh," she said, "there he is."

One of the waiters, without bothering to even consult him, seized a spare chair from a nearby table and planted it opposite him.

He removed his hand and concentrated on his face, setting it to an expression slightly on the pleasant side of neutral.

Taylor sat and the maître 'd and his minions disappeared.

"So," David said. "Hi. I'm...you know, grabbing a quick bite to eat."

The dark woman did not greet him or otherwise reply and merely slid her hand into her jacket and withdrew a newspaper. She placed it on the table and slid it across toward her partner.

The periodical in question was The New England Inquirer, an obscure gossip rag which had made gains in popularity and circulation recently. His gaze darted directly to the author of the headline article on the front page before he even bothered to read the title. Jenny Ocren. His gut seemed to sink between his ankles. Ms Ocren seemed to have a grudge against him. Or a fixation on him. Perhaps both.

The title read: *Millionaire playboy stomps through East Village—the work of a secret twin brother?*

"Ah, yes." David adjusted his tie and cleared his throat. "You remember that business, don't you? I was in pursuit of that face-stealer who'd prowled around Manhattan appropriating people's identities and committing credit fraud. He tried to frame me at the last minute by attempting to beat up a little girl while imitating my face. I put a stop to it quite effectively."

His companion's ivory face remained impassive and her dark eyes stared. "Effectively," she acknowledged, "but loudly and blatantly. Clumsily. Once again, you imperil our entire operation by your difficulties with stealth and discretion. Our activities should not be fodder for the press."

While she scolded him, he read the article itself. Ocren had managed to snap a photograph of two men dressed in different suits but with mirror-image features, who tussled near a fire hydrant while a few onlookers gaped in shock. She concluded the piece by suggesting—and offered no real evidence—that the youngest Remington had an identical, possibly-insane twin brother whom the family had kept locked away for years.

"Hah!" He scoffed and pushed the newspaper away. "Taylor, I'll allow that perhaps I could have waited until he passed through a dark alley or something to make my move. But I doubt we have anything to fear from the press in this case."

"This case, Remington," she retorted sharply and tapped a red nail on the paper, "is the second time she's reported on you this month alone. And that's in addition to her coverage of the fiasco at the demolition derby a while back."

David exhaled slowly. For a moment, he wished he'd not chosen to use Remington Davis as his professional name. Right now, he had a hard time shifting from David-off-duty to Remington-on-duty. "The Inquirer is a bottom-of-the-barrel gossip sheet which only the most bored or deluded of conspiracy theorists read. Didn't they once suggest that one of our city councilmen was an oversized fae, only for the rest of the world to respond with deafening silence?"

The woman ignored all he'd said. "Is this why you've avoided me, lately?" She raised an eyebrow. "I noticed that every day, you've departed my house well before my shift begins at dusk."

"Now, now." He wagged a finger. "It isn't always about you. I have other business-related matters to take care of once my shift is over, hence leaving early to visit the places before they close. Some of us have to take business hours into consideration, you know."

Before she could respond, the maître 'd and another waiter sidled up, armed with food and wine, which they set before the woman.

"Here you are, madame," said the maître 'd, "the finest in the house." He turned to David. "Sir, we're terribly sorry, but your order is backed up in the kitchen. However, we will have it to you as soon as possible."

"Right." He coughed. "That will do."

They hurried away.

Taylor looked at the provisions set before her. "Interesting. They know who I am but not what I am. I'll have to teach them how to make a Historical Bloody Mary if I come here again." She pushed the Filet Mignon and Pinot Noir toward David.

He shrugged and picked his knife and fork up. "You can survive being shot, stabbed, gutted, and so forth. Does this mean that steak is fatal?"

She frowned. "Solid food makes me sick and my body tries to expel it via the quickest route. That can be…inconvenient, especially in public. Although I suppose I'll have a small sip of the wine to keep appearances up."

David continued to eat while she poured about two ounces into a crystal glass for herself and filled a second almost to the brim for him. "Now," she inquired, "tell me about these business matters you've been pursuing in the afternoons."

He smiled around a tasty, tender piece of the meat cooked to medium-rare perfection. "I've been looking for office space," he admitted. "For us, I mean. If the agency is going to expand, we can't continue to conduct all our business via a PO box like you've done for years. We need to be presentable."

"No," she stated. "Low-profile is best. We've already had more business lately and as much as the two of us—and

Presley—can handle. And you have yet to change my mind on this matter of taking mundane cases on. We should specialize only in matters that deal with the preternatural world."

He knew her kind of people disliked the word supernatural, and he'd adapted accordingly.

"You're partially right." He dabbed his mouth with a napkin. "The thing is, with the website having been improved, we're already bringing in more potential cases than we can handle. There's a backlog of queries you haven't even seen yet."

She was rarely surprised but she tensed a little now. He'd managed to tell her something she truly did not know.

"What we need," he went on, "is a real workspace—and a team. At least a room somewhere with a desk in it and a person to sit at the desk and handle the Frequently Asked Questions."

The waiter returned, this time with his pasta and merlot. He blinked in confusion when he saw the already half-finished steak.

"Oh," she explained with a slight gesture of her hand, "it's quite all right. I ate earlier. But thank you for the wine."

The man nodded and arranged things on the table to the best of his ability before David dismissed him with a polite nod.

He sighed when he looked at the gleaming white fettuccine. "I'll have to lift weights and spend time on the treadmill when I get home, I suppose. Anyway, what do you say? About the prospect of an office and a secretary."

Taylor drummed her fingers on the table, her icily beautiful face set in the placid expression she always assumed when thinking.

"I will consider it," she responded after a pause. Her dark eyes locked with his and focused. "But first, there is a case I need you to solve."

He took a swig of his wine. It proved to be exceedingly dry but in a good way. "It must be one hell of an important case if you need me to deal with it singlehandedly. At least that means it probably doesn't involve storming a fortified mansion and burning it down."

Her gaze flicked around and it occurred to Remy—he always reverted to that name when agency business was under discussion, so even his subconscious had apparently accepted the transition—that maybe he'd said that a little too loudly. She pointed to him and then the surface of the table.

"Put that glass down."

Instantly, he obeyed. The wine sloshed within the crystal and barely fell short of escaping to the tablecloth below. She'd used her command tone on him.

"That's enough drinking for tonight," she went on, her voice lower, "unless you're quite confident you can be more discreet."

His mouth crinkled as though he'd bitten into a raw lemon. "Yes, Mother," he quipped, although she was right.

"Good." She retrieved a pen and wrote something on a scrap of paper. "I want you to investigate some recent incidents involving a Dwarven shipping cartel with which I have dealings. I have no reason to suspect any skullduggery on their part—I've known them for a long time—so the problems must be the work of an outside party."

Remy nodded. "I see. What kind of problems are we talking about here?"

"Some of their shipments have gone missing of late." She finished writing and put her pen away. "And within this last week, the employees escorting a shipment have completely vanished. The obvious suspicion is that they've been robbed and killed. There are no ransom notes yet, nothing like that. Of course, there remains the possibility that the escorts absconded with the goods themselves but we simply don't know."

He almost reached for his wine glass but stopped himself before he made it obvious. "And how will my pending success affect your consideration of my proposal?"

"If," Taylor said, "you can find out what's happened to these personnel of theirs, I will be more open to a new office." Something in the set of her mouth suggested she was smiling, albeit so subtly that only someone who knew her would have caught it.

His response was his biggest, flashiest, most obvious grin. "Deal. I'll have them found within a day. Or, like, a day and a half, at most."

He patted his mouth with a napkin, pushed his chair back, and stood. "It's been a pleasure, Taylor, but I ought to leave and get to bed shortly. It sounds like I have my work cut out for me tomorrow."

She ran a finger around the rim of her wine glass. "Indeed. I'll have Presley gather the information you'll need. Good evening, Remington."

With a brief nod, he strode away.

As he passed through the indoor landscaping, his mind went over the list of requirements presented him months before by his family.

One hundred million in assets. A three-million-per-month positive cash flow. And zero unpaid debt with any of the businesses in which he owned stock. That was how the other Remingtons had defined the term "independently wealthy." Once he had fulfilled these conditions, he would be back in their good graces, both socially and financially.

He was...getting there. Slowly but surely.

And, he gloated, as he stepped out into the wet and gleaming New York night, *with the agency growing so fast and gaining so many new clients, we can expect an exponential increase in profits. What could possibly go wrong?*

CHAPTER TWO

Fluttershire Fairy Colony, Fort Washington Park, New York City

The morning was bright and cool as David drew his Lincoln into his usual space outside the park. He turned the keys and sat in the silent vehicle for a moment, put his game face on, and rehearsed his pitch.

First, he needed to begin to think of himself as Remington Davis. That had become his professional name, stage name, and street name. The fairies found it amusing to call him "Remy." He still found having two names—both equally important—a little confusing but introduced himself as that whenever he worked with the preternatural.

Last night, at the restaurant, he'd allowed himself to be David Remington again. Now, however, the vacation was over.

"All right." He sighed and climbed out of the vehicle.

Winter was overdue. The autumn had been long and

warm, and a white Christmas was by no means guaranteed. Not that he particularly minded. Having to wear a hat outdoors always left his hair looking ridiculous.

He stretched across to the passenger seat and retrieved a little something he'd brought, hidden within a brown paper bag. It was fairly heavy but he didn't have far to go. His destination, reachable only by foot, was a subtle roll in the earth at the edge of the shade beneath the George Washington Bridge.

Remy trudged past the usual assortment of joggers, dog-walkers, and possibly insane homeless people, one of whom eyed his paper bag with salivatory curiosity. He sent the hopeful a death-glare and the man backed away.

Soon, the two entrances to the colony of the Fair Folk were in sight.

"Halt!" a tiny voice insisted somewhere to Remy's left. He obeyed and wondered how it was that the guards always managed to see him before he could see them.

"Hi," he said tentatively, "it's Remy. Remember me? Riley's…er, friend."

Another high-pitched voice snapped at him from the right. "We know who you are. And we have our suspicions of why you've come."

Both speakers floated toward him and entered his field of vision. They were humanoids but small enough to fit in his hand, with gossamer dragonfly wings and sparkling eyes, and their skin was tinged with odd colors. The one on the left was bluish, whereas the one on the right boasted a bright orange hue.

Remy smiled in a pleasant, inconspicuous way. He tried

to quickly deduce what the hell they might be talking about but came up with nothing certain. Then again, the fae were notoriously fickle and their thought processes often outside of human comprehension.

"I only wanted to speak to her," he said. "Riley. May I please be permitted to do so?"

"Hah!" the blue one scoffed, drifted closer, and gestured toward him with a fist. "Yes, exactly as we suspected. Once again, trying to lure her away."

His gut tightened at the open hostility in the thin little voice. During his very first assignment with the Agency, half the colony had ended up beating the crap out of him. A man's psyche never entirely recovered from losing a fight to a horde of squealing little pricks the size of gerbils.

"Yes," the orange one added and swooped closer as well. "She spent too much time with you, grew too infatuated, and now, she acts and even thinks too much like a human. You have corrupted her with your malign influence."

He sighed and kept the paper-bagged object hidden behind his back. "I am merely interested in once again paying for her services. On behalf of the entire preternatural community, including yourselves, I have an important investigation to conduct, and I need someone who can magically track and locate people. Riley is the best. Besides, she likes me."

"Likes you?" the blue one raged. A few other fairies, by now, had wafted up from their lair to observe the commotion. "You—"

"Here," Remy interrupted and held the bundle up. He stripped the paper bag off in the same motion.

All the fae gasped, frozen in midair, and their faces went slack with ecstasy.

He allowed himself a smirk. "One entire half-gallon of honey," he announced. "Pure, unfiltered elixir directly from the beehive, courtesy of the men in the white suits and facemasks. The pound I'd need to pay for a week of Riley's help is included, and the rest is a gift for your colony."

Instantly, he was swarmed by cackling fairies. At least ten of them seized the jug and lifted it, then carried it with some difficulty toward the nearest hole in the ground.

"You're a great person, for a human," one of them remarked.

"Yeah! Come by more often," added another.

The honey-convoy disappeared beneath the earth. The other fairies trailed nearby, giggling and panting. One of them called back over his shoulder, almost as an afterthought, "Riley will be right out."

Remy nodded and glanced around. No other humans were nearby, which was just as well. Most people could not see the preternatural—which meant, if they'd been observing, they would have seen him speak to thin air, followed by a jug of honey that floated by itself toward what they probably assumed was a gopher den.

He waited and swelled with confidence—he'd pulled this off. The only possible hitch was that Riley herself might try to argue with him. Still, he knew he could handle that as well.

Perhaps two minutes passed before a single tiny, fluttering form rose from the nest.

"Remy." A soft, feminine voice sighed.

He waved. "Hi, Riley. Good to see you again. You're even wearing the dress."

She flew toward him, thankfully not too fast. "Do you still like it? I chose it based on what you said you liked originally." She raised her arms and twirled slowly in the air, which gave him a nice view of her miniature cleavage, legs, and buttocks.

"Yes, I remember." His palms began to sweat. Riley had been flirtatious with him from the get-go, but the fact of her being five inches tall and a member of a different species had buffered him against her advances.

Of course, that was before she'd demonstrated that she could magically grow to the size of a human woman.

He cleared his throat and imagined himself in an ice-cold shower. "So," he began, "I could use your help again. You saved my ass several times when we worked together before. Are you in the mood to do some tracking?"

"Sure," she replied with a grin. "As long as I get to do it with you."

Surrly Lending, Chelsea, New York City

Remy paused at the door. "Is this the place?" He cocked an eyebrow at the fairy.

"Well, yeah," she responded. "It says his name right on the door." She pointed.

"I see that. I simply meant, do you smell dwarf in here? Do you…uh, sense anything suspicious I should be aware of?"

Riley shook her head.

Satisfied, he pushed his way in. A bell attached to the

door heralded his entrance. It was deeper and lower than the tinkly ones most shops used, halfway to a gong. He supposed that was more appropriate for a dwarf.

Within, the place appeared quite normal. Or, at least, the small, cozy lobby was. No other customers were waiting, and behind a window, an apparently human receptionist wearing a burgundy sweater and butterfly glasses studied them curiously.

"Hello," she said cheerfully, "how can I help you?" She'd clearly seen Riley but wasn't fazed by her in the slightest.

Remy slipped two fingers into his front shirt pocket and produced a business card. "Hi, I'm here on behalf of Moonlight Detective Agency to see Surrly. Is he in? He requested our help." He showed the front of the card to the lady.

She squinted at it. "Mmm, yes...we were expecting someone else but let me inform him that you've arrived. Wait here, please." She hoisted herself from her chair and disappeared into a back room.

Once the receptionist had gone, Riley floated to Remy's ear and whispered, "I think he was expecting Taylor."

Feeling the fairy's breath on his ear like that brought stirring memories of her at five-feet-three and one hundred and twenty pounds, and naked. He clenched his teeth and made himself think, instead, of other dwarves he'd seen and what they'd look like similarly nude. That cut off the distraction rather effectively.

"Well, of course," he said. "It's not as though Taylor has had any other employees besides herself for...I don't know, a few decades? Centuries?"

"Oh." She sounded dejected.

Remy cursed himself for being needlessly snarky again. "Don't worry, not everyone is an ace at detective work, and you've always been useful in other ways."

He saw her smile out of the corner of his eye.

The receptionist returned and stood at the window. "Mr Surrly will see you, although he's not happy about the bait-and-switch. Go through that door to your right when I press the buzzer."

"That sounds simple enough." He nodded, walked toward the door in question, and turned the knob in time with the obnoxious buzzing sound. Beyond was a short, dim corridor that branched off to both left and right.

"Go left," the woman's voice called.

Remy did and the fairy trailed a little behind his shoulder. He stepped into an office that, at first glance, he mistook for a treasure vault in a Renaissance castle.

A big, broad hand appeared almost directly in front of his face, palm outwards. "Hold!" a voice grunted. "You're not armed, are you? I don't expect you're that stupid, but one can never be sure."

He raised his hands reflexively, mainly because the dwarf aimed a blunderbuss pistol at him with his other hand. The fairy had tensed and seemed poised to employ some kind of defensive magic but waited for any signal from her partner.

The dwarf blew warm air out of his lips, fluffed his huge mustache, and patted his visitor down with a hand that felt like a tennis racket encased in concrete. "Good. And the fairy can relax. I mean you no harm unless you mean me harm." He spoke with a gravelly brogue and rolled his R's.

"I don't," he stated. "May I have a seat?" He glanced toward the guest chair opposite the dwarf's massive oaken desk.

"Yes. I am Surrly, as you might well have guessed. And who might you be?" He raised his thick iron-gray unibrow and holstered his bizarre gun.

He wiped his sweaty palms on the back of his pants. "Remington Davis, Taylor's partner. It seems she forgot to inform you that I'd be the one handling your case. And this is Riley." He gestured toward the fairy.

"Hello!" she chirped.

Surrly frowned at them both. Even by dwarven standards, he was squat and solid and dour-looking, visibly aged but still spry and strong. He stomped over to his leather chair and sat, shaking the floor a tad, and put his fists together under his beard.

Remy pulled the other chair out and settled into it. Riley perched on his left shoulder.

"Now," the dwarf began, "Taylor and I are longtime associates, and I have been a client of hers in many cases. It seems to me that there is no good reason she should not take care of this herself. I do not know you. In fact, I've never even heard of you. With such a long working relationship between us, she owes me the satisfaction of being able to trust her competence."

Instinctively, he bristled but inhaled slowly through his nose and tried not to insult the man.

Riley spoke for him. "He's legitimate," she insisted. "I've been with him to Taylor's house, and we both helped her against those werewolves. You heard about that, didn't you?"

Surrly grunted. "Yes. I've no reason to mistrust you, young lady, but this man is an unknown quantity. I'm a moneylender. I specialize in knowing my quantities." He waved a bricklike hand.

The rest of the office was piled with valuables. Now that he had a moment to study them, the dwarf's itchy trigger finger made more sense. His hasty examination revealed bars of gold and silver, crates full of precious gems, sacks of gold dust, and even *objets d'art* made of similarly precious materials. One entire wall was lined with steel safe boxes, but half of them hung open. They must have caught Surrly in the middle of an inventory session.

All these things were the kinds of currency popular in the preternatural community. Paper money had never really caught on, except with humans.

Remy straightened. "As it so happens," he explained and raised his voice a little, "it is precisely my competence that led Taylor to take me on as a partner. She asked me to handle this mission personally and I have her complete trust. And that business with the werewolves? I killed one myself. I've already leapt through fire and emerged unscathed. Oh, and the fairy helped. With us on the job, success is guaranteed, as surely as if Taylor were handling it herself." He smiled.

Surrly snorted. "You're cocky, I see. But you don't seem to be lying. Perhaps exaggerating. Nonetheless...I will give you this job, provided Taylor understands that I will hold her accountable for any failure of yours." He pointed at the investigator's face with a finger almost as thick as one of his gold bars.

His smile did not falter. "You won't be disappointed,

good sir. I recently foiled an identity-theft scam run by one hell of a clever face-stealer. Among other things."

"Yes, yes." The dwarf, scowling, had already reached into a drawer of his desk and now withdrew a manila folder. "Allow me to brief you, then. Our cartel often deals with the import of raw, uncut diamonds. Do not bother to ask me exactly how we acquire these diamonds. I will give you an answer so vague as to be pointless."

"Understood," he said and ignored Riley's hiss of confusion.

Surrly continued. "A shipment recently arrived in the United States. The escort crew checked in with me immediately after they left the boat here in New York. Then... nothing. It was no tremendous shock since we have been targeted with a series of thefts lately. But this was the first time that our people disappeared, along with the merchandise, and that deepens my concern."

The blocky face, already far from pleasant, drooped now in a mixture of grief and anger. Remy knew dwarves to be a tightly-knit group. An attack on one, unless he'd gone rogue, was an attack on all.

The dwarf opened the folder. "I recommend you begin at the pier where their ship arrived. Your small companion should be able to aid you to find subtle traces, I imagine. Here is a rundown of the information we have, as well as a picture of one of the missing dwarves—a man who worked directly under me on many similar jobs."

Remy accepted the documents—two sheets of paper with details typed in a list format and a full-size photo scan. "Thank you, Mr Surrly. We will hurry to the piers at once. I ought to have something to call you with as early as this evening."

Surrly nodded. "Good. Leave a message on the office phone if we're not here. And one more thing..." He pointed again and his unibrow lowered over his deep-set eyes. "If you get into any trouble, you know nothing about me. Not even my name."

CHAPTER THREE

Pier 88, Western Manhattan, New York

Riley, stretched on the dashboard, pulled her skirt up a little higher. "Do you think it looks better like this?" she asked. "Or the way it was? I suppose it's more…suggestive when it's pulled all the way down."

"Whatever you think is best, dear." Remy tried to ignore her. It was, however, difficult. "We're almost there, by the way, so get back on the clock. My God, why does this city have so many piers?"

She shrugged. "I don't know. People probably need places to land their ships, and—"

"It was a rhetorical question." He interrupted her and she pouted. "Check that note from Surrly. He said Pier Eighty-eight, right?"

She breezed over to the file folder on the passenger seat. "Yes." Her eyes bright, she darted up toward his face. "And I can detect a little of his essence—the dwarf we're looking for. He was here recently but we'll need to get closer, though."

"Good, yes." He turned off of 12th Avenue in search of somewhere to park. Of course, he had to drive a good quarter-mile deeper into the city before anything presented itself. There was a great deal of bustle in the area and cars hunched evilly in every nearby space.

Finally, he brought the vehicle to a stop in a parallel space alongside a hardware store. No signs specifically indicated that parking was for customers only. "Riley, be a good girl and enchant my car so no one can steal it, or destroy it with a crowbar for fun, or place a parking ticket on the windshield. I have no idea how long we'll be here and I'm down to my last three quarters."

"Okay," she agreed cheerfully.

He climbed out, shut and remote-locked the doors, and waited for the fairy to work her magic. She swooped around the Lincoln in a circle, gestured with her hand, and released bright silver-hued sparks to cascade all over its surface. It glowed subtly in the building's shade.

"Thanks," he said.

Remy turned toward the piers and immediately settled into a fast walk along the noisy streets. His tiny companion flapped along behind him. He had no fear that normies would notice her. The overwhelming majority of them could only perceive the preternatural if they'd been "touched" by it in some way.

Besides, this was New York. Half the locals would probably simply shrug, swear under their breath, and get on with their business.

They jaywalked carefully across 12th Avenue, weaved between gridlocked, honking cars with glowering drivers, and found a place to cross the Hudson River Greenway. As the pier itself came into clear sight, he stopped and his jaw sagged.

"Whaaaat the hell?" he drawled.

"Oh, wow," Riley commented.

Luxury cruise ships were docked all along the pier. The surrounding area looked like a goddamn carnival. Nothing in sight gave off much of an industrial vibe. As a result, he immediately double-checked his list of notes from Surrly to make sure they had the right place.

"Yeah." He sighed. "This is it. Eighty-eight. Did our supposedly fastidious moneylender make a numerical error? Somehow, I don't see cruise ships as likely candidates for an underground cartel's illicit diamond-smuggling operation. Honestly, look at some of these ridiculous people."

He waved a hand to indicate the people, most of whom were dressed like tourists.

Despite the moderately chilly and overcast weather, half or more wore sundresses or open-collared Hawaiian shirts, along with goofy hats and sunglasses or even glorified bathing suits. Heaps of luggage rested against inert legs or dangled from overtaxed arms. Some of them shivered visibly.

Remy shook his head. He'd seen enough preternatural phenomena by now to wonder if, perhaps, they'd struck a snag in the space-time continuum and these people had been warped there from August when New York became a giant sauna.

Riley raised her hand. "Maybe they're going to the Bahamas."

"Well," he retorted, "they're not there yet. They ought to

at least wait until they've boarded the ship and exited American territorial waters before publicly making fools of themselves. But, plunge onward we must. The dwarf's musk is still lingering in the air, isn't it?"

The fairy zipped a few yards ahead to sniff and survey the pier. "Yes, he was here," she assured him. "I can even see some of his footsteps, although it looks like he retraced his steps a few times in some of the same places, so that makes it hard to tell which of the tracks are older."

He nodded and strode into the melee.

It was far too crowded for the two of them to hold any significant conversation. He didn't want to attract undue attention by talking to someone no one else could see, not to mention that the general racket of shuffling cargo, footsteps, and burbling voices would have drowned out Riley's attempts at speech.

Instead, he caught the fairy's eye and signaled different places with his gaze. She fluttered along the pier, counting footsteps and pointing in different directions. Usually, the place she indicated required him to push through a gigantic mass of humans.

"Excuse me," he muttered. "Pardon. Coming through. Terribly sorry. Excuse me..." Many of these people probably came from outside the city proper. They therefore expected an actual apology when someone shoved past them in a crowded area.

Remy checked his notes. The departed dwarf was named Rimbledon, and his weight was estimated at barely shy of three hundred and fifty pounds. This became less and less mysterious as they followed his faintly glowing footsteps around the pier.

"I do believe," he mumbled when they emerged into a relatively open area, "that we've now visited every food stall around this pier. We were definitely at that hot dog stand twice."

Riley tapped a finger to her lips. "Do you think he was buying food for his friends?"

"Possibly." He shrugged. "Then again, I used to know this really neurotic girl with an eating disorder—an overeating disorder, that is—who used to go out of her way to go to different restaurants and snack stores in the neighborhood at different times to disguise her activities."

"Why?" the fairy asked.

"Oh, never mind."

The waters were cold and gray when they departed the pier itself and moved along the waterfront. Remy was not terribly surprised to end up in front of a public restroom.

"He went in there," his companion said. "Wait—it has an Out of Order sign that looks like it was hanging there even before he arrived but he went in anyway. That doesn't make sense."

He pinched the bridge of his nose and shuddered. "If we cannot find clues anywhere else, we'll come back here and investigate. But let's save that as a last resort, shall we?"

From there, the trail led to a pub cleverly disguised as a refreshment stand and half-hidden near the base of the greenway's embankment. He noted a few preternaturals among those crowded near the bar—another dwarf, a gnomish couple, a humanoid who looked a little like an alien gray, and a hairy lady who probably enjoyed the moonlight too much.

"Hmm," he observed. "We might be able to actually ask

these people about our guy." He retrieved the photo print of Rimbledon's broad, puffy face and stepped toward the bar.

Ahead of him, the gray struggled to order a margarita in a voice that sounded like someone mumbling through an old-fashioned walkie-talkie. Remy briefly made eye contact with the bartender—a human male with an impressive scar along his jawline—and considered simply barging in and demanding information.

He could always pretend to be an undercover cop, after all, or simply name-drop Taylor.

Before he could act on the impulse, Riley tugged at his ear and pointed. He looked quickly. Hanging just beside the bar was a huge poster with the words **DO NOT SERVE** printed at the top in bold black letters. Below them was a picture almost perfectly identical to the one in his hand.

"Goddammit," he snapped and turned away from the stand. "I guess that answers that question. Lead onward, fair companion."

She continued to illuminate Rimbledon's tracks. They led through a small, half-hidden tunnel which took them under the greenway and back into the city, and they finally emerged near the edge of what seemed to be a bowling alley. Around back and beside the dumpster was an almost invisible, narrow staircase.

"He went down there," the fairy stated.

"I'm not sure how he fit down there," Remy quipped, "but okay."

At the bottom, a gruff-looking man with heavily tattooed forearms opened the door and asked them what the password was.

He held up his business card. "The password is Taylor Steele. Have you heard of her? I'm her partner. We're looking for this dwarf, Rimbledon, on behalf of Surrly the moneylender."

The guard blinked and fell back half a step. "Yeah, yeah. Come in. But don't cause us any problems."

"Of course not." He chuckled and held the print up. "Have you seen this guy?"

The man squinted. "He was in here maybe two days ago but only long enough to place a bet on one match before he hustled out. He said he had to meet with some guys. I thought maybe he only wanted to drop a load, though."

Remy nodded. "That is possible. May we step in?"

The basement of the bowling alley hosted an obviously illegal sporting event, which he at first assumed to be dogfighting but turned out to be gremlin-fighting.

A fat gnome jumped up and down next to the pit. "Rip his bloody colon out through his abdomen! Yesss! That's my boy." His plastic cup of piss-colored beer sloshed over his hand and spattered on the dirty floor.

Other patrons also were going wild and uttered curses, encouragement, or wordless howls of bloodlust as a cacophony of shrieks and snarls rose from the circular depression in the center of the floor.

Remy gestured toward the spectacle. "Do you care for some high-class entertainment, Riley?"

She blushed. "I don't really like gremlins."

He ignored her and strode up to the nearest spectator who didn't seem hysterical—a skinny female elf with black tearstains tattooed beneath her eyes. A few feet beyond was the dirt-filled pit, where two knee-height creatures, scaly and ugly and green, snarled and tussled.

The investigator tapped the elf on the arm. "Excuse me, ma'am. Have you seen this dwarf?"

She turned toward him with a disdainful expression that was, somehow, all the snootier for how hard she tried to hide it. Her eyes disapproved of his suit and tie and generally clean-cut appearance before her gaze moved to the photo in his hand.

"Not if I can help it," she said.

Remy moved on but none of the other patrons were any more helpful. Riley illuminated a few more of Rimbledon's footsteps, but they simply circled the pit and crossed to the bar and back a few times. Nothing surprising or any way out of the ordinary was revealed.

"Well," the fairy said when they stepped outside and ascended the narrow staircase, "it does seem like he kept walking after this—deeper into the city. That way." She pointed.

"Into Hell's Kitchen," he confirmed. "The place has mostly been gentrified all to fuckery these days, but some parts still possess that quaint, old-fashioned, demilitarized-zone type of charm."

She led them down sidewalks, along fences, and through alleys into parts of town that seemed to grow progressively more dilapidated. Crowds thinned and the bustle of the city became background noise rather than immediate reality.

"Where the hell are we?" Remy wondered. "I've never been here and I don't think I've even heard of this street."

Evidently, no one else had either, since there was not a

single moving vehicle in sight. Most of the shops were boarded up and the housing projects looked like dormant military fortresses.

Soon, Rimbledon's tracks led to the abandoned road and into a dried-out sewer tunnel.

Riley stopped abruptly and hovered in midair. "I don't like the look of this place," she admitted. "There are numerous strange smells in there. Next time, I expect you to take me to nicer places when we go on a date."

"That's nice, dear," he quipped. "I don't seem to have a flashlight, though. Illuminate the place, would you?"

With a dramatic sigh, she produced an expanding beam of silver light from her fingertip that spread throughout the rusty, circular space. Remy stepped in.

He didn't like the looks of the place, either. Still, at least it wasn't an out-of-order waterfront bathroom.

"I suppose," he commented in a low voice, "that this would be the place to smuggle diamonds. They could easily stash them overnight or something while the couriers scatter. I don't think even the junkies have found this place. Did we wander into New Jersey while I wasn't paying attention?"

"Hmm," the fairy responded. "I don't think so. It's really dirty, though. I wouldn't have worn this nice dress if I'd known we'd go someplace like this, even if it does show my features off while covering enough to be a tease like you said."

It occurred to Remy that he'd never banged a chick in a sewer tunnel before.

"I must say," he admitted with a small smirk, "your features looked rather...nice...when magnified so I could have a good look at them. At your normal size, it's harder to appreciate the jiggle physics of—"

He stopped and both of them froze when a sudden bend in the tunnel revealed its contents before them, horribly sprawled in total silence.

The dwarven escort crew was there, but they would not be going anywhere else ever again. A ventilation fan in the tunnel ceiling above had funneled the stench upward and now, repeating patterns of light and dark moved over the remains in time with the spinning blades.

"Oh no." Riley gasped.

With mounting horror, Remy realized he might not even be able to count the bodies. The pieces had been scattered too much. It was difficult to tell which limb and which lump or shred of flesh had belonged to which dwarf.

He swallowed, adjusted his tie, and wiped his hands on the back of his pants before he withdrew his phone from his pocket. "Riley, we need light on...that. All of it."

She squirmed with discomfort but did as he asked, and the carnage grew horribly clear under the bright silver radiance. He woke his phone up, tapped the camera button, and snapped a picture.

As the click faded, he recognized the familiar face of Rimbledon amidst the massacre. The dwarf stared blankly at the ceiling and dark crimson ribbons and part of a spinal column trailed below the beard. The rest of his body was nowhere nearby.

Remy focused despite his revulsion and noticed a large number of guns. Some had fallen, while others were still held in the frozen grasp of dead, nerveless fingers. He saw a few bullet holes in the surrounding masonry. "What the hell could have done this? It looks like the work of a rabid animal. Whatever it was, they tried to kill it but obviously failed."

Maybe, for all he knew, these dwarves were terrible shots but he somehow doubted that. They looked tough, and Surrly had said they were experienced. Whatever had slaughtered them was nothing even remotely ordinary.

The fairy pointed at something on the other side of the scene. "Look."

He complied and his gaze identified a misshapen lump. Cringing in disgust, he stepped over and through the bloodied remains toward the object.

It was a fist-sized sack and it was filled with strange, clear stones, almost like chunks of glass.

Riley drifted over and peered into the bag. "Uncut diamonds," she explained.

Squinting, he asked her, "Are you sure? They don't look like any diamonds I've seen. Then again, those were probably cut."

The fairy shrugged. "Diamonds are a girl's best friend."

"Jesus," he remarked. "In that case, this is the cargo they were transporting. Whatever attacked them didn't even rob the poor bastards. It was simply murder for the sake of murder."

"That's awful," she exclaimed. While she was as sickened as he was, she seemed to have already recovered somewhat from the shock. "We should take those diamonds, though. Surrly will want them back, won't he? And they're a clue."

Remy nodded. "I agree." He picked the bag up. It was heavy, despite its small size.

"Oh," the fairy added, "I also have a spell that can show what happened during his last moments—Rimbledon's, I mean, since we have his trail already. Like a human movie."

He squirmed in place. "I'm not sure I want to see that... but it might be useful to know. We need some kind of a lead." He took a deep breath. "Do it, then."

The fairy nodded, and her eyes glazed over as she waved her arms slowly up and down in alternating patterns, then clapped sharply.

Remy fell back a step and jerked with tension when moving figures sketched in pale light appeared in the middle of the tunnel.

Both he and the fairy watched in sick fascination as the phantasmal holograms reenacted the slaughter. At first, they saw the troupe of dwarves marching through the tunnel. A humanoid form leapt on all fours like a great cat and collided into the dwarf on point to drive him out of sight. He screamed and the others yelled in response as they drew their weapons.

Guns blazed as the group tried vainly to defend themselves. Rimbledon was knocked off his feet by the attacking blur and, for an awful few seconds, he watched as their assailant ripped one of his friends apart, limb from limb, using a strength beyond anything Remy had seen.

"What the hell?" The investigator gasped.

They saw the attacker clearly at that moment, but his appearance made no sense. His face was obscured as if by gold-colored fog and a strange marking, like a cattle brand, glowed with light of the same color on his chest.

Rimbledon raised his weapon and fired but the faceless man vaulted upward and out of sight. More bodies tumbled in the shadows at the sides and screams echoed. The dwarf cursed and aimed into the darkness near the ceiling.

Finally, the assailant dropped from high on the wall, somehow zig-zagged in midair, and struck with a powerful grasping blow that turned the whole scene red. Everything spun, and then, presumably as Rimbledon's head came to rest on the ground, it grew still when the eyes glazed over and he stared at his own body.

The vision disappeared and silence reigned in the tunnel.

Riley was biting the side of her hand. "That was even worse than I thought it would be." She moaned.

Remy assented. "We should get the hell out of here and contact Taylor. I don't think she realized what she has sent us up against."

The fairy enchanted the sack to lighten its weight, and he carried it over his shoulder through the tunnel. He tried not to startle at shadows or panic at every little noise, but it took a certain degree of effort.

He didn't know what they were up against, yet, either.

CHAPTER FOUR

Harrison, Westchester County, New York

The Lincoln eased its way slowly up the winding drive that climbed the wooded hill to Taylor's estate. The door to the massive garage opened automatically in time for the car to proceed without stopping into its usual space.

Remy inched the Lincoln between two of her black Teslas and pulled far enough ahead to be clear of the door, which closed behind him once he had stopped.

Riley slumped on the dashboard but stirred when the vehicle came to a halt. "Remy," she said, "I didn't want to mention this before, but there was…a really bad smell back there. In the tunnel."

"I know," he replied. "Dead bodies get like that after they've been sitting out for a while." He pulled his key out, opened the door, and exited. She zipped after him.

"No," she protested. "Not only that. I mean…something smelled evil. I couldn't recognize it but I don't think it was anything normal that did that. Even normal by preternatural standards, I mean."

He opened the side door of the garage and let the fairy through before he ambled toward the mansion's front door. "I was afraid you might say something like that. We'll talk to Taylor about it. It pains me to admit it, but she's probably smarter than I am."

While he tried not to shudder, the charnel scene he'd photographed and the desperate last stand they'd watched reappeared constantly in his mind. Especially the dead eyes of Rimbledon, the very dwarf he'd tried to track.

Taylor's house was built more or less into a low rocky cliff that emerged from the crest of the hill. It was located at the back of a labyrinthine, old-money neighborhood. The mansion was only two stories tall but still significantly large and possessed an ornate elegance that many of the area's *nouveau riche* would envy.

He mounted the steps to the front doors. The right one opened before he could knock and he stepped over the threshold.

"Hi," he droned, not feeling up to any further conversation at the moment.

Presley, Taylor's butler, closed the door behind him and accepted his jacket. The retainer noted the presence of the fairy but declined to comment.

Remy had once been surprised to learn that the elderly English gentleman was, in fact, a lycanthrope. He'd never seen him transform into a wolf-beast but he had seen other werewolves do exactly that, so there was no reason to doubt that the old boy could pull it off.

The butler stood a moment as if he waited and braced himself for something, but there was only silence as the new arrival trudged to his usual chair in the antiquated foyer.

"Sir," he asked in his dusty yet dignified old voice, "is something wrong? Usually, you incorrectly refer to me as 'Jeeves' and make obnoxious comments of some kind. You don't seem at all yourself."

"Uh..." He drew a deep breath and loosened his tie. "It's been a long day, Presley. Or Jeeves, whatever. Let's simply say we found some clues but it's the kind of thing that makes me think maybe Taylor should handle this one herself."

The man's eyes widened. "Oh dear. That does sound dreadful, then. May I fetch you something to drink? Any honey for Ms Riley?"

Both man and fairy replied in unison with, "Yes, please."

With a quick nod, the butler strode toward the kitchen. Dusk wasn't too far off, anyway, so Remy supposed he'd have to prepare Taylor's red salt tea, as she coyly referred to it.

Riley settled herself on his shoulder, her shapely legs draped over the edge so her feet dangled slightly above his armpit. "Thanks for saying I have nice features back there." Her voice was soft and cooing. "I could show you them at your size again if you want."

Freezing water. Instinctively, he attempted to visualize the thought. *A glacier in Alaska is melting and I'm standing right under it.* In truth, it was entirely unnecessary. The gruesome and depressing spectacle in the tunnel had definitely killed the mood.

"You're welcome," he responded. "Some other time, though. After what we found today, I suspect we'll be busy with serious work for a while. Ugh, as if I didn't already have enough things to worry about."

"Worry about?" the fairy protested.

Remy sighed. "I don't mean worrying about you. I meant dealing with the aftermath of that massacre on top of all the work I'm doing expanding our business. You're fine, fear not."

"Oh." She folded her tiny arms over her chest. "Well, I guess I believe you..."

He leaned his head back and allowed the house to reassure him with its familiarity. It was an old, dark kind of place and furnished in a way that didn't even try to be modern, but everything was tasteful, even sophisticated, and Taylor and Presley kept it clean and functional.

Across from him, a small table held a pile of books. Taylor was always reading in her spare time—usually scientific or esoteric stuff but sometimes music theory. He supposed a person got bored when nothing except highly specific types of violence could kill them. Least of all, time.

The butler emerged from the kitchen with a broad tray that held a teacup and saucer, as well as a tiny sauce dish half-filled with honey.

"Sir," Presley began, "I added a touch of brandy to your tea if you don't mind. I'm afraid I got the impression that you could use it."

"Quite right, Jeeves," he replied and perked up slightly. He seized the cup and drank half of the steaming beverage in one gulp.

Meanwhile, the retainer set the tray with the sauce dish on the end table. He'd broken a single tine off a plastic fork, Remy saw, for Riley to use as a utensil. The fairy, beaming with joy, fluttered enthusiastically toward her meal.

The butler clasped his hands behind his back. "Let me know if you need anything further. I'll be in the sitting room until Ms Steele awakens, which ought to be quite soon."

He wasn't wrong. When the last of the sunlight beyond the windows died and ceded space to the darkness, something stirred in the crypt below Taylor's basement.

The investigator finished his spiked tea with slow sips while he listened to the barely audible sounds as Taylor glided up the stairs, pushed the cellar door open, and moved down the hall.

"Remington," she greeted him. "No business today, I see." She wore a black silk night robe that flattered her greatly, albeit in a classy sort of way.

He cleared his throat. "The business you sent me on was quite enough. I have some fairly important things to share."

She nodded. "Let me have my first sip of tea and you can tell me all about it."

While he didn't particularly feel like waiting, she was a difficult woman to disobey.

By now, he'd finished his tea and Riley, her honey. Taylor vanished into the kitchen for three or four minutes before both she and Presley strolled out to the parlor. In her hand was a teacup, the interior of which was stained a deep rusty-brown color and which, at present, contained a steaming crimson liquid. Her eyes flashed subtly red when she drank.

"Now," she began and seated herself in the armchair across from him, "tell me everything."

He tried not to waste too much time on the basics of his visit to Fluttershire, his brief meeting with Surrly, or their jaunt around the piers in search of Rimbledon the dwarf. The important thing was, of course, the conclusive evidence that the diamond couriers had been butchered to the last man. He even showed her the picture he'd taken on his phone and tried not to look at it himself.

Taylor nodded. "I see." She betrayed no particular shock.

His jaw and gut tightened suddenly with the beginnings of anger. "You don't seem surprised. Did you expect this? Did you know you were sending me after…I don't know, some rabid monstrosity that was able to kill half a dozen heavily-armed dwarven mercenaries?"

The woman remained calm. "I did not know anything for certain," she answered, "but let us say that I considered this as an unlikely worst-case scenario. In any event, you're still in one piece, and so is Riley."

"True," he conceded.

"And you said that whoever attacked them didn't steal the diamonds?" Taylor went on. "Where are they now?"

"Correct, it wasn't a robbery, after all. And the diamonds are in the trunk of my car, of course. I concluded that your garage was about as safe as anywhere else, especially with you waking up soon."

The vampire finished her version of tea. Her face grew distant and placid as she considered his words, arranged information into branching trees of possibilities, and sifted through various courses of action.

It took only a moment. "I will take the investigation over from here," she stated.

Remy blinked in surprise. He had expected that she would simply tell him to get more third-party help, suck it up, and try not to die. "Oh," he stammered, "that's…uh, probably for the best, to be honest…" He inserted a finger into the top of his shirt around the neck and loosened his collar.

"However," Taylor continued, "your role is not entirely concluded."

He braced himself and decided he wasn't sure he liked the thought of that. But he was good at poker so put on his least-expressive face.

"In the morning," she said calmly, "I want you to take those diamonds to Surrly. He was expecting us to retrieve them, of course." She lifted her empty cup and saucer and Presley stepped forward to take them.

Remy exhaled with relief. He couldn't help himself. Something—some primal fear—had wormed its way into him when they'd found the dwarves' bodies and now, in a single instant, he was liberated from it.

"Yes," he agreed, eagerly, "that sounds fantastic. I'd be happy to. The bag isn't really even all that heavy, at least not after Riley magically reduces its weight. And Surrly is a tremendously pleasant gentleman to do business with."

Taylor almost smiled. "The moneylender will reward you for the return of his merchandise. When he does, you may take that and use it to make a down payment on whichever office space you think is most suitable for our new, expanded operation."

The evening simply kept getting better and better. He grinned and re-buttoned the collar of his shirt. "Excellent. I'm glad to know you've finally come around to the wisdom of having a front, of sorts. Like the mob. Only we truly are a legitimate business, more or less."

"More or less," she agreed.

Remy forged ahead. "I thought perhaps something half-way-ish between your home and mine. So that I don't have to drive so goddamn far every day—no offense—while still being a reasonable distance from your lovely estate here. Upper Manhattan or Washington Heights, perhaps, or even Yonkers or one of the more tolerable parts of the Bronx. I don't know. I'll look into it."

The vampire waved a red-nailed hand. "Do so. It sounds like you'll have fun. But keep yourself available. I will handle the more dangerous aspects of the Surrly case but I may still need you to do important auxiliary work."

Riley, who had listened quietly until now, took wing and perked up. "Does that mean we'll still work together?" she asked and gestured at her human crush.

"Probably," he said. "It never hurts to have someone around who can deflect bullets. And your company is moderately pleasurable, as well."

"Yay!" the fairy exclaimed.

He stood and dusted himself off. While he wasn't looking, Taylor pointed at his fae companion and issued a silent command, ordering her to linger in the house a moment after Remy took his leave. Her eyes flashed with surprise but she nodded.

"Well," he said, "I really ought to get something edible and actually eat it. And sleep, of course, after a little research and a few other chores. I'm glad to have helped with the whole diamond business."

Taylor stood as well. "You're welcome. Good evening, Remington. Be careful."

The young man turned, retrieved his coat, and saw himself out the front door. The fairy, meanwhile, remained in the foyer. She floated toward Taylor.

"Riley," the woman began, her dark eyes almost enveloping the small form, "I assume Remington has already paid for your services, but I want you to stick by his side, regardless. Even if you have to stretch the terms of your formal bargain a little. For me…as a favor. I'm trying to keep him out of too much trouble, but it's possible he'll need your help soon."

Riley nodded with a vigorous motion and brought her tiny fists toward her chin. "Oh, yes, of course, Taylor. I wouldn't want anything to happen to him. Some of the other people in my nest might get mad again if I spend too much time around him, but I can always say you told me to."

"I did," the woman observed. "They'll certainly respect that. Now run along before he drives off and forgets that you're not with him."

The fairy waved goodbye and darted toward the door, opened it with magic, and flapped out into the early-winter darkness. The door drifted shut behind her.

Taylor stood where she was and took a few moments to listen to the sounds the night made, all of them audible even within her creaking old mansion. Presley stepped up behind her.

"I must say," the butler ventured, "it's fortunate that he didn't investigate that little disappearance any sooner. Granted, it might have allowed us to reach a conclusion more swiftly, but it's likely we'd be permanently deprived of a fairly useful employee."

The vampire turned to look at him. "Do I detect a note of criticism in your tone, Presley? Oh, you're right in a way, I suppose." She sighed. "But then again, his luck is in itself almost a preternatural ability. It ought to see him through while I deal with the worst of things in the meantime. Besides, I'm taking every reasonable precaution to keep him safe."

"Quite," Presley agreed and paced across the foyer, "and that is commendable but not entirely accurate. Every precaution except removing him from the case and putting him in protection for a time."

She laughed softly. "He'd protest that and probably find a way to sneak off, anyway. He's positively high on this idea of transforming us into a more traditional business. I still have my doubts. You and I have run things smoothly for all these years, only the two of us. But our current situation makes me think that perhaps it is time to expand and step up our game. We still don't know exactly what we're dealing with, but the world is growing more dangerous."

The butler nodded. "Shall I contact one of our allies and have them watch over young Remington, then?"

A red nail traced its way around the vampire's lips.

"Not yet," she said.

<u>Surrly Lending, Chelsea, New York City</u>

This time, the receptionist recognized them and didn't give them the run-around.

"Oh, hello," she said when Remy strode in with Riley

fluttering along behind him. A heavy-looking sack dangled from his hand. "The gentleman from Moonlight Detective Agency, yes. Taylor left us a message last night explaining your findings."

"Good," he replied and gave no sign of his irritation at himself for having forgotten to call them. Between the horror of his discovery yesterday and the excitement of his coming payday, he had too much on his mind.

The lady waved them toward the far door. "Surrly is in. He's expecting you. And, ah...yes, I see you have the merchandise. Wonderful."

He grinned. "Isn't it, though? I promised him we'd have the matter resolved within a day or so." His smile drooped. "It's really too bad about the men, though."

The receptionist merely nodded. She pressed a button and the door buzzed until he opened it and stepped into the hall toward the dwarf's office.

"Come in, come in!" Surrly's voice boomed.

He was seated behind his broad oak desk and Remy noticed, with some relief, that the blunderbuss was nowhere to be seen. Most of the piles of riches had also been reorganized and removed from the floor, returned to their safe boxes, or perhaps taken away by the man's clients or partners.

"Mr Surrly," he declared, stood before the desk, and held the bag aloft. He was thankful that Riley had enchanted it again since in its natural state, it probably weighed at least thirty pounds. "I have located your lost shipment. Mission accomplished. Unfortunately, the men you had escorting it had all been dead for at least a day or so by the time we arrived."

He tried not to think about it, although it was difficult. He'd seen violence—he'd even been in a gunfight and killed a few men along with a werewolf—and as bad as that was, it still didn't compare to the awful scene they'd stumbled across yesterday.

The dwarf, huge except in height, nodded solemnly. "Yes, that is indeed unfortunate. But it's the cost of doing business. The darker the trade, the more this kind of collateral damage tends to happen. They all knew the risks. I can only hope we don't lose any more. Place that bag in the corner near the black safe, if you would, please."

Remy obeyed, although Surrly's words surprised him. And not in a good way, either. Yesterday, the moneylender had seemed almost heartbroken by the prospect of a group of his fellow dwarves—and loyal employees, at that—being murdered on the job. Now, he took the information in stride.

Part of him recoiled in disgust. He was tempted to turn and berate the dwarf for his callousness, but that would be both unwise and bad for business. Instead, he considered that perhaps this was some cultural response that humans could not understand. Dwarves might have different ways to express grief.

He set the bag down as instructed.

Surrly turned his chair toward the young man. "Of course, you will be rewarded for returning my property. The reward will be worth far less than the value of the merchandise itself, naturally, but you ought to find it to your liking. And stealing from me would have been profoundly stupid, anyway. You'd draw not only my wrath but Taylor's as well. I'm sure you know better than to make her angry."

Remy nodded. After Taylor had tracked down the leaders of the conspiracy against her two or three months before, she'd had to pull some strings to keep a lid on the sheer magnitude of the death and destruction she'd wrought. The general public never heard the details and it helped that she hadn't harmed any innocents. But a few conspiracy theories circulating on the Internet had posited that terrorists had successfully destroyed a CIA safehouse, or something like that.

"Right," he said. "She Shdoesn't do things by half-measures when she's pissed off."

Surrly chuckled. He was counting objects into another sack, and Remy wondered when he'd get around to writing the reward check. Then, to his surprise, the dwarf shoved the bag toward him.

"Here you are, my friend."

He blinked. "Okay? What is this?" He opened the drawstring and peered inside. An assortment of white and green stones gleamed at him.

"Your reward, obviously." The dwarf grunted. His mood was sinking fast and he seemed impatient for them to leave him to his work.

Remy took a deep breath as Riley—who'd examined a gold statuette somewhat distractedly—fluttered to his shoulder. "Well...thanks. But what the hell am I supposed to do with a bag of rocks?"

Surrly shrugged. Without making eye contact, he muttered, "That's your problem. I don't deal in human currency. But you're quite the intrepid detective. I'm sure you can think of something." He pulled out a calculator and a sheaf of papers.

Effectively dismissed, the investigator nodded again and gritted his teeth as he closed the drawstring and slung the sack over his shoulder. "But of course. It was great doing business with you, Surrly old boy. Perhaps we can help you again sometime." He turned and trudged out of the office.

As he and Riley traversed the lobby, the receptionist looked up. "Have a nice day," she said.

He gave her a thumbs-up without speaking or turning to look at her, opened the door by bumping into it, and strode out onto the sidewalk. A couple of guys brushed past and paid no heed to his bulging sack.

Riley floated beside his face. "What's wrong, Remy?"

They rounded the corner and he put the bag on the pavement once they were more sheltered from all the pedestrian traffic. "Well," he whispered, "I didn't expect my reward to be a portable rock garden. Money would have been preferable."

"Hmm." The fairy swooped down toward the payload. "Let me see."

He opened it for her, and she stuck her head in, wriggled around, and jostled the contents while her ass poked out the bottom of her dress. He looked aside and pictured Mr Surrly in skimpy lingerie.

Riley did a one-eighty, her backside now sequestered within the sack and her head out the top, and draped her hands over the edge. "Holy shit!" she exclaimed and stared at him with eyes that practically glowed.

"What?" Remy asked. "Also, I don't think I ever heard

you say 'shit' before. Maybe you really are spending too much time around humans."

"Remy," she gasped, "this is a small fortune. These aren't merely rocks, they're gems."

He cocked an eyebrow and considered the new information. "Well…that's an improvement over simply being the beginnings of nice gravel lawn. The only problem is, where do we find a place that exchanges unpolished dwarven gems for cash?"

She shrugged.

A shifty-looking fellow in a stocking cap strolled past and studied the bag. Remy glared at him and the man kept walking. The investigator picked the bag up and headed to his car.

"Riley, we have extra time today. I think we ought to pay a little visit to one of my other…er, contacts upstate."

Farmer's Market, Tuxedo, New York

Remy sighed deeply and retrieved a handkerchief as he exited the freeway. "I cannot believe I'm doing this to myself."

Riley had poked around the passenger-side cupholder where he kept his coins and now read the years on them out loud. She stopped at his comment and regarded him curiously. "Doing what?"

"Committing myself to nasal torture. I think the Inquisition used to do stuff like this to heretics." He shuddered. At least he'd stopped in Hackensack, New Jersey, bought some allergy pills on the way upstate, and taken two of them immediately to fortify his sinuses against the punishment to come.

The fairy was confused. "Why would you do that?" She dropped the dime she'd been admiring and floated to the windshield to look around.

"Because I have no choice. I'm allergic to cats." He could almost feel his nose tickling already, but it was probably merely psychosomatic suggestion. Irritably, he pushed all thoughts of feline dander from his mind.

Riley folded her arms. "Isn't this where they have the Renaissance Faire? I have cousins who took me to that once. It was great fun, actually—seeing all the drunken humans acting sensibly for once."

Remy bit his tongue to keep from barking with laughter at that. "Sensible isn't the word I'd use, but fair enough. Anyway, RenFaire is in the summer, if I recall. No, we're only going to the market."

Outside of town, he took a turn down a dirt road and his Lincoln rumbled along the muddy ruts. He'd have to go through a carwash later, he thought morosely.

They arrived at the perimeter of a rustic farmers' market. Most other humans who stumbled upon it would notice nothing even slightly odd, nor would they know that the ongoing event was hosted and managed by a peculiar commune based nearby, right on the edge of Sterling Forest State Park.

What he didn't know was how much longer they'd be open. Already, it was getting late in the year. He'd have to ask someone if they planned to shut down for the winter.

He pulled his car into an open space on the dying grass between a rusty pickup truck and a soccer-mom-esque

SUV. Then, breathing a deep breath of the air in his car—still uncontaminated by cat-filth—he clapped the handkerchief over his face and stepped outside.

It was a grey, moist, chilly kind of day, although still warm enough for him to get away with going hatless. He waited for Riley to exit the vehicle, retrieved the bag of gems, and slammed the door.

"Now," he mused, "where the hell is Ishmapps? His stand always seems to be at the complete opposite end of the market from wherever I park. I swear he does it on purpose. It's almost as if he doesn't like me."

"What?" the fairy asked. "I can't understand you with that cloth over your mouth."

He lifted a corner of it to tell her, "Don't worry. I'm talking to myself."

They pushed into the heart of the market. Remy had been there for the first time on one of his early assignments and perhaps three times since, although it had been at least a month since his last visit.

With the weather deteriorating, there were only about half as many sellers as there had been during high autumn and perhaps a third as many buyers, even with tarps to keep out the worst of the rain and cold. The smaller crowd made it easier to study the stands from a distance.

Riley grew excited as they weaved down the makeshift aisles. "Remy!" She all but panted. "They're selling organic honey over there. Ooh! And over there, sweet potato pie. I love sweet potato pie."

Afraid that the fairy was about to rocket off and try to apply the five-finger discount, he said quickly, "Yes, we'll get some, I promise."

"Really?" She beamed and her eyes were on the verge of glistening with tears of joy.

"Really. As soon as I have some actual…you know, money." He jostled the sack in his hand. "We'll pick up some honey and pie on our way out. You have my word."

She clapped her hands around the left-side base of his jaw and kissed him on the earlobe. "You're the best, Remy."

"Don't mention it," he quipped. By now, he'd noticed a few of the sellers eyeing both her and the sack with subdued curiosity. He was not alarmed, however. The farmers there looked perfectly normal but were not, in fact, human.

On the plus side, the allergy pills seemed to be working. So far, he'd had only a few tickles in his sinuses and a few half-sneezes and false alarms. Nothing catastrophic.

In the extreme rear of the market grounds, half-hidden behind a picnic table and a garbage can, he finally located Ishmapps' stand. It was little more than an end table with a few handmade trinkets atop a plain cloth covering, although he also had a portable shelf behind him that was completely covered with a light throw-rug. A locked case rested near his feet.

Before the man could notice him and try to escape, Remy jogged toward the little stand, waved with his handkerchief, and grinned with all his might. "Maps Cat!" he exclaimed.

The seller's head snapped toward the sound and his eyes blazed with an odd, yellowish vibrancy. He was a thin, gangly man in early middle age, with shoulder-length reddish hair and a short, scruffy beard of the same hue.

When he caught sight of Remy, his jaw tightened and

his shoulders slumped. "I told you never to call me that again," he snapped.

"Ha, ha, good to see you, buddy!" He laughed and pretended not to have heard. "Riley, this is Maps Cat. Maps Cat, Riley."

"Hello!" the fairy said and waved. "I thought you said his name was Ishmapps, though."

The red-haired man gritted his teeth visibly. "It is. What do you want, Remington? What's in the sack?"

"Explosives," he said. "Nah, I'm only messing with you, Maps Cat. It's dwarven gems I wanted you to have a look at. Say, your stand looks almost…empty. It's almost as if you're not really here to sell much of anything. Well, you know"—he chortled—"aside from—"

"Medicinal plants." Ishmapps cut him off. "You know that. Stop pretending to be an idiot. Humans, in their infinite wisdom, have made certain things illegal, even if they grow like any other vegetable and have well-proven health benefits. At least, for customers I can actually trust."

Remy gestured to the man and looked at Riley. "They're vegetarians, you see. All of them. The old thing about vegan pets dying of malnutrition is clearly bunk."

Maps' left eye bulged and an off-kilter, throaty yowling sound began to emerge from his mouth. "I'm not a goddamn pet, Remington."

"Whoops! Sorry," he replied. "Right. You're a farmer. But what with your long list of discerning customers, some of whom are influential in multiple industries, you strike me as the type of man who'd know how to exchange some of these things for real money." He set the bag down on the table.

Ishmapps stared at him and for a moment, his pupils were vertical slits rather than round black dots. Finally, he looked into the sack.

"Yeah," he murmured, "these are dwarven gems, all right. Valuable too. What do you expect me to do, though? I'm not a bank."

Remy glanced at the strongbox resting on the grass. "Wellllll...if you know anyone who'd buy these things you could, like, take them off my hands and give me the cash equivalent from your personal stash there."

The man's eyes narrowed again. "I need cash too, Remington. Finding a buyer might take a little while."

"Aww," he protested. "Could we trade for part of the gems? Enough for me to buy some honey, a sweet potato pie, and an office building. Please, Maps Cat. I'm counting on you."

"Stop calling me Maps Cat!" The man almost snarled the protest. For a second, it seemed that red fur covered his entire face and body and whiskers extended from his nose. Remy swore he could see a red tail swaying behind the chair as Ishmapps puffed himself up momentarily and seemed to grow larger. He hissed.

The fairy's eyes widened. "Oh, werecats! I haven't seen any of you guys in a while. I didn't know you were all vegetarians now, though."

Ishmapps returned to normal, although he still looked cantankerous.

She turned to Remy. "You're being kind of mean. Maybe he'll help us if you stop making fun of him."

He raised a finger. "On the contrary, Ishmapps deliberately stonewalled me the first time I met him, even when I tried to be polite. He only seems to cooperate when I name-drop Taylor and remind him of how displeased she'll be if he continues to act like a mangy, bad-tempered stray."

Remy planted a fist on his hip, risked the exposure of his nose and mouth to all the atmospheric werecat-dander, and stared philosophically into space. "Yes, and Taylor was saying something recently…about needing a new fur coat, wasn't it? Wait, no—she wanted a pet cat. One that had human levels of intelligence so it would be more fun to play fetch with."

Ishmapps continued to glower and he chuckled again. "The best way to do that, she said, would be to use some really, really evil magic to make sure this hypothetical smart-cat can never, ever change form and has to remain a cute widdle kitty forever—"

Maps threw his hands up and sighed in defeat. "Fine. Whatever. I'll appraise the damn gems and trade you some of them for some of my cash."

Remy smiled a cheery, glowing smile. "Great! Some of them now, you mean, and the rest later. Call me when you find a buyer. The sooner, the better."

The werecat counted the gems, estimated their weight by hefting them in his hand, and jotted numbers on a pad of notepaper. As he did so, Riley buzzed around in joy.

"Honey and sweet potato pie! Thanks, Remy."

He nodded. "Don't thank me, thank Maps Cat." Then, he sneezed.

CHAPTER FIVE

Bushwick, Brooklyn, New York

Remy almost rubbed his hands with glee. His head pivoted and his gaze darted like a bird or lizard to take in the sights of his new office. The leasing contract lay on the desk before him, and the leasing agent held a pen out.

"Actually," he told the man and snatched the pen, "before I sign, I do have a few questions."

The agent was a small, dark, wiry man who gave off a slight air of desperation, and he almost frowned. Remy could see the effort it took to maintain his game face. "Oh, right, of course. Questions. Ask away."

He stood and made a show of surveying the premises while he tapped his lips with the head of the pen. "Hmm..." He knew what he wanted to ask but stalling the guy was a good intimidation tactic. "Could we do one more quick tour? I forgot half of what you told me earlier. Sorry! I was thinking about the money."

The agent—his name was Khachaturian, he recalled—

grimaced and glanced at the nearest clock. "Yeah, fine. But do me a favor and pay attention this time, okay?"

"But of course."

They strolled through the halls and offices as the man quickly summarized the essential features of the real estate once again. Remy nodded every few seconds to show he was paying attention—which he was.

The place was almost perfect. It had stood empty for a while so it could use basic maintenance, cleaning, and perhaps redecorating, but it would serve nicely. It came with desks, chairs, functional utility infrastructure, and basic equipment like a push-chart, paper cutter, and even a nice red stapler.

There were no computers, though, but they'd probably only need one or two to start with.

"So," Khachaturian rambled on, "you'll have to contact the power company yourself, and set up—"

"I have a question," he interrupted. "To what extent would you say the doors are reinforced? Like, how much punishment could they take before being broken down?"

The man blinked. "Uh, they're steel, I know that much. I dunno if they're reinforced, though."

Remy shrugged. "Steel is better than wood. Oh, also... how many other potential entries are there? Extra routes by which someone could sneak into this place. Including air ducts and stuff like that."

Khachaturian's mouth moved for a second before any sound came out. "Only the front entrance and the fire escape. I dunno about air ducts. That seems a little far-fetched. Listen, Bushwick's safer than it used to be. It ain't exactly Chappaqua, but I mean—"

"Right, safer," he went on. "Still, what do we have here in the way of security systems? Obviously, I'd have to install one myself after the power is turned on, but are there any for the entire block?"

The agent frowned. "I'd have to call and ask the landlord. But a private system would probably be your best bet."

He chewed on the tip of the agent's pen as they walked toward one of the larger offices. "Another question. Local ordinances. What kind of rules does this neighborhood have on loud noises in the middle of the night? How…uh, fastidious are they about reporting suspicious figures prowling around?" He paused. "Oh, and are the walls bulletproof? I'm merely curious."

Khachaturian now actively squirmed. "Why are you asking me all this stuff, man? You're not planning to run some kind of illicit business here, are you? We don't want to be involved with that shit."

Pretending to be surprised by the inquiry, he protested, "Of course not. We simply deal with highly sensitive information on behalf of our clients, which might be susceptible to identity theft, blackmail, and that kind of thing. Not to mention good old-fashioned burglary since we sometimes handle large sums of money. For example…"

He fished in his pocket and produced a massive wad of banded cash and set it onto a desk in front of the agent, who stared at it.

"That," he stated, "ought to completely cover the down payment. Plus, I could be mistaken, but I believe there's a little extra, as well. Why don't you take all of it?" He smiled.

Khachaturian's thick eyebrows again rose in surprise, although of a more pleasant kind. "Yes, sir, Mr Davis."

Once he'd pocketed the money, Remy told him, "I think we're ready to sign that lease contract now."

The agent shrugged. "Okay. I hope it works out for you. Whatever problems you might have, well, the place isn't my problem anymore."

Soon, he departed, along with the signed forms, the money, and even his pen. Remy stood in the center of the lobby, basked silently in triumph, and imagined how the location would look once he was through with it.

He remembered something. "Riley," he called, "you can come out now."

A file cabinet creaked and shuffled as one of its drawers opened. Seconds later, the fairy hovered before his face.

"It's all ours now?" she asked. She'd put on a little weight after all the sweets she'd eaten recently, but it hadn't really affected her figure. If anything, she looked cuter.

"All ours," he replied. "Well, technically, we're only renting it, but close enough. Ours as long as we don't miss a payment or fuck anything up and make them come over here to actually enforce the rules."

Riley rocketed toward the ceiling and raised her arms over her head like a ballerina. "That's great." She soared around the building's interior, darted from one room to the other, circled the lobby, and swooped down the halls.

Remy quickly gave up trying to follow her and instead, sauntered into the office he'd claimed for his own. It was the second-largest—the biggest one, he assumed, would either be storage or a kind of conference room for schmoozing the clients or potential big-shot business partners.

He settled into the chair. It was a standard office-supply-shop one, serviceable for now but could stand replacing. To the left stood a black file cabinet and atop it perched a coffee mug with "World's Greatest Middle-Manager" printed across the front.

With a wide grin, he took the cup and upended it on the surface of the desk, marking it as his own. *I could get used to this. Mr Remington, Chief Operations Manager. Mr Davis, Lead Systems Analyst. Some important-sounding shit like that.*

As he sat, Riley fluttered in. "Which office will be mine?"

"Hmm." He looked around. "This one seems like a good candidate. It's also my office, but you have the advantage of not taking up much space, so we'll give you the corner." His gaze dropped to the coffee mug. "And this will be your desk. I'll see if I can find an old matchbox or something to use as a chair."

The fairy drifted to the surface, settled her rump on the upside-down mug, and leaned back so that her breasts pointed skyward. She'd crossed her legs, but uncrossing them would provide an unobstructed view of—

"I get to work with you," she purred. "In the same room, at your side. Day in, day out. In and out."

Remy swallowed a glob of saliva. "Indeed." He glanced around. "Come to think of it, this office could accommodate two human-sized persons. At least for half an hour or so. Better yet, an hour. Fuck, I forgot to ask that agent if the walls were soundproofed."

Riley only half-comprehended him. She'd turned and

now pushed the cup so it sat directly between Remy's chair and the doorway. Her buttocks swelled nicely beneath the hem of her dress.

In the same moment, he remembered that he'd promised Taylor he'd call her about the new office. Sucking in air, he made himself imagine the floor giving way beneath his chair to plummet him into the waters of New York Harbor. Which, at this time of year, would be damned cold.

Focus returned. He pulled his cell phone from his pocket.

"Hey," Riley said, "don't you want to help me set my desk up?"

He waved a hand. "In a minute. I have to be a good business partner."

No sooner had he said this than the front door to the building opened.

Tense with alarm, Remy bolted to his feet, thankful that the collapsing-floor daydream had worked. He emerged from his chosen office and sidestepped down the hall toward the lobby and the entrance. Footsteps moved steadily closer to him.

He rounded the corner and gaped at his partner.

"Taylor," he gasped and ran a hand through his hair. "Jesus. I was worried we were already being robbed, or suicide-bombed, or whatever. I was about to call you."

The woman wore sunglasses and a black hat and scarf, he saw. In order to have arrived here this soon after dark, she would have had to leave her house well before twilight. He'd never seen her do that before.

She nodded to him and strode past, her black clothes

swishing lightly in the air. Aloof and purposeful, she barely even bothered to examine the place as she traversed it. He almost wondered if she'd been there before—she certainly acted as though she already owned it.

"This will do," she proclaimed over her shoulder. "I'll see you in my office in five minutes." She made a beeline for the largest office in the back corner, stepped into it, and closed the door.

Remy sighed. So much for his conference room idea. He noted the time—6:26—and returned to his office, determined to play along and wait exactly five minutes.

The fairy stared in bug-eyed surprise when he arrived. "How did she get here so fast?" she wondered.

"Hell if I know," he replied. "She must have set an alarm clock and put on a ton of sunscreen. At least we get to keep this office for ourselves."

At 6:31, he stood outside the large office, knocked on the door, and waited for a response.

"Come in," Taylor said after ten or twelve seconds.

He turned the knob and entered. His partner had already ensconced herself behind the large, black desk in the rear-center of the room.

She gestured to a simple, uncomfortable-looking wooden chair in the corner with a red-nailed hand. "Have a seat."

Remy grabbed the chair, carried it to the middle of the office, and sat across from her. "Well," he began, "I didn't have time to set us up with coffee machines yet, so I'm afraid I can't wait for you to offer me some and then accept."

The vampire almost smiled. "There will be more than

enough time for small luxuries. Assuming, of course, that we can actually afford this in the long run." She folded her slender hands before her.

"Aha," he said and raised a finger. "You wanted to talk business, specifically finances. Little did you realize that you haven't caught me unawares in that regard, even if I expected another hour or two before you arrived. You didn't get sunburned, did you?"

"Not really," she responded, "although I do hate driving when the sun is out. Of course, I might not have had to if you'd gone with your original idea of leasing an office in Yonkers. You must have been offered an excellent deal on this office to tolerate it being all the way down in Brooklyn."

"As I was about to say," he shot back and adjusted his cuff links, "I did get a good deal, and I've already crunched most of the numbers." He grinned.

Taylor nodded. "Let's hear the crunching, then."

Remy obliged with alacrity. This was his time to shine, and it quickly became apparent that he was impressing her. He suspected that she wanted to find fault with his math, his logic, or his business instincts, but he refused to make it easy for her.

Instead, he quickly recited all the figures he'd memorized and patterned the whole spiel on business pitches he'd overheard from his parents. He rattled off how much extra the agency would have to bring in to compensate for the cost of the office, how much income potential they were looking at for taking on only one mortal client per week, and the overall six-month growth projection for the business.

Taylor interrupted him. "Didn't you also say something about hiring a team?"

"Yes," he replied. "A receptionist is a necessity, really. You and I will be out on cases all the time, so someone has to hold the fort and deal with prospective clients, not to mention janitorial services and certified letters and all that crap. I've already included the labor cost in my estimate of how much we'll pay for the office, based on the current competitive average for white-collar employees in the Greater New York City area."

She was smiling pleasantly when he came to the end of his explanation. "You've done your homework. You might have even taught me a thing or two."

He accepted the compliment with a curt nod. "I suppose that, over the years, I absorbed more than I thought." He shrugged. "Spending one's entire childhood seated at a dinner table with rich people who always discuss money, one naturally picks up some of the knowledge, whether one wanted it at the time or not."

"Of course," agreed the vampire. "At my family's table, the most commonly discussed subject was war. The older aristocracy differed from the present one. In some regards, at least."

For some reason, that made him uncomfortable. She had never revealed exactly how old she was, and he wondered which wars her family had presided over. The Catholic-Protestant conflicts of the sixteenth and seventeenth centuries? The Wars of the Roses? The goddamn Crusades?

"Right," was all he said. "The Dow Jones Industrial Average is truly mightier than the sword."

She ignored the quip. "Remington," she asked and her demeanor grew darkly serious again, "have you noticed anything unusual in the last few days? Particularly since I put you on the Surrly case. Has anyone weird approached you? Anything?"

The past week had been a flurry of activity, but his brain had been in overdrive and he seemed to remember almost all the details. "No weirder than usual. I'm still new enough to all this preternatural stuff that my definitions might not be identical to yours but nothing stands out as really bizarre or sinister."

"I see." She closed her eyes briefly while her mind computed the information.

When she opened them again, they fixed on him and held him in place. "I want you to take the rest of the money you get from those gems and spend some time flashing it around the city. Spend it. Behave like your old self again—a real wealthy playboy."

Remy leaned back. His brow pinched in confusion. "That's rather an odd request. I'd ask if you're telling me to take a vacation, relax, and enjoy life more but I know that's not what you mean. This is some strategy of yours. May I ask what you hope to accomplish by having me toss hundred-dollar bills at cocktail waitresses and limo drivers?"

Taylor's face shifted subtly and she now looked almost concerned. "Let us say that you are half right. You have been working very hard lately and would benefit from having a little more fun."

"Fair enough." He ran a finger under his collar.

"But," she went on, and for only a second, she hesitated.

He perceived, somehow, that she'd stalled him for time and had only now thought of what to say. "There is also the matter of that obnoxious reporter, Ocren. If she's following you and you simply act like your old self, then that's not too suspicious. Business as usual. Again, we don't want attention from the press."

He nodded slowly. "That sounds sensible, in a way. But why do I have the impression that you're trying to avoid telling me something?"

A ripple of tension went through her. He'd struck a nerve, perhaps—or, maybe, she merely debated whether to continue arguing with him like a human or whether she ought to put an immediate end to his insubordination using her vampiric powers.

Remy did not relish the prospect of being compelled like a zombie. But something wasn't right and he decided to push his luck.

"So," he drawled, "you want me to act like my old, trust-fundy self. It will make me less suspicious to the media. Fair enough. But it will make me more visible in general. And since I started working with you...well, there are some creatures who probably don't like me very much. What kinds of potential threats can I expect from them?"

Taylor was stony-faced. "Little, if any. Thanks to my governance of the New York City area being preserved after Gabriel's little coup attempt, the rules are still very much in place. Preternaturals are not to harm or exploit humans. Then again, there is some gray area when it comes to humans who actually interact with the preternatural. So, it will behoove you to be cautious."

He laughed softly. "Cautious is my middle name. Wait,

no, it isn't. I could try it as a pseudonym, though. Still, what you said is awfully...vague. Do you have any information on specific parties who might be interested in me?"

It seemed clear that he was getting to her and that she was on the verge of simply commanding him to leave, yet for some reason, she didn't want to do this. He was narrowing down the range of her potential evasions.

She continued the charade, though. "You don't need to know about any specific parties, but I will say that someone might approach you with an odd set of requests or suggestions. It's very unlikely you'd be attacked. But if anything strange happens—anything at all—inform me immediately."

Somewhere in Remy's mind, a mechanism snapped into place. This was it—as close as he would get to outright confirmation of what he suspected. Now was the time to lay all the cards on the table and see how she reacted.

"I'm bait," he stated. "Exactly as I suspected. You're using me to lure someone out. Someone who couldn't resist approaching a man who has experience in both the preternatural world and New York high society. Gosh, I only hope nothing happens to me in the line of duty before you swoop in to make everything all better."

A subtle ripple of tension went through the woman, and her eyes sharpened. Then, she relaxed and for a moment, he even thought she might sigh with resignation.

"David," she said, "I don't want any harm to come to you. It's easier to draw someone out when you're not aware of what you're doing. I can see there's no way to fool you, however, unless I use compulsion or mindwipe, and I don't want to do either."

He pursed his lips. "Well, that's nice to hear."

"I will brief you on the situation." The corners of her mouth turned downward. "Don't make me regret doing so." She leaned back in her chair. "I have been tracking a certain figure in Israel…someone powerful and likely a fellow vampire. My kind don't get along with one another. We're territorial—like cats, you might say. This individual has made large, bold moves. And those with global ambitions always make their way to New York eventually."

Remy smirked. "So that's why I was born here, to begin with."

Taylor went on without missing a beat. "This vampire already has their fingers in several money-filled pots. Specifically, those linked to wealthy families who have…'problem children' and very loose pockets." She shrugged awkwardly, which was not like her at all. "That makes you the perfect lure."

He didn't speak at first. Somehow, he didn't consider it an honor to be regarded as ideal bait.

"So," he said finally, "how long have you tracked this mysterious Israeli vampire?"

"Months."

He nodded. "And how long, exactly, have you planned to use me as your lure?"

Something in her eyes hardened a little, although for the most part, her poker-face was intact. "The same number of months, approximately."

For whatever reason, that statement finally pounded like a punch in his gut. He blew the air out of his lungs and put a hand over his eyes. "Let me guess," he began, "this time period is also the same number of months I've worked for the agency. For fuck's sake."

Taylor actually sighed now. "Yes, Remington, you are an astute observer. And I mean that. You have the makings of a fine detective. I was already aware of our rival when I replied to your original inquiry about the company and arranged for us to meet at the Sotto Suolo. It's true I needed help with the workload and had considered expanding the business, but…yes, that was my original motivation. I have to do what I have to do, David. The world is a dangerous place. And sometimes, I must do questionable things in order to stop other people, or entities, from doing things that are even worse."

"Oh," Remy replied in a deadpan monotone. "Questionable. Yes."

Her eyes drooped slightly, and he realized that she truly looked…sad. Regretful, even. In the time he'd known her, it had never occurred to him that she might experience legitimate pangs of guilt or wistful sorrow.

Somehow, that merely made him angrier. His hands clenched into fists and his teeth ground together.

"David," she went on, "I'm sorry. That was my thinking at first. But despite your quirks, you've been a boon to me —professionally and perhaps even personally. I…feel like I've begun to break out of my shell. Please understand that—"

The sound of his chair scraping the floor as he pushed it back cut her off. He rose to his feet.

"Well," he said sharply, "I'd better get back to work. I have considerable shit to do. Money to spend and all. Very nice talking to you, Taylor."

Remy spun and stormed toward the door. He yanked it open and slammed it shut behind him. He'd felt Taylor's gaze on his back the whole time.

"David!" she called. He ignored her.

A few steps beyond the office door, Riley wafted up, her tiny eyes wide with concern. "What's wrong?" she asked.

"Bait duty." He adjusted his tie. "I'd better get on it. I'll need to get the rest of my cash stores out of the bank until Maps Cat comes through with the rest. Come along, and I'll show you how a Remington wastes money."

His grating tone of voice must have indicated that he wasn't particularly jubilant about this since Riley, to his surprise, did not cheer, nor ask him what he planned to buy her. They strode from the building together in silence.

CHAPTER SIX

Tenor Extended Stay Hotel, Queens, New York

Alexander Thomas was not a happy man.

Something bumped against the wall to his left and the thudding impact rattled the thin walls and created a shower of fine, powdery dust and plaster. A woman giggled and a man said something in a slurred tone, possibly not in English. Alex wasn't quite sure. With Americans, it was hard to tell.

He ignored it, though. Since he'd arrived, all kinds of the city's flotsam and jetsam had drifted through the rooms adjacent to his, sometimes minding their manners but more often than not leaving the place even worse than how they'd found it.

Which was an accomplishment, since this motel was already about as seedy as it got.

He paced constantly. "She's practically a queen or something," he grumbled under his breath and his hands clenched around each other behind his back while his feet maintained the steady pounding rhythm. "She's rich. You'd think she could afford to put me up somewhere nice, for God's sake."

As if in reply to his muttered complaint, the couple in the room to the left clicked a lighter and made sucking sounds, accompanied by the gurglings of dirty water at the bottom of some mysterious glass device.

"So classy." He drank tap water from a cheap Styrofoam cup. "At least it's been, what? Four days since the last time the police stopped by. That's encouraging."

While it still seemed unlikely given what he'd experienced, he'd heard and read that New York was far cleaner and safer these days than it had once been. Only a generation or two before, the city was often spoken of in almost apocalyptic terms. Sometime in the 1990s, it had begun to make a recovery.

And yet, Alex had also heard and read that Melbourne was recently ranked fifth on a list of the world's safest major cities. By contrast with his hometown, the Big Apple still seemed seedier and more dangerous than anything he was used to.

The fact that he was forced to huddle in this squalid place was merely one of many things feeding the vendetta that slowly swelled within him.

"Oh," he breathed, "I'm a loyal, loyal servant, make no mistake." He thought of the mark on his chest. "I would never dream of resenting the tasks imposed upon me by my glorious mistress. In her great wisdom, she knows exactly what I should be doing with myself at any given moment of the day. Or night."

But he knew things, too.

In the course of his service to the vampire Moswen

Neith, he had learned that she was not one of a kind. There were other creatures like her in the world, other entities whose existence was not even acknowledged by modern science or mainstream society.

Some of those might even be her equals in power. Some of them might be curious to know about her revival—and might even be willing to cut the leash she'd placed on Alex in exchange for that information.

Suddenly, his chest exploded in pain. His eyes bulged and the breath thrust from his lungs. It was as though someone had pressed a heated clothes-iron over his heart.

"Fuck!" He gasped, doubled over, and noted the faint golden glow that now emanated from the brand of ownership placed upon him. His teeth gritted, he sweated in agony and tried to purify his mind of any semblance of treason. This had happened before.

The phone rang—the landline phone that came with the room, specifically. It was so strange to hear its rambling, mechanical, slightly echoing racket in this day and age of digitized musical ringtones.

Alex's gaze snapped toward the archaic device. The pain in his chest faded to nothing as quickly as it had begun, but his tension hadn't diminished at all and fear had taken the place of pain. His mouth was dry and the palms of his hands wet. Since the beginning of this nightmare, he'd stopped believing in coincidences.

He extended a hand, picked up the receiver, and raised it to his ear. "Yes?"

"Alex," a female voice said. Somehow, it was both dusty and raspy on the one hand but rich and smooth on the other. She enunciated both syllables of his name with great care.

"Yes, mistress?" He swallowed the growing lump in his throat.

"I wish to hear your report upon your progress," Moswen instructed.

She had rapidly been learning English since her awakening and was mostly fluent by now, although she'd never be able to pass for a native speaker by the standards of any of the Anglophone countries.

"It seems," she went on, "that in all this time, your thoughts may have...wandered. I wish to return your focus to your servitude to me. Your mind should not wander into foolish places."

Alex's head slumped. Instead of a burning sensation in his chest, he now felt something like ice-cold acid pooling in his stomach. Thanks to the mark, he was reasonably sure the bitch could read his mind.

"Yes, mistress, I remain loyal and devoted to your cause." He sighed. "As for my progress, that task is done."

There was silence on the other end of the line for a few seconds before she spoke again. "Tell me more."

He hoped no one was listening in on this line, although he wouldn't be shocked if Moswen had some way to protect her communications from prying ears.

"I killed the dwarves," he explained. "They're all dead, with no survivors. And I made it good and messy, as you requested. The sheer brutality ought to send a clear message, I'd say. The Americans are used to people being shot left and right, but as soon as someone is ripped to shreds, they lose their minds."

"Good," she acknowledged, and there was a cruel satisfaction in her voice now that chilled him to the bone and beyond.

"Yeah. So..." He took a deep breath. "With that done, can I come home now? You never specifically said I had anything else to do here or that I had to stay after—"

"No." She cut him off. "You are to remain where you are. Your pledge of loyalty is unconditional. If I tell you to return to Israel and change my mind while you are flying back, you must leap from the plane and swim back to New York, if that is my will. Do you understand?"

Alex clenched his jaw but tried to empty his head of seditious ideas. "Perfectly, mistress."

"Good. This New York seems to be one of the present world's greatest cities—a center of tremendous wealth and influence. That means it is also a place of great power."

He nodded out of habit. "True enough. Not as nice as Melbourne, though. Then again, most cities aren't."

"Be quiet," Moswen snapped and he flinched. She went on. "I wish for you to spend time in this city and learn who are the most influential among the...what is the word they use?"

"Preternaturals," he replied. "They seem to think that supernatural would be bad for public relations."

Moswen paused, probably to inscribe the word in her brain for future usage. "Once you have identified the most important preternaturals among the community there," she continued, "you are to deal with them on my behalf."

Alex did not like the sound of that. "Mistress," he retorted, "I am devoted to carrying out your will, but is there any chance you could clarify that statement? Are you asking me to literally make deals with them, or euphemistically ordering me to kill them? It would be helpful to know."

"If," she countered, "you determine that they would be willing to accept me as their rightful superior, you may negotiate terms. I will accept tribute and pledges of loyalty. If they are not willing, destroy them. Either way, I will have this city. The great centers of wealth and power are the birthright of the powerful, and none who exist in our world today can match me. Those who fail to acknowledge this shall be punished. Do you understand?"

"Of course," he said. "Absolutely—definitely. You'll be pleased to know I already have a few leads, you might say. Names have been dropped. I can tell who the big players seem to be, the ones whom the little spackers serving as their underlings regard with fear and awe. The easiest way to get to them is probably through their human intermediaries." He almost clammed up momentarily as the brutal irony of this statement struck him. "That seems to be the way of things, doesn't it?"

He could almost hear her smirk through the phone. "It is well for you," she intoned, "that you do understand. Now, go. I will contact you again soon to hear how you have done. And remember your vow."

The phone clicked and went dead, the sound somehow as heavy and pitiless as the closing of a coffin's lid.

Alex hung up the receiver and stared at the phone. "Oh, I remember. It's fucking difficult not to, isn't it?"

For a moment or two, his thoughts slipped beyond the control of his conscious will.

They turned themselves over within his brain and

drifted to that awful day at the temple in the Negev and how happy and excited he'd been to participate in the excavation. How he'd leapt, oh so quickly, at that opportunity instead of doing something smart—like waiting another year until he could have gone, instead, to Peru or Ethiopia or Xinjiang. Anywhere but that accursed ruin in Israel.

He'd been lucky to be the only survivor of the massacre but he did not feel particularly fortunate. The only good thing about still being alive was that there was still the chance, however slim, that he might be able to escape.

All this internal dialogue emanated from his mind over the course of only a second or two, but that was enough to inflame the mark upon his chest.

"Shit!" He grimaced and clamped his hand on his torso when suddenly, it felt again like someone had stabbed him in the ribs with a hot poker.

In the next moment, it faded and was gone.

Alex collapsed on the bed and covered his face with one of the spare pillows to muffle the sounds of the potheads in the next room. They blathered and thumped around and he half-hoped that he might accidentally smother himself in his sleep.

He forced his thoughts to turn, instead, to the tasks at hand. They would not be easy.

"Yes, mistress," he muttered into the pillow. "I obey."

Por's Bar, Lower Manhattan, New York

The bartender climbed the wooden beam he'd installed to give himself access to his customers. With his small hands, he carefully set a cocktail glass filled with a wet martini down on the wooden surface before the man who called himself Remington Davis.

"There ya go, buddy," he grunted and hopped down to the floor to begin work on a lemon shandy for another patron.

Remy took the glass by its stem. "Thanks, Por. This is my third, isn't it? In any event, we'll say it's my last for tonight. I have a big day tomorrow and all." He raised it to his lips and downed about a third of the beverage in one swig.

"Whatever you say, pal," Porrillage called over his shoulder. "But keep an eye on your tab."

He paid no heed to this comment and sipped the remainder of the vodka and vermouth. His gaze lingered on the bartender as he drank.

On the off chance that an uninitiated normal person found this bar and wandered into it, they'd likely assume that Por was simply a little person. One had to look closely and have an open mind to the preternatural to discern that he was a gnome. It seemed to have something to do with the shape of his ears and the texture of his skin. His attitude was quite ordinary.

"Well, Por," Remy said, "I thought things were going better at the agency lately, but of course, I was wrong. Once again, things are headed back into the proverbial shitter." He swished the liquid in his glass.

The gnome raised an eyebrow but didn't look at him. He climbed onto the beam and pushed a shandy across to the morose-looking elven women who'd entered. "Is that a fact, Mr Remington?"

"Yes," the young man responded instantly. "Taylor still

doesn't have much faith in me except as a kind of patsy or something. Even after everything I did for her during the business with the coffin thieves breaking into her house and shit."

Por had a brief, inaudible conversation with the bar's waitress, who was tending to the patrons out on the floor. Once they were done and the woman hurried off, the gnome turned back to him.

"Didn't you say before that she wasn't actually in real danger there, and your heroics ended up mainly tying off some loose ends or something?" He had planted his fists on his squat hips and now looked at the human with a skeptical squint.

Remy swiped a hand through the air. "That's not the point. The point is, I demonstrated tremendous amounts of courage, daring, determination, skill, and so forth, and all of it because it seemed like she was in danger. And how do you suppose she thanked me? Well, uh...she did say thanks. But what do you suppose she told me about what her next big purpose for me is?"

"I dunno," Por threw back as he turned to rearrange some of his materials. "Gigolo work, maybe?"

Oh, I wish, he thought but did not say it out loud.

Instead, he explained, "No, she wants to use me as bait. Apparently, that's the main reason she brought me into the company, to begin with. That's even worse than hiring a female graduate with a PhD because she has nice boobs. It's a complete and utter waste of my talents."

"Huh." The gnome quipped, "I always assumed Taylor as a good judge of people's character and abilities. I guess even she can make mistakes though." He coughed.

He sipped his drink. "Absolutely. Over the course of however many centuries she's been around, she's been able to accumulate considerable skills and she's a smart lady, I'll grant her that. But no one's perfect. I'm in the process of trying to grow our business, so I've already demonstrated that my capabilities go beyond simply being her fishing lure."

Porrillage peeked out beyond the bar itself to scan the floor for anything that might require his attention. Business tonight was moderate and the crowd didn't seem too rowdy.

The gnome turned his attention to Remy again when he returned to his workstation. "I dunno there, Rem. It sounds like maybe you have too much on your plate at once. If Taylor wants you to draw out some enemy of hers, she has a good reason for it. It sounds dangerous, though. Are you sure you should be worried about expanding the business when you have something like that to focus on? If I were you, I'd take it one thing at a time." He grimaced.

So what he's saying is that the only way to impress Taylor enough that she'll let me focus on growing the business is if I go balls-to-the-wall with the conspicuous consumption and asshole playboy routine. Yes, it makes perfect sense.

"Por," he proclaimed and slapped a hand on the bar, "you're right. What I need to do is further prove that I can expand the agency's reach—and more importantly, demonstrate that I can kick ass with the best of them even when she has me on some dangerous, important duty I'm barely qualified for. But one thing at a time. Now, I merely need to remember which I ought to do first."

Remy barely noticed as he completed his final sentence

that the door had opened and another customer walked in. Now, the individual took a seat on the stool to Remy's right.

He glanced over. The newcomer was a tall, rangy, older man, although his posture was somewhat stooped, which made him appear shorter. He wore faded trousers and a brown trench coat that he'd probably purchased around the beginning of the Iraq War. Gray streaks were marbled all through his medium-length, unkempt hair and bristly beard stubble. His face was long and haggard.

"Evening," the man stated to no one in particular. He creaked and gasped as he attempted to make himself comfortable on the wooden stool.

Por glanced at him. "Hi, stranger. What'll it be?"

The crusty man made a low, ragged sound in his throat as he seemed to think about it. "Single whiskey, on the rocks, if you would, please."

"No problem." The gnome turned to his glasses and rapidly assembled the simple drink.

Remy had almost finished his own. The newcomer smelled a little ripe, so he was thankful for the excuse to leave post-haste. He drained the last of his martini and set the glass on the counter.

When he pivoted to climb down from his stool, the old man turned to him and spoke. "David Remington. I thought I might find you here. I've looked forward to the opportunity to finally meet you."

He paused and frowned at the fellow. "Do I know you or something?" Dimly, it occurred to him that this might be one of the suspicious characters whom Taylor had told him to keep an eye out for.

"Not yet," the man said with a pinched smile. He started to reach into his coat.

Remy slid off his stool and onto his feet and backed away slowly, his body tense and his hands raised to protect his chest and face.

"No, no." The man sighed. "It's only my business card. Relax, my friend."

Now that he could see the man's coat more clearly—courtesy of a shaft of light from above the bar—and there were no suspicious, weapon-like bulges. The man put two fingers and a thumb into an interior pocket and produced a laminated card, as promised.

He took it cautiously and examined it.

"Don Gannon." The newcomer introduced himself.

Remy could have read that himself. He also read, below the name, the fascinating information that the man was a reporter for The New England Inquirer.

A groan of exasperation worked its way out of his mouth even before his somewhat buzzed mind could contemplate how diplomatic he ought to be. "Oh, for God's sake. You people again."

"Don't worry," Don reassured him and took the card. "I'm not here to harass you with questions about your recent exploits. Not exactly. Rather, I have an offer of sorts that you might find interesting. Have a seat again and listen, Mr Remington."

The young man had to admit he was curious now. He repositioned himself on the stool as Por cast a sidelong glance at both men. The elven woman two seats to the left ignored them and sipped her barely alcoholic shandy.

Remy wondered if this Gannon guy could even tell that she was an elf.

"So," Don began, "yes, I'm with the Inquirer, and I can understand why you'd be less than happy with us. But hear me out. Things were not always as they are now."

"Ah," he said, "you wanted to reminisce about the good old days."

His companion shrugged. "In a way. You see, I used to be the paper's star reporter. I delved into things that received more extensive coverage by the so-called respectable press, not to mention a few things that the mainstream papers refused to cover. But the people ought to know regardless, even if only from a small publication like ours."

Porrillage placed the man's whiskey in front of him. He raised it, drank a good-sized mouthful, and crunched one of the ice cubes before he set the glass down.

"But," Gannon went on and returned his focus to the younger man, "I'm old now. I don't have the energy I used to, and my goddamn joints hurt too much to go literally chasing after leads. I can't keep ahead of the game these days and have the best stories scooped out from under me by the young upstarts like Jenny Ocren."

At the mere mention of her name, he pivoted toward the bartender.

"Por!" he shouted. "Another martini. And please hurry. This is an emergency." His teeth ground together as the gnome grumbled and reached for the vodka.

Don took another swig of his own refreshment before he continued. "So, then, Remington. What I'd like to propose is a deal. An exchange of information, to be precise. We can help each other. If you, in the course of whatever strange business it is you seem to be involved in, come across anything…interesting…that might make a good Inquirer story, you tip me off as soon as possible."

Por set the martini on the bar. Remy snatched it immediately and gulped. "Yeah," he muttered, "and what would I get in return as part of this hypothetical deal? Which, by the way, I haven't actually agreed to yet."

"Information," the reporter said. "Over the course of a long career in investigative journalism, you see, I've built up quite the list of contacts. I know most of what goes on in this city, even if I'm not as fast on the trigger these days. I know things, Remington—things you might also benefit from knowing. Information for information, a fair exchange, if you ask me."

Remy drank a little more and almost emptied his glass. The woozy rush made him feel slightly better about the whole Jenny Ocren thing. If he was lucky, he might even kill the brain cells responsible for remembering that she existed.

"Well, Don," he replied, "that does indeed sound fair. I'm not decided yet, though, since it also sounds like it might be a potential hassle and could involve the kinds of risks that my employer—er, partner—doesn't want to take. Still, I'll think about it."

Gannon smiled in an almost wistful way. "Please do." He pulled a pen from his pocket and wrote something on the dry part of his cocktail napkin. "Here's my number. Call me if you turn up a good lead or even if you only want to ask me a question. Leave a message if I don't answer. I promise it won't be long before I get back to you."

Remy accepted the napkin and stuffed it into his pocket. "Thanks." He finished his beverage and pushed the glass away. "I think it's time I called it a night, though. I'm dangerously close to the point where I'll be able to tell in the morning that I'd been drinking."

Don extended a hand. "Good to meet you, sir."

He gave it a cursory shake and noticed with something close to surprise that the old man still had a strong grip. He half-slid and half-hopped down from his stool, wobbled for a second, and turned away. "Por, don't do anything I wouldn't do. And yes, my tab will be taken care of directly. You know how reliable I am."

The gnome almost chuckled. "Have a nice night there, buddy."

Remy took two steps toward the door before he stopped. An idea had come to him, intruded upon his contented haze, and sharpened the edges of his thoughts. He turned toward Gannon.

"Don," he called. "How much does it cost to take an ad out in the Inquirer, anyway?"

CHAPTER SEVEN

Bushwick, Brooklyn, New York

Remy's index finger hovered over the page, seeking the line he'd last been on.

"M...kay," he said, "uh, that's four hundred fifty-four point seven eight, as of, let's see, eleven-fourteen, twenty-twenty..."

He cross-referenced the number from the invoice against what was recorded in their bank statements. So far, everything was kosher.

"You know," he said aloud, mostly to himself, "it's amazing that the IRS hasn't shown up on our doorstep by now. Usually, small businesses—especially ones that try to operate in semi-secrecy—have those assholes knocking on their door sooner rather than later. Granted, our paper-work seems to be in order. But still."

It occurred to him that perhaps, at some indeterminate point before he had ever met Taylor, the IRS had shown up only for her to have "dealt" with them.

He shuddered. As unpleasant as the government's tax-henchmen were, he didn't relish the notion of much of anyone being on the receiving end of her wrath.

"Then again," he mused, "she has that weird power to make people do whatever she says using that one tone of voice. I would think that even federal employees would have enough of a human soul to be moved by magic of that caliber."

It made sense, the more he thought about it. Far too many people with big guns and big connections would get suspicious if a number of IRS guys turned up dead. Simply using a Jedi Mind Trick on the tax collectors to get them to stop asking bothersome questions seemed much smarter.

Riley, meanwhile, was seated at her own "desk" made from the upturned coffee cup. Earlier, as he worked through the company's accounts and receipts and other such tedious documents, she had watched with curious eyes to get a feel for the process of accounting and had asked pointed questions here and there.

Now, at least, she had seemingly moved on to doing some accounting of her own. Her soft voice was barely audible even with him right beside her. "Sixteen... Seventeen..." She took a fragment of a once-round peppermint candy off the general pile and added it to the peppermint section.

The fairy was making good progress. The generalized heap of tiny sweets on the left had shrunk to about half its original size and to her right, multiple smaller and more organized piles were growing. Not only peppermint chunks, but also individual Skittles, pieces of chocolate bars, and candied peanuts were all now subject to a thorough inventory process.

Watching the fairy at her low-tech work, Remy sighed. They really needed to set computers up in there, and sooner rather than later.

The front door opened and footsteps entered the building. He perked up, slightly apprehensive but mostly curious. Whoever it was, they definitely wore high heels, judging by the clacking sound their footwear made against the floor.

He almost rose from his desk but stayed where he was when it became apparent that the visitor moved directly toward his office. The heels stopped outside his door and a fist rapped against it. "Hello?"

Remy glanced at Riley and made a fluttering motion with his hand. She scowled at him but obeyed and flitted away to hide in the narrow gap behind a file cabinet.

"Hi," he said to the door. "You may come in."

The knob turned and a woman stepped through. His eyes widened.

She was probably in her late twenties and possibly Puerto Rican, although with shoulder-length blonde hair and green eyes half-hidden by huge black lashes. She wore a green dress, low-cut up top and about knee-length at bottom, along with matching heels, and carried a brown pleather purse.

Her most striking features, though—two of them—were located between her shoulders and her abdomen.

"Hello," the woman said again in a voice that sounded like a teenager's, although huskier.

He blinked, cleared his throat, and forced his eyes upward to the new arrival's face. "Uh…" he began and cleared his throat again. "Hello there, ma'am. Can I help you?"

"Yes." She smiled. "I'm here replying to the ad about needing a secretary?"

Remy had momentarily forgotten that he might receive applicants any day now and would therefore have to conduct proper interviews. "Oh, great…perfect, yeah. Pull up a chair and have a seat." He gestured and smiled.

The woman pushed an extra chair away from its place against the side wall and toward his desk. He tried not to wince at the scraping sound and hoped she hadn't damaged the floor.

She sat, crossed her legs, and fluffed her hair. Her cleavage was directly in front of his field of vision and commanded his full attention.

"So," she said. "Hi. My name is Roberta Diaz. You can call me Bobby, though. Everyone else does." She laughed and extended a slender hand.

He stretched across the desk and took it, again struggling to keep his eyes level with her own. "Nice to meet you, Roberta. Or Bobby. I'm Remington Davis, Vice President and senior co-agent here at Moonlight Detective Agency."

For now, he decided not to mention that everyone called him Remy. In his mind, it didn't sound professional.

"Hello, Mr Davis." She returned the smile. "So, yeah. I have references, and of course I also wanted you to tell me, like, what duties I'd need to perform. I have some experience with this type of thing, so I bet I'd be perfect."

Remy nodded as he tried to organize his thoughts. There was a slim chance that what Ms Diaz had said about experience was some kind of coded signal about the preternatural...but probably not. She didn't come across as all that bright.

"That is possible," was all he said. "You say you've run a reception desk before? May I see your references?"

She continued to smile as she opened the flap of her purse. "Yeah, sure. Oh, crap." She withdrew a manila folder and seemed surprised to discover that it was bent at the center.

Her smile faded. "I didn't think it would crease. I didn't really fold it, only kind of rolled it a little to fit it in my purse. Something must have jostled it—people bumping into me and stuff. Sorry!"

He chose not to comment on that. Instead, he accepted the folder, flipped it open, and thumbed through the references and work-history documents. Bobby had indeed held several receptionist jobs.

"Hmm." He rubbed his chin. "This looks good, for the most part, but it says here that you were dismissed from your position at the university office. May I ask why that was?"

Her head moved down a notch and her shoulders up as she cringed in slight embarrassment. "Oh, yeah. I guess you could say I misjudged my audience a little in that case. Ha, ha. I would have thought a science department would have more open minds."

Remy arched an eyebrow. "Go on. I'm curious."

"Well," Roberta began and re-crossed her legs. "They said I was weirding out the staff and students because I kept talking about things you'd think they ought to be curious about. You know, mysterious stuff—the paranormal and supernatural and all that. Sure, some people think it's...uh, BS, but maybe that's only because it hasn't been investigated properly yet, right?"

With a slow, underwater-like motion, he nodded. "Yeah...you might be onto something there, Bobby." He scooched forward an inch or two in his seat and leaned toward her across the desk. "Tell me, do you know what it is we do here?"

"Kinda," she answered him. "The ad said you guys do private investigations for clients who want good discretion. So, like, I guess confidentiality agreements and whatnot. I have no problem with any of that. My aunt hired an agency once to see if my uncle was cheating on her." She paused and squinted as she looked around. "Can I chew gum in here?"

"Certainly," he said. "Wrap it and put it in the trash when you're done."

She withdrew a stick of gum from the purse, unwrapped it, and popped it into her mouth. "I guess I'd have to deal with the walk-ins and take the phone calls and stuff, so you wouldn't have to clue me in on all the gruesome details, anyway, if it's too sensitive. At the university, they said I was fantastic at that kind of thing but they didn't feel I was a good fit for their 'culture of inquiry.' Even though I inquired about stuff all the time."

"Right," Remy concurred. "Those academic types have a somewhat narrow definition of inquiry. So, if I may ask, where do you get your information on all these...paranormal subjects?"

She made an excited "ooh" sound and dived into her purse to surface again with a rolled-up newspaper.

"Right here," she announced. "The New England Inquirer. Mostly, it's stuff about local celebrities, but in every issue, they have a column about unexplained occurrences. Like when that rat the size of a pit bull came out of the sewers? They had one of their science guys test the water trail the thing left behind. It was full of chemicals he traced all the way back to the Pentagon."

"Wow," he droned. "Fascinating. I didn't hear about that, but it definitely sounds like something a university science department ought to look into more."

"That's exactly what I said," Bobby responded and almost bolted from her seat in her enthusiasm. "Someone ought to request a grant for stuff like this. We might have government bio-weapons living right under our streets. And then there's all the stuff with remote viewing and how they're trying to weaponize auras…"

Remy continued to nod until she momentarily ran out of steam. He injected another question.

"So, Roberta…clearly, you're the curious, observant type. Now, we don't want you getting too curious since we respect the privacy of our clients, but overall, I'd say those are desirable qualities."

He paused for effect and the woman smiled with pride.

"Since you pay so much attention to the preternatural," he went on, "does that mean you could tell if an alien craft was buried under this building? Or if it was haunted? Or if a fairy was hiding behind that file cabinet over there? This place seems to have something of a reputation, honestly. That might be why we got such a good deal on it. I haven't seen any ghosts myself yet, but it might be useful if someone else were alert to things like that."

She'd ceased chewing her gum and her mouth had dropped open. Her eyes were wide and enthralled.

"Holy crap," she blurted. "That's really interesting. But...uh, no, this place seems perfectly normal to me so far. I'll keep that in mind, though."

Remy leaned back in his chair. "That's encouraging to hear, Bobby. I wouldn't want our work to be interrupted by those malicious Fair Folk or any vampires or anything." He chuckled.

She responded to this with an exaggerated laugh, which caused her bosom to heave in eye-catching fashion.

The interview proceeded, with him determining that the young woman possessed some basic computer skills, experience with managing an itinerary, and decent customer service abilities.

"Well," he pronounced when they reached the end of the process, "I'd say you're hired, Ms Diaz. I think you'll do fine here."

Her face lit up. "That's great! Thanks, Mr Davis. Remington, I mean. Where will my desk be? When do I start?"

He pushed his chair back and stood. "Come with me, I'll show you. As for your starting date, it will be soon but I'll have to consult with my...ah, partner before I can give you a definite answer."

Remy took her out front and flourished his hand at her desk and chair before he quickly reviewed the procedure for greeting customers—whether in person, over the phone, or via email—taking messages down, and so forth.

In the middle of his spiel, a door in the far corner opened and Taylor strode out.

Both Remy's and Bobby's eyes snapped up as the other woman glided toward them, aloof and elegant in her black dress and jacket.

Bobby extended a hand. "Hi, I'm Roberta Diaz, but you can call me Bobby. Mr Davis just hired me."

Taylor accepted the hand. "Hello, Roberta. I'm Taylor Steele, the agency's owner and Remington's boss."

His teeth scraped against each other and a muscle along his jaw rippled.

The vampire turned toward him. "Remy, may I see you in my office ASAP, please?" She spun on a heel and was already halfway across the floor before he could even think to respond.

Remy decided to cut Bobby off before she could ask any further questions. "Taylor's busy right now so don't mind her. She's a nice person to work...with. But yeah, welcome aboard. We'll say this interview is concluded for now, but we'll get in touch with you shortly with more details."

"Great!" She turned away to spit her gum discreetly into its original wrapper and looked around for a trash can.

He held out an open palm. "I'll take that."

Smiling awkwardly, she dropped the wad in his hand. "Okay, thanks. If you don't need me to do any paperwork yet, I'll get going. I'm looking forward to your call! Oh, is it okay if I read the Inquirer and maybe some fashion magazines when I'm not busy?"

"When you're not busy, sure." He shrugged.

She thanked him again and ambled toward the exit, the clacking sound of her heels diminishing as she left. He hoped Taylor wasn't about to override his hiring decision and force him to deliver the bad news.

No sooner had the woman shut the door behind her than Riley zipped out of their shared office.

"What was that?" the fairy demanded with a pouting expression. "It sounded like you were about to ask her out on a date. And you couldn't keep your eyes off her chest. I was watching. I saw the whole thing."

Remy shrugged. "She'll make an excellent face for our organization, I'd say."

"You weren't paying attention to her face!" Riley hovered in front of him and planted her fists on her hips. "Instead of calling her Bobby, you might as well call her 'Boobs.' Plus, I heard that humans sometimes call someone a 'boob' when they think they're stupid—which she obviously is."

"Oh," he retorted as he walked slowly toward Taylor's office, "I found her quite charming. She's a clever and multi-talented girl, really. Not many people can chew gum and talk about mutant pit bull rats at the same time. Now, please wait while I speak to Taylor."

She hovered where she was and glared at him when he knocked on the door.

"Enter," Taylor said.

Remy stepped in and closed the door, entirely confident that Riley would press her ear to it momentarily. He lowered himself into the chair in front of the lady's desk.

"Remington," she began, "I am...perplexed by your choice of secretary. Well, I can see how she'd appeal to human males, but I expected better of you."

Her demeanor, he decided, was cool but not yet icy. She was giving him a chance to explain his reasoning. He waited to make sure she was finished before he spoke.

"Why would you want another mortal involved in our business?" she went on. "And Boobs there doesn't seem like the sharpest knife in the drawer. Riley and I were right in front of her and she suspected nothing."

He gestured emphatically with his right hand. "Exactly. Boobs—er, Bobby—is completely harmless. She'll be pleasant to the customers while failing miserably to uncover the secrets we want to stay secret. While she claims to believe in paranormal or supernatural shit, everything she believes is completely wrong."

Taylor's gaze drifted to the side while she digested his words.

"If she were herself a preternatural," he continued, "we'd have to worry about hiding her nature from mortal clients. Or cops, the landlord, or whatever. And if she was a savvy human, we'd have to go through the whole process of initiating her. As is, she won't betray any sensitive information, and you could waltz right past her, sip from a blood bag and turn into a bat, and she wouldn't suspect a damn thing."

He smiled, then furrowed his brow. "Wait—can you turn into a bat? I never thought about—"

"You have a point," Taylor admitted and cut him off. She had folded her hands atop one another on the desk but now, she detached the left one and rested her red nails on the surface. "We'll give it a trial. As per usual, though, anything that goes wrong is on you."

Remy adjusted his tie. "But of course."

She relaxed her posture a little. "The subject of our new secretary-receptionist is not the only thing to discuss, however. I also wanted to ask you something far more important."

"I'm all ears," he replied and spread his hands.

Drumming her fingers on the desktop, she queried, "You haven't done anything careless, have you? Such as, for example, trying to hunt whoever killed those dwarves on your own. The other day, you seemed quite agitated after we spoke about the whole bait issue." Her expression softened. "I understand that. I should have been more honest with you and at an earlier point in time. But any lingering resentment you might have is no excuse to do anything stupid."

"Since when," he scoffed, "have I ever done anything stupid?"

Taylor didn't look much amused. "This...individual, this entity we are tracking—the mysterious vampire in Israel—is incredibly dangerous. I do not yet know their exact identity, but I can say with certainty that they are powerful and not someone to be trifled with, Remington."

He sat stoically, endured the lecture, and met her gaze.

She drummed her fingers on the desk again. "Let me put the situation into perspective. You know that I am not to be trifled with, either. And yet, even I am worried. I'm playing it safe. I understand and respect that this is an adversary who poses a real threat to me. I mean no offense to you as a mortal, David, but you are not in the same league. You don't even have one human lifetime under your belt. Attempting to face this rival of ours by yourself would be the height of foolishness. And I really would rather you not die. Believe me."

"Well." Remy sighed. "I suppose I'd rather not die either, to be perfectly frank."

"Good," Taylor riposted. "In that case, do as I told you previously. Go out on the town and spend money. Be loud and visible about it. Put yourself in places where numerous people will see you and perhaps even want to talk to you. And, again, pay attention to anyone suspicious who approaches you with strange questions or requests."

He immediately thought of Don Gannon, but he was sure that didn't count. There was nothing especially suspicious about a journalist who worked for a gossip rag begging for leads and offering half-assed promises in return.

With that thought tucked away, he cleared his throat and straightened his tie. "I haven't tracked the dwarves' killer on my own. And when I get my next cash installment from Maps Cat, I swear I will immediately go out and be my old asshole self again. It shouldn't take long at all to begin attracting all kinds of weirdos who suddenly want to talk to me again."

Taylor's dark eyes regarded him for a moment. "All right. I am glad to hear that. You've worked hard on expanding our business so in a way, this could be the break you need, anyway. Be careful, Remington. I mean it."

Smiling, he saluted her with two fingers. "Yes, ma'am. Speaking of which, I'm almost done with today's round of stuff, so I'll depart shortly. At least my apartment in Manhattan is closer to this place than yours in Harrison, ha. Sorry about that."

She said nothing but nodded to him with a wry, almost

sour expression. He turned and left, closing the door behind him.

Riley was waiting for him and fluttered around his shoulder almost immediately. "I overheard most of that," she reported. "Sorry. I didn't mean to listen in but I couldn't help it."

"Of course you couldn't." Remy adjusted his cuff links. "Don't worry, though, none of that conversation was anything shocking, I'd wager. Let's finish up and go home, shall we?"

He walked toward his office and the fairy trailed close behind. "Boobs already left," she pointed out. "Were you hoping she'd stick around?"

"No," he countered. "I dismissed her myself, didn't I? At this point, I simply want to rest and prepare for tomorrow. And if we do bring her back and give her the job—which we probably will—it will be for purely professional reasons. Don't worry, Riley. You're still my number one sidekick."

"Hmph," she scoffed and folded her tiny arms over her chest. "That had better be true."

Remy completed a few minor pieces of paperwork and returned his files to their folders before he locked his office. Riley hitched a ride on his shoulder as he strode out the front door and into the street.

"Oh," she quipped, "I'm surprised also you were bold enough to actually lie to Taylor about not investigating those murders. Usually, she can see right through people when they lie."

He half-frowned at this. "I didn't lie, actually. What I said was technically true because I said I hadn't tracked the perpetrators. In other words, I used past tense. We won't be going after leads until tomorrow."

The fairy pursed her lips as she considered this. The street lamps reflected golden sparkles off her iridescent wings. "You have a point there," she admitted.

CHAPTER EIGHT

Industry City, Brooklyn, New York

Remington piloted his Lincoln down the street, hemmed in by the blocky, uniform buildings of one of New York's biggest light manufacturing and warehousing districts. The day was cold and bright, somehow bleak despite the sunshine. The sparse white clouds looked lost in the blue sky.

"Riley," he began, "keep an eye out for this V-Electronics store. My phone app can't seem to make up its mind as to exactly where this place is located. I suppose that's a good sign, in a way. It means that the place is weird and weird is exactly what we're looking for."

"Okay," she agreed. "I'm still not so sure this is a good idea, though."

He flapped a hand dismissively. "Nonsense. We'll be fine. After all, our information comes from a disheveled guy we met in a basement tavern whose father probably kept asking him when he was going to get a real job until the day he died. What could possibly go wrong?"

It was true. Already, he had begun to benefit—or so he hoped—from his burgeoning professional relationship with Mr Don Gannon. How useful the reporter's tip had been would remain to be seen.

Remy had called the man the night before after he'd arrived home from work. Don had picked up after only two rings and seemed excited to hear from him.

"Yes, so happy you called," he'd gushed in his wheezing and gritty voice. "If you have any kind of lead for me, anything at all, give it here and ask me any question you like. I can't promise I'll know the answer but let me tell you that I can almost certainly point you in the right direction if nothing else."

He decided the best thing to do was throw the man the equivalent of a stale bread crust—edible and nourishing enough to a starving man, but not something that he would particularly miss if he shared it.

"Well, Don," he'd said, "as it so happens, there is—or was—this underground casino in Lower Manhattan near the financial district that was raided by the cops a couple of months ago. In addition to the basic illegality of gambling, it seems they had an episode of violence that finally pushed them into the limelight. A guy was even killed. But wait, there's more. Some witnesses reported that they'd seen odd, uncanny things there. The types of things some people might even describe as supernatural, we'll say."

The reporter had been almost panting with excitement while he listened, and Remy could hear, over the phone, the sound of him jotting this all down on a scrap of paper.

Then he had asked his question.

"Tell me, Don. Have you heard anything about diamonds or other gems being smuggled secretly into the country? Probably by strange, short individuals, mostly with beards, I'd guess. Does that ring a bell?"

It had. Gannon refused to say much on the grounds that he didn't know much, but he did drop the name of V-Electronics in Industry City. And that was that.

The car glided along the avenues but Riley still seemed nervous. She bit her fingertips as she glanced around in search of the store.

"Taylor warned you," she pointed out. "She said that whoever's responsible for those murders is not someone to mess around with, didn't she? And she's not the type to lie about something like that, Remy. Not only that, we both saw what happened to those poor dwarves."

He ignored her, although he heard her words and understood them, of course. The truth was, he simply didn't prioritize them. All he could think about was Taylor's half-embarrassed admission that he was bait. Merely bait.

No matter what, he would show her that he was far more than that.

They reached a cross-street and around the corner to the left, both Remy and Riley located their goal at the same time.

"V-Electronics!" she shouted jubilantly, her wings flapping.

"Got it." He turned the Lincoln toward the building. Like much of Industry City, it was blocky and nondescript although small and squat as though it crouched between the other edifices.

He sighed with relief when he saw it had its own parking lot. When he turned the car in and chose a space near the front entrance, though, he realized there were no other vehicles present.

"Shit," he muttered. "This is a prime business hour and on a weekday. Let's go read the text on the door, shall we?"

"Okay," Riley agreed.

Remy shut the engine off and stepped out into the vacant lot. He couldn't put his finger on exactly what it was, but something impressed him with a feeling of abandonment and even desolation.

He wondered if the place had recently gone out of business. There were no broken windows, and no For Sale sign out front so that much was encouraging.

They approached the door and he peered at the establishment's listed hours.

"What the hell?" he exclaimed. "This place must be run by six different people who all have sleep disorders."

V-Electronics was open a grand total of eight hours per week. And at widely scattered times on Mondays, Wednesdays, and Fridays only. Today was a Thursday.

"Aww." The fairy pouted. "It looks like we're out of luck. Unless you want to try to break in?"

He grimaced, then rubbed his hands together. "Yeah, I think I do want to try to break in. Well, before we actually break anything, I might as well attempt to…"

With little real expectation of success, he gave the door a shove. To his pleasant surprise, it swung inward without resistance.

"Well, then," he stated. "No destruction of private property necessary."

The fairy wafted in behind when he slipped in, and the door swung closed without a sound.

They both stopped and examined their surroundings. Immediately, he realized that he'd been incorrect about the place going out of business. Still, he had been in the right ballpark, so to speak.

Everything about the interior bespoke a pending move. The entire place was disassembled and in the state of chaos between its former equilibrium and the coming new order in which everything was packed away and shipped off to be reassembled elsewhere.

Riley floated beside his ear. "Weird," she whispered, so softly he almost didn't hear her. "It's like a wrecking crew came through."

"Except there's no crew to be seen," Remy observed. "Maybe they're out to lunch?"

They inched forward, poked their way through the mess, and tried not to make a noise even though they'd already announced their presence quite clearly.

The shelves were standard for an electronics store—cheap but reasonably sturdy perforated metal, mostly in a dull off-white color. They were empty, however, and not a single product remained on display for any potential customers to see. Only a few spare, forgotten hooks dangled from the racks.

What wares still remained in the business had been hastily and haphazardly stuffed into a vast assortment of cardboard boxes, plastic tubs, and metal crates.

Bluetooth headsets lingered in a half-full box and protruded from a sea of azure packing peanuts. Motherboards and circuit boards were packed between layers of bubble wrap within metallic cubes. The floor was covered with small traces of debris.

"Hmm." Remy scratched his head as he looked around. "There's not much of interest here. The proprietors are closing shop, I suppose. Still, there might be a clue around. Riley, stay near me for now, but once we get to the other end, fly higher and scan for anything suspicious-looking."

"Sure," she concurred.

They crept between a vacant shelf on one side and a line of heavy tubs on the other and into an area more deeply shadowed. It lay far from both the front window and the nearest overhead light. He emerged from the aisle and glanced toward the far wall.

Then, air rushed and something hurtled toward his head.

He threw himself forward, ducked, and rolled, acting on instinct even before consciousness could involve itself. And as he came out of the roll, he saw the black head of an iron hammer swing through the space where his skull had been.

Before he could come up in something resembling a fighting stance, the hammer's owner was on him. A short, stout, blocky-headed form tried to shoulder-ram him before his assailant swept the hammer up once more.

Remy stumbled back a step but braced himself on his feet and caught the handle of the mallet to twist and yank at it. The dwarf grunted and snarled.

"Short-ass son of a bitch!" the investigator yelled and pulled the weapon toward him. "Give it up."

"Like hell, you preening woodpecker." His assailant cursed and shoved forward with his stocky frame.

They struggled against one another and spewed insults that both probably would have been embarrassed about under other circumstances. The dwarf thrust forward gradually with his solid strength while the human stepped over or around him and tried to disarm him from different angles.

Riley flew up. "Remy! Are you okay? Who is that?"

"He's not fat," he shouted and the sweat on his hands made it harder to retain control of the hammer. "He's big-boned."

"I didn't say *fat,* I said *that!*" the fairy retorted.

The dwarf growled. "Shut up, pencil-dick. Take your miniature escort and get the fuck out of here."

Riley watched the two of them struggle with a mixture of captivation and disgust before she finally sighed and shook her head. "Okay. Clearly, neither of you are mature enough to play with that thing."

She pointed her finger and a silver flash erupted from the hammer, momentarily blinding both men so neither of them saw the heavy tool suddenly elevate before it hurled itself across the floor to the complete opposite side of the building.

"What the hell?" the dwarf demanded.

Remy rubbed his eyes. "Ah, yeah, she does stuff like that occasionally. Sorry! At least now, maybe we can talk like civilized human beings. Or dwarves, whatever. I'm not here to kill you so there's no reason for you to try to find another hammer and hit me in the head with it. I only wanted to ask a few questions." He brushed himself off, put on his game face, and examined his new potential friend.

The dwarf still bristled with subdued hostility but he

had begun to calm. "These are not good times to ask questions of strangers," he murmured.

For a dwarf, he was actually kind of thin, although still wide and strongly-built in contrast to Remington. His deep widow's peak, long mustache, and short beard were all a dark reddish color, and his skin was coppery. Something in his eyes suggested a sense of humor and relative lack of typical dwarven uptightness, which Remy hoped would make itself known once he was less agitated.

"Strangers," he mused. "You make a good point. Allow me to properly introduce myself. I'm Remington Davis, with Moonlight Detective Agency. I'm Taylor Steele's equal partner. You might have heard of her." He slipped a business card out of his jacket and extended it.

The dwarf's bushy red eyebrows shot upwards. "Taylor, yes. I didn't know she had a partner now." He accepted the card and gave it a cursory glance.

"Well, she does. We're currently helping Surrly, the lender—if you know him—with a little issue that's befallen him." He dimmed the brightness of his smile now. While he wanted to come across as open and pleasant, he also wanted to convey the gravity of the situation. This individual, whoever he was, had probably heard about the murdered dwarves.

"Oh," the fellow responded, "I see." He paused and seemed hesitant to say more. "My name is Andrew Volz. I own this establishment. I thought it might be better for business if I relocated to Philadelphia. I have to go where the money is. Hence the mess."

Remy nodded. Volz was clearly willing to play ball but

also tried to find out more about him before he revealed too much.

He also noticed that Riley still floated nearby. She watched the dwarf suspiciously and seemed ready to intervene should he become violent again. It was unlikely that would be necessary, though. Volz was no longer angry.

"So," he asked the dwarf, "are you connected with Surrly's cartel, at all? Don't worry, you're not in trouble. We're simply trying to get a better idea of what the hell is going on lately."

Volz eyed him and almost smirked. "You think highly of yourself, don't you, Davis? Nothing scares you much, does it?"

Remy shrugged. "Some things do."

"Well," he replied, "to answer your question, I am not, and never was a member, but I know of them and worked with them, yes. They used to contract me for technology installation, troubleshooting, and general expertise. They were good, reliable, steady customers. Until a few days ago."

He adjusted his cuff links. "Really? What happened?"

Volz frowned. "They suddenly started acting like human teenagers during a citywide riot. A whole crew of them burst in as I was closing up for the day, shoved past me in a mad rush, and looted my store. Actually looted it! They grabbed everything they could carry, bowled me over when I protested, and left in one hell of a tremendous hurry. It seems they were fleeing the city."

His hands clenched and unclenched as he recounted this tale. Remy didn't blame him for being pissed. That kind of behavior was even less tolerated among dwarves than it was among humans.

"So," he continued, "after being robbed in that fashion by people I considered to be on my side, no less, you can imagine how I might be a tad concerned about strangers coming into this place at odd times."

Remy waved a hand up, then down. "Oh, think nothing of it. I've had large hammers swung at my head before. I completely understand."

The dwarf uttered a short, barking laugh. "Somehow, I don't doubt the veracity of that statement."

He smiled. "But seriously, though, your…ah, friends were probably fleeing whoever it was that killed a group of their co-workers in a tunnel a few days ago. Did you hear about that, by chance?"

"Vaguely," Volz admitted, "but I almost preferred to avoid the details."

"Yeah, well," he countered and while he allowed his tone to become gruff and cynical, he maintained a pleasant expression so the dwarf might feel like he was being included in a secret. "Unfortunately, the details will come looking for you. Wait, that doesn't make sense. You know what I mean, though. There's trouble afoot."

Volz nodded curtly. "That much is obvious. Perhaps it would be best if you filled me in."

Glancing around, Remy saw a crate that was almost at pelvis height. "Do you mind if I take a seat?"

"Not at all. I think I may do the same."

Both men now sat, and Riley, meanwhile, had fluttered into the rafters to poke around. He let her go for now. There seemed to be no danger.

He explained the situation to Volz. While he left out some of the more specific details to be safe, he started at the beginning and made it clear that someone had slaughtered a group of dwarves to send a message—and without even robbing them of their diamonds.

The dwarf shook his head slowly as the human reached the end of his story. "We live in strange times and New York is a stranger place. I'm sure you want to know what I know about the whole business. And the answer to that is nothing. I got the impression that Surrly was occasionally involved with shady characters, but I have no honest idea who ordered the hit."

Remy studied the dwarf's face as he spoke. Between his own experience dealing with smarmy high-society types and a few things Taylor had taught him, he could usually tell when someone was lying unless they were exceedingly good at it. Volz seemed to be telling the truth.

"Too bad," he quipped. "I was kinda hoping we could wrap this entire case up within the next five minutes after you confessed." He smirked.

"Hah!" Volz laughed. "For someone with all the strength of a limp scarecrow, you do have some measure of balls, as humans say. I like that. Too bad I can't be of any help to you unless you're in Philadelphia and require—"

"Actually," he cut him off, "I might be able to offer you a job. Working with myself and Taylor, I mean, so it'd be safe. You'd probably be more secure under her wing than you would in Philly. Think about it. Everyone heard what happened to those assholes a few months ago who fucked with her, right?"

His companion rubbed his beard with a thick hand. "I did. And your offer intrigues me. Tech work, I presume?"

The human nodded. "We need a computer network set up at our new office. For that matter, we need computers. Our operation is basically analog at this point. Vintage."

Riley fluttered down. "Are we getting another employee? He tried to knock your head off."

Remy tried not to roll his eyes. "It was a slight misunderstanding. You would have done the same in his position. Besides, for a short guy who looks like he bounces for a dive bar where you have to be under five-foot-two to get in, he seems smart."

The dwarf made a flicking motion beside his nose. Remy assumed it was an obscene gesture. "I won't, at least," Volz stated, "be the shortest one around. Look at her. I could step on her if I'm not careful." He chuckled when Riley lowered herself to face level.

The fairy's eyes narrowed. She did not look amused.

"Besides," Volz went on, "I can smell money on you, Remington Davis. And especially at a time when a quarter of my stock has been subject to random larceny, that is my favorite smell." He smiled.

CHAPTER NINE

Bushwick, Brooklyn, New York

"Volts!" Remy called and strode toward the squid-like mass of wires and cables where the redheaded dwarf squatted. "How's it coming?"

The short figure turned his head and glared at him from under bristling brows. "My name is Volz. Don't make me start calling you Rammy. Would you enjoy that? I'm not German. The last letter of my name should be pronounced according to the standard English rendition of the letter zeta. Or 'zee,' as modern Americans call it."

He stretched his face in mock surprise. "Wow. *Volzzzzz*," he drawled slowly and stretched the sound as if hearing the name for the first time. "I promise I'll try to remember that."

"Good." The dwarf grunted. "Smarmy bastard. Anyway, it's coming along fine, barring some concerns about exactly how good a network you want. But I have the basics well under control, so I'd estimate an hour or so before you're online."

"That's great to hear," he responded. "Keep earning that pay, my diminutive friend."

Volz snorted. "I'm only diminutive on the vertical axis. You're disturbingly small on the horizontal."

Remy beamed. "That, too, is great to hear, since I've actually put on at least five pounds since summer. Being off drugs, you remember to eat food."

"Good for you. You don't seem too curious about the concerns I mentioned, though, nor did you answer the implied question."

"I was getting to that." He watched as the dwarf fiddled with a screwdriver. "Tell me these concerns and I'll answer your questions, implied or otherwise."

The dwarf had been sprawled on the floor. Now, he sat and took a deep breath.

"All right…well, for starters, like I said, you'll have working computers with basic Internet in very short order. But I'll need to order stacks if you want to get a powerful private server running. A proper, serious business really ought to consider that, I'd say. Of course, setting one up costs both time and money." He looked sidelong at his new employer and cocked an eyebrow slyly while he waited for a response.

"You," Remy said, "would make a good salesman, Volz. Our own super-powerful private server sounds awesome. Do it, I say. Spare no expense."

To illustrate that he meant what he said, he dug into his pocket, produced a fat wad of cash, and waved it seductively before the dwarf's gleaming eyes.

Maps Cat had sold another load of the dwarven gems—the bulk of them by now, in fact. The profits, in this case, were even beyond what he had hoped for. He could more than afford a couple of nights on the town as part of Taylor's bait operation. And he could afford to have their new office hooked up with every possible advantage.

Volz almost trembled as Remy put the money back in his pocket. "That's the kind of attitude I like to encounter," he stated. His voice was gruff but he grinned openly now. "It's good to know someone values my skills highly enough to want to put them to good use. Yes, Mr Davis, there are many things I could do with this place—for the right price, of course."

"Go on," he instructed.

The dwarf glanced around and fondled his mustache.

"For starters, internal and external security cameras. Closed-circuit television. With the nature of your business, you can't be too careful. I could also get you extra surge protection, layers of insulation for the wiring, and other such things that will reduce potential fire hazards. An updated central air-conditioning system might be nice, at least before next summer. Maybe an artificial fireplace."

As the dwarf came to the end of his extensive sales pitch, the door opened and in sauntered Ms Roberta Diaz.

"Bobby!" Remy exclaimed and turned away from Volz toward her. "It's such a pleasure to see you." It was true—she wore a fairly low-cut blouse with the top button unfastened. "I bet you're excited for your first day of work, aren't you? Well, it's only a half-day, but still."

She grinned a little sheepishly and fished around in her purse for her gum. "I'm definitely excited, Mr Davis. Ooh, who's this? The janitor?" She'd seen Volz and now stood over him and gawked with curiosity like a child who'd stumbled onto an ostrich at the zoo.

Volz made a barking, snorting sound that rapidly transformed into a proper laugh. "Tech guy, actually," he corrected her in his deep, rough voice. He didn't sound angry, though.

"Ohh," Bobby marveled. "I guess it would help if we had computers and stuff. I know how to use them but am terrible at setting them up or fixing them. Will you be around for a while? It might be helpful to have you here in case anything gets screwed up."

"Probably," the dwarf said. "It depends on how much the boss here wants to pay me, though, of course."

Remy smiled for the benefit of them both. "Like I said, spare no expense. By the way, Bobby, this fine gentleman's name is Andrew Volz. Volz, this is our receptionist and I suppose also my personal secretary, Roberta Diaz."

"Call me Bobby," she interjected.

The dwarf set his screwdriver down. "Bobby. I like that. So tell me, Bobby, if you're not a technology person, what kinds of things do you find interesting?"

"Oh," she replied and seemed to search for the right words as she pulled a chair toward the reception desk. "Haha, I don't know, really. Well, the paranormal, but you probably don't want to talk about that."

Remy bit his tongue to hold his laughter in check. *This ought to be good. She thinks he's merely a short, stocky guy with an epic biker mustache. I wonder what the dwarves think about the government rat-mutants?*

"Hmm," Volz began. "On the contrary, that sounds like it might be a diverting subject. At least as interesting as stacks and servers and what Remy is willing to pay for them. Go on."

Bobby did. Since Remy and Taylor weren't really advertising for customers to come to their new office yet, there was almost no actual work for a receptionist at this point. He had merely thought he ought to bring her in for a few hours to get used to the place, fill out all the payroll documentation, and maybe run through a couple of exercises on how to deal with their clientele. Plus anything Taylor might specifically want to talk to her about, of course.

But, without customers to deal with, the girl still had considerable time to regale the dwarf with all the exciting material she'd gleaned from that most august and important of publications, The New England Inquirer.

"The experts are now about, like, ninety-eight point four percent sure that, because of all the genetically modified organisms—that's what GMO stands for—in our food, we may be opening ourselves up to subversive influences through the astral plane. See, 'cause organic food contains stuff that naturally helps us block out all those negative energies. But the GMOs inhibit the formation of psychoreceptors, which means people with harmful intent, like curses and stuff—or maybe even aliens or demons—can broadcast signals directly into our brains. That's probably why there's been a spike in mental illnesses recently…"

Remington had the young woman fill out payroll forms gradually while she spoke, but he made no particular effort to stop her from regaling Volz with her theories. It certainly enlivened the workday for all of them.

The dwarf, for his part, chuckled and shook his head. "I suppose you make a semi-convincing argument there but forgive me if I'm a skeptic." He glanced quickly at Remy. "I don't believe in any of this supernatural or paranormal shit." He sighed. "There isn't any evidence for it. If it were really as prevalent as these so-called experts say, we'd see some of these strange beings walking around every day, wouldn't we?"

Remy kept a straight face. Back in college, he and the boys had pulled off quite a few beautifully executed practical jokes on the more gullible of the freshman, so he had experience in playing along. Not to mention his skill at poker.

"But," Roberta protested, "how do you know we don't see supernatural beings walking around and we simply don't recognize what they are? I mean, you'd think they'd have ways of disguising their true identity."

"Hah!" Volz scoffed, although he kept his tone friendly. "Next thing, you'll try to tell me that dwarves exist and have their own secret network here in New York. I'm sorry, but it's too much to swallow."

Remy continued to chew on the side of his tongue as the two of them argued. They both seemed to be enjoying themselves, at least.

"Look," Bobby urged and again, her hand disappeared into the depths of her purse. "Here's the latest issue of the Inquirer. You really should read this if you don't already. They have a column about Unexplained Occurrences. Right now, they're talking about an upcoming exhibit that'll be at the Solomon R. Guggenheim Museum—occult objects that supposedly carry great power. Some of them have even set off highly delicate instruments in ways that science can't explain, like when people tried to measure their—"

"The Guggenheim," commented Volz, "is an art museum, and art—pleasing though it might be—is mostly fiction. If it were being hosted at, say, the Museum of Natural History, I might be inclined to take it a little more seriously."

The conversation petered out when he proved intractable and Bobby grew increasingly distracted by the rigors of filling out forms. Taylor hadn't made an appearance yet, and Riley had gone home to the Fluttershire Colony for a night off—protesting even as Remy insisted she take a brief vacation.

That left him with nothing to do but watch the dwarf work. Which got boring really, really fast.

"I think," he announced, "that I'll be going shortly. I need to run a little investigation of my own—something personally requested by Taylor."

Bobby looked at him and her mouth formed a perfect "O" shape.

"Wow, that sounds exciting," she remarked. "Even though it's almost dark."

"Exactly," he countered.

Somehow, tonight seemed like the appropriate time to spend the money Ishmapps had paid. As the boss had said, he needed to engage in conspicuous consumption, the more conspicuously the better.

After that, he simply had to see who happened to show up to say hello.

. . .

Times Square, New York City

Remington stood bathed in neon light. "Ah," he proclaimed, "the night is young and Maps Cat is a kind and generous provider." He thrust a hand into his pocket and fondled the wad of cash secured by his money clip.

Justin, standing a few feet to his left, smirked and drank from a flask. "Fuckin' A."

Craig, who stood a few feet to his right, popped a pill surreptitiously into his mouth and sighed happily. "And a beautiful night it is. Heh, heh."

He was not worried in the slightest that either of them would ask who Maps Cat was. Even if he told them, they'd simply laugh and ask what he was on and where they could buy some of it.

Of course, he'd lied about the night being young. It was actually 3:17 am already, but by his old standards, that was early. The goal, after all, was to act like his old self again.

He'd therefore drunk a cup of coffee before setting out and meeting the boys—to be safe since lately, he'd been on the type of sleep schedule befitting an adult with a real job.

Now, the three of them staggered down the sidewalk and forced aside the bodies of all who crossed their paths as easily as they had summoned their attention.

Justin cackled and drained his flask of its final drop of booze before he flung it in the general direction of the nearest trash can. "Ooops!" he shouted. "It looks like I missed."

"Gosh," Remy intoned and his mind slid easily into the thought patterns he'd established before he'd attempted to improve himself, "I hope some salaried peon doesn't have to actually clean that up. God forbid the little people have to earn their pay."

Craig snickered and the sound broke into a snort for a moment before it resumed. "Hey, look. Sexually mature female organisms at ten o'clock." He gestured in the appropriate direction.

Remy squinted. The man's observation was correct. As they marched along the rim of Times Square, the trio rapidly approached two attractive specimens. One of them wore a fur coat and even looked vaguely familiar. He had no idea who the hell the other chick was.

Not that it mattered.

The two young women were talking to each other about some or another bullshit and aggressively ignored everyone else in the universe on their stroll. Especially guys. Remy saw this as a challenge, albeit not a very difficult one.

He looked directly at them, cupped his hands around his mouth, and bellowed, "Hey!"

The girls looked up, half-shocked and half-amused. They didn't stop walking but at least they slowed.

Remy had their attention. He shoved his hand into his pants, produced the money clip, and held it and its contents up for all to see. "Do you girls wanna buy stuff?"

That settled it. Soon, the five of them crisscrossed Times Square, left large-numeral dollar bills wherever they went, and made no effort whatsoever to keep their voices down.

Of course, Remy, Justin, and Craig had begun the night with several overpriced drinks. That helped ensure that, admittedly, he was having a good time so far, even if this was technically a work assignment. It was good to be back.

Wasn't it?

When he'd first made the calls, both of the boys responded with excited incredulity. It had been three months since he'd so much as spoken to Craig and more like five months in the case of Justin, probably since the man tended to break shit—and not only empty liquor bottles.

"Holy living crap," Craig had gasped over the phone, "this cannot be. *The* David Remington actually wants to go out on the town again. We all figured you were fucking dead." He'd broken off into snickering at that, as though it amused him to think that David must be deceased if he wasn't partying and attention-whoring and setting money on fire.

Although he had only requested the presence of Craig and Justin, he had explicitly instructed them to tell as many other people as they wanted that he was back. Word needed to get out. Anyone who wanted to watch the shit-show ought to be in the vicinity of Times Square tonight.

They had money to spend, egos to bruise, and memories to create. Taylor had instructed him to be publicly visible. And what place was more public or more visible than the Center of the Universe?

Already, they'd bumped into a few old acquaintances who, satisfyingly, had lingered to gossip after the three of them moved on.

Yeah, between tonight and my appearance at the Hidden Garden, all the beautiful elite ought to be aware of me again very soon. Maybe that Ocren chick and her stories will even help.

They took their two new female friends out for even more booze, then invaded a drugstore for the sake of going somewhere that sold merchandise at this hour and bought random pieces of cheap crap with no intention of keeping it.

"I say," Justin exclaimed in a really bad fake British accent as he pulled a foot brace off the rack. "It appears this medical device is only in the thirty- to forty-dollar range. With useful implements at such a low cost, I fail to see why there's any debate over health care for the poor in this country."

The two girls cracked up at that.

Remy led the posse to the counter, where a tired-looking young woman tried to ignore their jokes and the excessively personal questions they probed her with. Her expression resigned, she rang up the foot brace. Remy paid for it easily.

The quintet stumbled into the street.

"Justin," he ordered, "I'm holding you to your word. About health care for the poor. I hereby command you to donate that piece of crap to whichever homeless person happens along next." He gestured vaguely toward the street.

"Okay," the man agreed. He hauled his arm back with a dramatic flourish, grunted as if in slow motion, and tossed the brace, still in its packaging, across the pavement, where it clattered against a shuttered storefront.

Guttural, spitting laughter erupted from them all.

Craig, who had the lowest alcohol tolerance of the three, put a hand on Remy's shoulder to steady himself.

"Shit, man," he drawled. "It's good to have you acting like your old self again, David. It really is."

His gut tightened a little at that. It stung.

I really was this bad, wasn't I?

He pushed the concept from his mind and continued his rampage.

Soon, dawn began to break and some of the businesses reopened. More tourists and shoppers, workers, and other random humans began to swell the avenues.

"Hey," Justin suggested, "let's do more charity. I think I saw a news camera somewhere over there."

They invaded a fast-food restaurant, demanded enough food to feed a dozen people, and stumbled out into the square where they loudly distributed the sandwiches and hash browns to anyone they happened to come across and especially people who didn't look rich.

"There, there," Remy proclaimed and raised his voice to almost a shout, "don't worry, hungry little worker bee. The Remingtons will see to it that you don't go without nourishment today." He shoved an egg-based concoction into the mitten-covered paws of a guy who looked like he probably worked for the Road Commission and who accepted it with a few blinks but without complaint.

Next, they bought the two bitches an assortment of needlessly expensive cosmetics at Sephora and some high-end athletic shoes for themselves. Finally, they selected jewelry for all.

"Justin," said Craig, "you were right. There is a news camera. Let's monopolize their time."

By now, several people had actually stopped to watch the posse, laden as they were with bags and trinkets and given their obvious inebriation and general loudness. Remy was surprised they hadn't had an encounter with the NYPD yet.

The camera was attached to a three-person crew who were conducting lame slice-of-life interviews with random New Yorkers—or visitors to the city—asking them what were probably banal questions designed simply to fill time on the morning news.

He spearheaded the charge. Before the news crew even knew what hit them, he and his entourage had barged directly in front of the camera, displaced the guy they'd been talking to, and shoved him aside.

"Hey!" Remy yelled, "check this out!" He grabbed the fur-coated chick's arm and lifted it so that her bag, overflowing with pricey makeup, dangled in front of the lens.

The lady doing the interview mouthed wordlessly before she attempted to intervene. "Excuse me," she said sharply, "this is live. We're doing—"

Justin interrupted her. "We're doing good works. Canadian bacon sandwiches for all." He doubled over, giggling.

Craig added, "Never let it be said that the New York elite don't care about the common man." He snickered.

Remy realized he had to top them both. "Yes," he pronounced, "it's true. From our own pockets, we have fed the hungry of this great city and also donated a foot brace to a nearby sidewalk. But fear not for our own finances, because all that crap cost like, I don't know, one percent of what we spent on this."

He held out a big-ass jewel set in a gold ring between his thumb and forefinger. "Seriously, look at this thing. I don't know what kind of gem it is, exactly. But it cost a ton, so it must have been worth it."

"Okay," the newswoman snapped, "that's enough. We're leaving. Charles, kill the camera."

Remy held his companions back as the news crew closed shop and tramped off toward the other side of the square. Suddenly, he didn't feel like any of this was all that funny anymore.

"Fuck," said Justin, "it's been way too long since we had this good a time."

Realizing that they hadn't eaten any of the food they'd previously purchased, they agreed to get breakfast at a higher-end establishment. Justin led the two girls into the restaurant first, and Remy lingered in the rear and pulled Craig aside.

"Hey," he began in a low voice, "I'm not feeling that great, to be honest. I think I need a couple more minutes of fresh air. Go ahead without me and I'll be in shortly, okay?"

Craig, still mostly drunk, stared at him for a second before he smiled. "Okay, David. You're on a roll, though, seriously. Don't disappoint us now." He turned and disappeared into the building.

Remy's nostrils flared as he inhaled the cool air. As soon as the last of his companions was gone, he turned and hustled down the sidewalk, cut across to the next street at the earliest opportunity, and continued to put distance between himself and his temporary crew.

"God," he muttered. "I went out of my way to act like a really bad caricature of my old self, and they ate it up with relish. I don't even know who my old self is anymore at this point. Ugh."

He almost wished he could simply disappear. Or, like the face-snatcher he'd tracked down not long ago, adopt a completely different appearance and identity.

But that was impossible. Instead, once he reached an area where there weren't quite so many humans around, he looked for a taxi. Even with all the other bullshit he'd purchased, he was fairly certain he could afford the ride back to his apartment. It wasn't too far.

A yellow cab approached and the driver's demeanor suggested he was looking for reliable fares. Remy looked toward the windshield and raised a hand in the universal gesture for "I need someone to drive me the hell out of here."

Instead, someone pounded into him.

"Oof!" The impact knocked the air out of his lungs and him off his feet. His head spun while his body careened forward. The city and its buildings and traffic all became rapidly darting, brightly colored blurs and in horror, he realized that he was hurtling directly into the middle of the street.

Horns honked and cars swerved. The taxi he had tried to hail pulled out into traffic, almost T-boned a Chevy, and the driver accelerated and sped away.

Dark, wet asphalt loomed, and Remy struck in the next second. Painful waves of shock exploded in his wrists, shoulders, and part of the right side of his face. He rolled along the pavement. More car-horns blared.

In the midst of a roll, he glanced up dizzily and saw his attacker.

It was a man—or something shaped like a man—clad in brown boots, dark-blue jeans, a black hooded sweater, and a black ski mask. He was average-sized and nothing about him was strange or suspicious aside from the mask.

"Shit," Remy groaned as another car raced toward him.

He rolled back the way he'd come and narrowly escaped the path of another oncoming cab as brakes and tires squealed. The vehicle rumbled over a pothole to swerve around him and displaced traffic in another loud eruption of horns. A car on the other side of the road veered halfway onto the sidewalk before it righted itself.

Before he could find his feet, the masked man was on top of him.

"Hey," he protested when the dark figure's arms clawed at him, "do you know who I am? I work for—"

"Yeah," a voice rasped, and the man's hands caught him by the shoulders. "I do know."

He shoved and Remy catapulted wildly most of the way across the street, his arms and legs flailing desperately.

"Fuck!" he cried. Again, he crashed onto the asphalt and tumbled head over heels and again while cars honked and drivers wrenched at their steering wheels and slammed on their brakes.

The masked man was somehow airborne. Remy crawled to the sidewalk and dragged himself upright using a lamppost, but his assailant had vaulted over the entire street in a single superhuman bound.

They sent a goddamn vampire or werewolf, was all he could think. *Taylor thought someone working for our enemy would approach me. Instead, it looks like they'll kill me.*

The plan had worked a little too well.

Moving so fast he could barely follow him, the masked man reached his side. "Hold still," he commanded.

Remy did not hold still. Instead, he snatched up an orange traffic cone and swung it toward his attacker. It really was a shitty weapon, but there wasn't anything else nearby and he wasn't about to go hand-to-hand with someone who clearly had preternatural abilities.

His assailant was already gone before the traffic cone could touch him. He dodged instinctively to the side and from somewhere behind him, the man's fist lashed out and struck the lamppost he'd used for support. The metal shrieked and bent.

"Oh, crap," he gasped as the dark form lunged toward him again.

He half-tripped over his own feet and fell into the street, directly into the side of a moving car. It wasn't moving very fast but an object with that much mass still had significant velocity and kinetic force behind it.

Remy was flung off his feet again and spun as the car tried to stop, the brakes screeching. The vehicle wheeled to block traffic. The driver, a woman who was on the verge of total panic, attempted to unbuckle herself to check on him but she seemed to have frozen.

A shadow moved and the mysterious attacker loomed over his prostrate form. He was, by now, feeling the fact that he'd had his ass kicked by both man and car and could barely move. The assailant would succeed.

Sirens had blared distantly for a moment already but now, out of nowhere, they seemed almost on top of them. In one corner of his vision, Remy saw flashing red and blue lights.

The masked man hesitated. A tremor of rage and frustrated will to action rippled through him and his blue eyes blazed. In the next instant, he seemed to blur and was gone.

Remy lay where he was in the street near the curb. An SUV had stopped in front of him, so he was momentarily safe from being run over unless some other vehicle rear-ended the SUV and knocked it into him. The lady driving the other car behind him finally managed to loosen her belt, opened the door, and stepped into the street.

"Oh, my God." She moaned. "Are you okay? I didn't see you I swear, I didn't see... What were you doing?"

He coughed and tasted blood on his lower lip—hopefully from the lip itself and not from his lungs or stomach. "Hailing a cab," he replied.

A police car drew up alongside him and cast its rotating lights of scarlet and azure over the curb. Judging by the still-growing blare of sirens, at least one more cruiser was on its merry way.

The woman froze again as the doors opened and two cops emerged.

"Wellllll," a voice began. "Mr Remington. It's been a while since we've had to respond to one of your various disturbances. Old habits die hard, don't they?"

Remy groaned and tried to sit but failed. "Good morning, officers. And yeah, they do."

CHAPTER TEN

Times Square, New York City

Alex staggered around a concrete corner, seeking the concealment of the alley's shadows, and slipped easily into their deceptive darkness. He could move faster than other humans. It was one of the perks that came with the otherwise shitty job of being Moswen's slave.

A trash dumpster appeared before him as he bolted down the alleyway. Without even slowing his stride, he leapt high, soared over it, and struck a rattling metal fence beyond.

His hands and feet linked into it and for a second or two, he hung there as if perched and debated whether to climb over and keep running or vault himself upward and climb to the top of the building to the left.

"Keep it simple, stupid," he gasped to himself beneath his ski mask and swung over the fence. He landed lightly on the ground beyond and sprinted deeper into the darkness. By now, the voices and shuffling bodies and police sirens had already faded away behind him.

He paused to catch his breath in an especially gloomy corner.

"Fuck," he muttered after a couple of gulps of air. "Fuck, fuck, *fuck*. None of this is going like it should. How the hell was I supposed to know the cops here have such a good response time? Or did the prick simply get lucky?"

He'd tailed Remington for a little while now. It hadn't been too difficult to track his movements. The spacker always seemed to be accompanied by his pet fairy, though.

With her around, any kind of attack was far too risky. Despite their small size and harmless appearance, the Fair Folk, as Moswen had mentioned, possessed enormous magical powers, which they sometimes used to protect mortals who paid for their services or whom they simply happened to like.

Last night and this morning were the first time he had seen the man without his little preternatural companion. Now, he'd decided, was the time to strike.

Even then, he'd waited for the proper moment. The rich prick had completely surrounded himself with people. Even with his augmented abilities, Alex might have had trouble abducting the man with his mates hovering by his side and dozens of witnesses nearby. He'd skulked and watched and waited until at last, the two of them could have a brief moment alone.

But he'd failed.

"Fuck," he cursed one last time. He sprang toward the nearest building, seized the external metal staircase, and used it to hurl himself upward to cling to the wall. The morning sun hadn't reached his position yet. No one would see him unless they somehow expected to see a man climbing a tall structure the way a lizard climbs a rock.

He supposed that transporting this Remington guy would have presented problems of its own—the man certainly had a big mouth. But the risk would have been worth it. He was Taylor Steele's assistant. Some of the rumors even suggested they were lovers.

"God," he muttered as he clambered past curtained windows and felt the breeze grow stronger with the elevation. "I don't know what she sees in him if that's the case. Who knows?"

What all the rumors agreed upon, though, was that Taylor was one of the most important individuals in New York's preternatural community. Maybe even the most important.

With her human boy toy as hostage, Alex could have lured her into a trap. Moswen would be very pleased. She might even finally allow him to return to Israel—or better yet, to Australia, although that seemed unlikely since he'd pledged his entire life to her.

"I need to find another way," he rasped. The top of the building was in sight. From there, he could scout his path back to his shitty motel room. "Another way to get at that vampire bitch. Taylor, I mean, haha. Something that will grab her attention."

He scrambled onto the roof and kept himself low so as to not be silhouetted against the morning sun.

"And then," he said, "I need to find a way out."

As soon as the words left him, he almost panicked. Anyone who happened to be reading his mind could interpret that in several different ways.

"A way out of trouble with the cops," he added hurriedly before the burning pain in his chest could rise. "Of course."

NYPD Times Square Precinct, New York City

Remington rubbed his temples and blinked to ease his eyes. He didn't think he'd really drunk all that much last night, but perhaps exhaustion had made it worse. After all, he'd been up all night and passed out for only a couple of hours after the arresting officers deposited him in a holding cell.

He sighed, a long, ragged sound like something an old dog would make. "How long now," he wondered out loud, "has it been since the last time I was in one of these places, anyhow? I can't fucking remember."

Of course, he'd been to jail many times. At least ten or twelve, something like that. But it was difficult to recall many of the details.

This was, however, the first time that he did not know for an absolute fact that his parents' lawyers would be along to bail him out any minute now.

As he continued to massage his head to try to jump-start its contents, the guy on the cot across from him shifted his position and seemed, for a moment, like he was about to get up and tell him to shut his mouth. Fortunately, he merely grunted and fell back asleep.

"Oh, good," Remy quipped as the man returned to unconsciousness. "I don't feel very sociable right about now."

He returned his thoughts to the question of when he'd

last been incarcerated. Most of the times it had happened, it had been while he was blackout drunk or severely high and in the process of doing something so stupid that his sober self wouldn't have believed such tall tales, anyway.

That played tricks on one's memory. A substantial chunk of his life, he now realized, consisted of urban legends that other people knew better than he did and which he had no way to verify. David Remington, mysterious doer of asinine deeds.

It could not have been all that long since his last stay, though. Judging by the way the officers on guard behaved, this was merely another round of business as usual.

"Heyyy," one of the cops exclaimed in the same tone of voice he'd use to greet an old friend he might bump into at the bar, "it really is Dave Remington. Shit, buddy, we were starting to miss you." With a huge grin, the man stood from his chair and sauntered toward the cell.

"Hi, yeah," he responded and hoped he didn't sound too irritable or too slurred. "I guess it's good to be back. I mean, as opposed to having my head run over and used to patch up the goddamn avenue or being torn apart by that asshole in the ski mask. You guys saw him, right? And someone saw him jump across the entire street in a single leap, moving faster than a speeding bullet and so forth?"

The guard, a younger Chicano gentleman, simply laughed. "The officers who picked you up saw something, that's for sure."

"Cool." Remy coughed again. There was no blood this time so the bleeding hadn't been internal. If it was, he'd probably be in the hospital rather than jail, anyway. "That means they're not blind. I greatly respect the NYPD's non-discriminatory hiring practices, but I have to admit it's encouraging to know that the guys responsible for finding out who did this have functional powers of vision."

The cop laughed again. "See, this is why we kinda like having you here. You make an effort. Most guys merely cuss at us or beg for their mothers or some shit."

"I try," he riposted. "Then again, I might beg for my mother if I actually knew what the hell even happened back there. Are you allowed to tell me that or is there some kind of stupid law against it?"

The officer took a step or two back and leaned against the wall. "Eh," he mused. "It looked an awful lot like you got into a drunken-ass, drug-fueled brawl with some crackhead out in the streets. That's what they're saying. You, however, have the right to remain silent."

"Now why would I do that?" he demanded. "Like you said, I need to make an effort to keep you guys entertained on the job. If I pass out, though, this guy might be able to handle the task." He gestured to the heavy, snoring form of the dude passed out on the other cot.

The cop rolled his tongue around in his cheek. "Doubtful. I'm not even sure that guy can talk."

Remy glanced at his cellmate. When the man woke up, perhaps he'd get to the bottom of the issue. He looked at his guard. Another cop, a middle-aged black guy, wandered in with two steaming paper cups of coffee.

"Oh," the first officer continued and snapped his fingers, "that reminds me. There was some FBI agent called about this case before you woke up. Some chick named Gilmore. She was really vague and wanted to know what the official report was so far, but definitely name-dropped you. Fun times."

The second cop uttered a rusty belly-laugh as he set down his dual beverages. "The FBI? Oh, Lord. What the hell did David Remington the Great do this time? Ha!"

He rubbed his eyes and exhaled slowly as he climbed to his feet. "You know, officers, to be perfectly honest...I have no frickin' idea."

For a brief moment, he reflected on the possibility that this might be bad—the Feds getting involved with things usually was. But he hadn't really done anything. Disorderly conduct, maybe, and the owner of the car that bumped into him might try to sue him for a new paint job or some shit.

But he wasn't too worried. In his experience, he tended to get away with things.

I'll be out in no time. I'm not sure how, but I'll manage.

The first officer took one of the paper cups of coffee from the second and turned back toward Remy. "Yeah, well," he stated, "if she wants to come in here and question your ass, there isn't much we can do about it. So be a good boy if she does, hey?"

The second man laughed again before he downed half of his coffee in one gulp. "Rolling around in the middle of the street and bouncing off cars. I wish I coulda been there to see that, haha! Oh, Lord, have mercy,"

Remy smiled, although without much mirth. He was merely a clown to these guys. That, he realized, was what most people saw when they looked at the old him.

The younger man took his leave and the older black man replaced him as guard. Remy settled into a seated position, rubbed his eyes, and breathed in and out while the last of the booze cleared itself from his system.

He turned to the guard. "Hey, man, do you know what time it is?" Since beginning work at the agency, he'd grown overly conscious of whether the sun was up or not at any given time.

The man glanced at a wall clock which was slightly out of the detainee's range of sight. "Oh, it looks like it's juuuust about six o'clock. You've been here damn near all day. Do you want your phone call? Your public defender ought to show up tomorrow, I think."

"Eh," he responded, "I'll give it another hour." He somehow suspected that news of his apprehension and incarceration would have spread quickly.

Half an hour passed.

Remy's guts curdled when he noticed that, by now, the weird guy across from him was on the verge of regaining consciousness. And with business hours mostly over, he was seriously looking at the prospect of spending the night there.

"So," he said to the guard, "what's that guy in for, anyway?" He gestured to his cellmate.

The middle-aged officer looked up from the fishing magazine he'd been reading and peered over the tops of his glasses. "Oh," he began and blew air between his lips, "birds of a feather, I guess." He waved his hand vaguely.

He nodded. "Drunk tank. Disorderly conduct and other such bullshit offenses. Got it. Hopefully, he didn't try to shove some other individual into oncoming traffic."

The guard lifted the magazine back over his face. "I can check the report if you really want me to." His tone suggested that he would have to be very insistent to get him to follow through.

"Oh, no, ha." He chortled. "That's fine."

He looked at the man across from him on the opposite bench. His cellmate was a big, slobby, heavy guy in an oversized coat, not in good shape but probably strong, with unkempt hair and stubble that was on the verge of becoming a proper beard. He smelled like cheap vodka, Swisher Sweets, and dirt sealed to the skin by a layer of dried sweat. His eyes fluttered open.

First, he uttered a long, grunting sigh and rubbed his eyes. Then, he glared. "You lookin' at something, pal?"

"Not at all," he answered. "Merely staring into space. I forgot you were there since you were sleeping, you know."

He struggled into a seated position. "That's cute. Are we in jail?"

Remy spread his hands. "Where else? It's so warm and safe here. I, for one, am comforted to know that the people of this city are concerned enough with our fate to provide us with such an excellent facility."

The guy coughed and spat on the floor. "What are you, a fuckin' college professor? Who bought you that suit?"

Before he could concoct some smartass answer—which, he later admitted, might make the situation worse—a door opened and two pairs of footsteps entered. One sounded like it belonged to a small, light person.

A cop barked, "David Remington! Someone to see you."

Remy sighed. He estimated it was about 6:40 now, meaning there was still twenty minutes until he would have broken down and demanded his phone call.

"About time," he commented.

The heavier pair of feet turned, left, and closed the door while the lighter pair approached the cell. The guard set his magazine down and stood to observe.

Taylor wore a rather stylish black velvet jacket and had sequestered her hands in its pockets. She stood and looked at him as though perched atop a mountain to watch all the little ant-sized humans scurrying by below.

He waved a hand toward her in a highly exaggerated manner. "Hi, Taylor."

"Remington." Her voice was flat. "Are you all right? Poor dear. Actually having to pay the consequences for your actions." She shook her head a little while her dark gaze remained fixed on him.

His abdomen tightened. What she'd said might mean that she was only there to scold or even mock him and planned to leave him there to rot—at least for however many days it would take for him to see a judge and have this minor-ass case dismissed.

"Wellllll," he drawled with an overstated tone of casual arrogance, "I seem to recall that my taking time off and having a night out on the town was your idea."

The faint shadow of a sharp little smile passed over her face. "Which is why I'll bail you out. This one time. You're far more useful to me free from the penal system but not free in the slightest from your debt to me for saving your ass."

The grungy gentleman on the opposite bench burst out in snorted laughter. "Haha, who is this? Your mom? Is she single?"

Remy adjusted his tie at his throat and pointedly

ignored the man and his charming commentary. "Thanks," he stated and looked at Taylor.

The officer chuckled in a slightly nasty way as he fished through his keys and opened the cell. "It's good to know someone out there still cares about him. For all the times he's been arrested, this is the longest stretch he's ever spent in jail. Almost a full day. I was kinda expecting to see his family by now."

Taylor stood unmoving with her hands still pocketed and looked at Remy with an expression that was mostly her usual resting face—cool, aloof, neutral, and almost unreadable. But he could read a trace of something else.

Sardonic amusement, he decided. On some level, she found this really goddamn funny.

He stretched his arms and legs, rolled his head on his shoulders to crack his neck, and sighed before he stepped out of the holding cell. The guard, meanwhile, kept his eyes on the hefty, unkempt detainee while he closed and locked the door.

For his part, the man remained on his cot and only glowered and muttered things under his breath.

Taylor and Remington strode to the door and quickly found themselves in the brightly lit hallway, where the officer who'd escorted her a moment ago rejoined them.

He was an older, broad-shouldered white man with a red lumpy nose. Judging by his voice, he drank his whiskey on literal rocks rather than ice and crunched and ate them after he'd drained the glass of liquid. "Ms Steele. Between you and me, we're not charging your boy there with anything serious at this point."

"Good." She now walked beside the cop and he followed the two of them. "He was, after all, attacked, so I would think the majority of the blame would fall on his assailant. Of course, I'm certain he put himself into a situation that made it much more likely that something of this sort would happen."

Remy remained silent but his mind groaned. The ride home would definitely be unpleasant.

Somehow, he had the distinct impression that Taylor would hold this incident over his head until after time itself came to an end.

It took a few more minutes before they were free of the precinct building. They had to stop at the front desk and complete more paperwork. He had to sign release forms and answer a couple more basic questions so the arresting officers could complete their reports.

He didn't pay much attention. It felt like the whole process was being expedited—as if his companion had some means to circumvent the usual protocols and hurry things smoothly along. But he could not remember the details of the previous times he'd been into and out of jail with much clarity, so it was hard to contrast the experiences.

Outside, the evening was bright with electricity and busy with noise and motion. Seeing Times Square again suffused him with an odd, uncomfortable mixture of both nostalgia and loathing.

Taylor gestured toward the nearest non-handicapped parking space. "This way, David."

He followed her toward a familiar-looking black Tesla. A couple of goons—who almost resembled Craig and Justin—ambled down the walkway. Both turned to stare lecherously at her as she passed, their mouths open as they formed stupid comments on their tongues.

She sent them a quick, sharp glare and they turned their heads forward and kept moving.

Remy chortled. "Those guys are smarter than they look."

To his mild surprise, she opened the back passenger-side door for him before she climbed into the rear driver's side.

As he slid in and strapped himself in, he glanced toward the front. Presley sat behind the wheel.

"Good evening, sir," the old man greeted him. "And madam. I'm very glad to see that things didn't take too long."

Taylor smiled and crossed her legs as the engine started. "Not long at all. Remington can't even have himself charged with a proper crime. Disorderly conduct, mainly."

"Come, now," he retorted, "disorderly conduct is better than nothing."

Presley maneuvered the car into the flow of traffic and began heading south and east. They were going to the office, then. Somehow, he would have been concerned if he'd started driving north toward Harrison. It wouldn't have been professional.

"Remington," Taylor said and turned toward him, "tell me about this person who attacked you. I already persuaded the police to tell me most of what they'd heard, but I want to hear your firsthand account."

He cleared his throat and tried to clear his brain. "Well, he—and I'm almost positive it was a man—came out of nowhere. Somehow, he snuck up on me on a busy street in broad daylight."

The vampire nodded. "Go on."

"He wore a black sweatshirt and a black ski mask and looked...average, I guess, nothing unusual. His eyes were bright blue, though. I remember that much. He also hit like a truck and jumped like two or three pro basketball players combined. My first thought was that he wasn't human. Fair enough, I was drunk but not that drunk. Some of the shit he did wouldn't have been possible for a mortal."

"It's unlikely," she mused, "although not impossible that he was a vampire. We can act during the day with sufficient protection. There are other possibilities, as well, however. A lycanthrope, or a shapeshifter, or a normal person who'd been...augmented. What, exactly, did he try to accomplish by attacking you?"

Remy shrugged. "Murder, I guess? Well, he probably could have simply torn my head off instead of throwing me around as much as he did. I don't know."

"Hmm." Her dark gaze went distant. "An intimidation beating—or perhaps a bungled kidnapping."

"Oh," he added hastily, "I just remembered. He said he knew who I worked for."

The vampire nodded again, more sharply this time. "David...what were you thinking, wandering around without backup? Where was Riley?"

He frowned. "Her week was up so I gave her the night off. Besides, I don't need a babysitter."

"Evidently," Taylor cut in, her voice almost a hiss, "you do."

Now, he began to get pissed. "I did exactly what you

asked, Taylor. I went out in public and spent a ton of money and acted like an asshole. You were busy, apparently, so that's one source of backup I had to cross off."

She seemed about to retort, so he forged ahead. "And Riley would have probably misunderstood what was going on and done something attention-grabbing. Imagine if she'd levitated me out of that guy's way while he attacked. Way too many people would be claiming to have seen some weird, weird shit."

Her face drooped with mild exasperation. "I could have mindwiped them if need be. That would be a hassle, but your death or capture would have been even worse."

"I'm glad you care," Remy retorted, "but next time you tell me to take a working vacation, give clearer instructions, perhaps."

She grimaced slightly, her manner suddenly cool and distant again as she turned her face away and declined to speak. Her slender hands came together in front of her and the red nails of the left drummed in sequence upon the back of the right.

Remy waited.

Presley, up front, asked, "Shall I put some soothing music on, madam?" He received no answer.

Did I beat her in an argument? He marveled at the thought. *Is such a thing possible?* He tried to contain his glee and avoid jumping to that conclusion too soon.

He was about to mentally declare victory when Taylor broke the silence.

"I will let it go, for now," she stated. "That does not mean you are correct, only that there are more productive ways to spend our time than arguing. We have other things to discuss."

Goddammit, he cursed inwardly. *So close...so damn close.*

"After the impressively melodramatic display you put on last night and this morning," she elaborated, "I believe we can declare 'mission accomplished' as far as the whole business of getting attention goes."

"Ah," he countered, "so you've been forced to admit that I succeeded at the task you gave me. We both knew I would."

"Oh, you more than succeeded, Remington." She turned her head partway toward him. "There is no further need, at this point, to tramp through the city flashing your money and acting like an insufferable prick alongside your loyal companions. Anyone who is the slightest bit interested in your activities will have gotten the point by now."

He forced a smile and nodded.

"I want you to stay around the office until further notice," she went on. "If you must go home, bring Riley with you and arrange for her to meet you in the morning as soon as possible. At least until I track your assailant. It's possible he's connected to the current case, but it might be something else—a leftover supporter of Gabriel's, perhaps. In any event, stay out of danger."

Remy neither agreed nor disagreed. He merely raised his eyebrows to indicate that he'd heard her speak and avoided answering.

The rest of the drive was peaceful. Soon, they arrived at their headquarters in Bushwick.

Presley waited while they unbuckled themselves. "Good

evening to you both," he said. "I will return before dawn unless instructed otherwise."

"Thanks for the ride, Jeeves." Remy climbed out.

As he and Taylor strode toward their office, he decided to make more conversation now that his anger had begun to fade. "So, have we decided on things like an Office Hours sign yet? Or how to deal with official inquiries into anything we're investigating?"

She unlocked the door and they stepped through. The lights were still on since Volz was present, tinkering with their security camera setup. He waved to them.

Taylor glanced at Remy. "I will let you know soon."

"Good." He adjusted his tie. "Oh, that reminds me, one of the cops said some FBI agent was asking about me. I must be really interesting. Or the guy who jumped me crossed state lines to do so, who knows."

She stopped and folded her arms over her chest and her eyes again took on that far-flung, contemplative look.

"Hmm. Another player on the board...fascinating." With that, she spun on a heel and glided toward her own office.

He stood and watched her go, and his skin crawled with irritation. "What the hell does that mean? Did you know about this already?"

Once again, she'd left him out of the loop.

Resolute, he clenched his jaw. As far as he was concerned, that meant he ought to keep pursuing leads on his own—and he might not even need to leave the building.

CHAPTER ELEVEN

Tenor Extended Stay Hotel, Queens, New York

Alex sighed and ran a hand through his hair, which had grown shaggy and disheveled. The cannabis enthusiasts next door had departed, only to be replaced by a music lover of sorts. Now, a seemingly endless barrage of Cardi B, Eminem, and other such American artists assaulted him any time he was in his room at all hours of the day between about eleven am and sometime after midnight.

He used a pair of scissors to cut a cotton ball in two and stuffed one half into each of his ears. Then he settled at the tiny, scuffed desk the motel had graciously provided and fired his laptop up.

Moswen had provided the device but she hadn't been particularly gracious about it.

Grumbling, he waited for it to boot and squinted in aggravation as he typed in his password. The thing was so cheap and basic. Didn't he deserve something high-end—or at least middle-end—for his months of loyal servitude?

Once the pitiful excuse for a computer booted up and concluded its clumsy search for the motel's Wi-Fi signal, he settled into the evening's task—doing research on Taylor Steele and her mysterious organization.

He'd already heard of the Moonlight Detective Agency and put two and two together. They didn't exactly advertise much, but neither was their existence a secret. They even had a website.

Alex snorted. "Jesus, Mary, and Joseph in a low-rent strip club, this is fucking awful."

For an apparently influential business, they had one of the crappiest websites he'd ever seen. It looked like some secondary school kid had thrown it together as a project for an Introduction to Web Design class and barely achieved a passing grade.

"Well, at least it has the basic information," he muttered. "Although I already knew most of this stuff. They have a new office in Brooklyn…interesting. And they're accepting new clients."

For a moment, he contemplated simply going in and posing as a customer. Remington hadn't seen his face. If they suspected him, though, that would be an excellent way to end up languishing in an American prison—which was the best-case scenario. Other scenarios included Moswen burning his heart out for failing her. Or Taylor, if she was as scary as everyone said, ripping his skull off and using it to play football.

"Excuse me, soccer," he corrected himself and allowed the sarcasm to drip nice and thick. "Over here, football is that game with the deformed ball and yards instead of fucking meters."

He browsed around the hideous website for a few minutes in search of any kind of information beyond the vague description of the services they offered as well as the address, phone number, and email. There wasn't much.

Scoffing, he murmured, "It makes me wonder how profitable their little venture is if they can't even afford to hire a decent designer. Maybe they're operating at a loss?"

His attention turned to doing a few searches with the idea that he might determine if Taylor had any prominent references, social media presence, or whatnot.

There was virtually nothing. No woman named Taylor Steele turned up in any list of university alumni, nor were there any legal records and professional accolades, nor did she have a LinkedIn profile. The Moonlight Detective Agency had a Facebook page, but it was sparse and mostly a launching pad to their lame website.

"Remington," Alex muttered. "It looks like once again, I have to go through that arsehole to get to Taylor." He continued to grumble while he recalibrated his search.

The difference was like that between night and day. David Remington was practically a local celebrity.

"So much for Remington Davis, like the website says. It's clearly the same guy under an alias. You'd think he could have come up with something less obvious—like, I don't know, Mikhail Jigoro, maybe." He shook his head.

The strange thing was, nothing about the abundant information on Remington suggested that he was a person to be taken seriously and was merely some spoiled, rich, idiotic party boy. And yet, there he was, clearly working for Taylor's agency.

Running a thumbnail over his lips, he considered that

Taylor might be using him as part of her front for the benefit of the general public. Remington might even be funding her entire operation with his family fortune.

It was the only thing he could think of that made any sense. The rumors, the down-low pieces of advice, and the unspoken implications that he had gathered were almost unanimous votes for his final conclusion. Taylor was one of the—if not the most—dangerous beings on two legs anywhere near New York. And Remington acted as her assistant and did some of her dirty work.

Alex hadn't wanted to face such a powerful vampire unprepared and unaided. He didn't know how Taylor compared to Moswen, but if they were anything alike, he knew not to fuck around.

And yet, he hadn't learned enough, hadn't found enough leads, and hadn't made enough progress on the mission his mistress had given him. Some kind of action, even if hasty and risky, seemed imperative.

That was why he'd targeted the human. Now, he might well have squandered his one and only chance at capturing Remington. Obviously, he couldn't entertain the notion that Moswen would tell him that everything was okay, pat him on the head, and say that at least he'd tried his best.

For only a moment—a fraction of a second—another possibility entered his head. It was one of the types of ideas he was not supposed to have, and while he'd tried to bar such things from ever entering his brain, his prevention system was not yet perfect.

What if I went to Taylor for help? A creature as powerful as she is might be able to help. What if I asked her to remove the brand, and protect me from—

The immediate response was as if someone lit a blowtorch in front of the left side of his chest.

"Aagghh, fuck!" he cried and his hands shook as he clutched the glowing mark over his heart. The agony commanded most of the attention his brain could summon, but with what little remained free, he broadcast thoughts of how stupid it was to even consider seeking Taylor's aid, and how he would never betray his beloved mistress.

The phone rang, and the pain faded.

Gasping, he leaned forward and picked up the receiver to raise it to his right ear with a hand that still trembled.

"H-Hello?" he said. He suddenly remembered the cotton in his ears and snatched the wad out of his right.

It took a second before Moswen spoke. "Alex. I have changed my mind and decided to call earlier than planned. Please tell me of your progress."

He was somehow relieved that at least she wasn't overtly angry with him and so far, hadn't made any veiled threats. The burning sensation had already done most of the talking, after all. Still, there was that hot, dusty menace to her voice. He knew better than to get comfortable or complacent with her.

"Mistress," he began, "I have more information on the… ah, situation here and have made some strides toward carrying out your will."

"Have you?" She sounded skeptical. "And what is that terrible music?"

Alex cleared his throat. "The neighbors. I simply continue to do what I do and try to ignore it. Anyway, I've learned more about this vampire, Taylor Steele. I think she, more than anyone else, is the person we need to focus on. Almost everyone in the preternatural community here has heard of her, respects her, and even fears her. She's one of the most powerful creatures in the city. It seems her role here is to act as the enforcer of the rules—she keeps the other creatures from misbehaving and drawing the attention of the human authorities."

"That is interesting." The vampire considered this in silence for a moment as she turned the facts over in her mind. "She cares about humans. It would seem she enjoys playing in the mud."

Alex recalled Moswen's previous orders—that he was to identify the top preternaturals in New York and either convince them to become her vassals or eliminate them.

Before she could speak again, he elaborated.

"Taylor seems like she might be open to negotiation, but it's hard to say. Many of the people—entities, beings, creatures, whatever—whom I've spoken to have said she's fairly reasonable but then again, there was some incident a couple of months ago when she destroyed a group of would-be usurpers who tried to remove her from the picture. From what I heard, she killed them all and burned the ringleader's mansion, so she's not someone to be taken lightly."

Again, somehow, he could hear Moswen smile.

"I would do worse," she stated.

He did not doubt that.

"So, anyway," he continued to explain, his words coming in a rush now, "I tried to capture her human errand boy, this poofy fuck named Remington since I thought I could lure her into a trap that way. The idea was to set up negotiations with the option to kill her if she wasn't accommodating. But he's usually protected by a fairy and the goddamn police intervened immediately on the one occasion when she wasn't there. No one really saw anything aside from a random fight, it seems, but—"

"Silence," she snapped.

Alex shut up at once, and his mistress continued.

"Your excuses do not interest me, but I want you to put that task aside for now."

He cocked an eyebrow and hoped momentarily that she'd command him to return to base but wasn't overly confident in such a glorious possibility. She probably wanted him to do something even worse than deal with Taylor—like kill the president of the United States and start a nuclear war with China. And without even a reservation at a decent hotel. He clamped down on these thoughts instantly before his chest could flare again.

Moswen made a deep throaty sound and it somehow occurred to him that she might have just eaten.

"There is an object I require," she told him. "I have been trying to procure it by...acceptable means for some time now."

Alex tried not to wince. "Tell me more, mistress."

"My buyers have already attempted to purchase it. Several times, in fact, each time making larger and more generous offers. But success has eluded me. Those who possess it now are not willing to part with it at any price."

He basically knew what was coming.

"I need you to steal it," she said. "It has a name but these ignorant humans never seem to use it. Crudely and unimaginatively, they merely call it the Egyptian Black Cat Idol. As though it were the only one." She broke off speaking to laugh, the sound like a sand dune collapsing over an oasis in the middle of a dust storm.

Alex coughed. "Where is this idol now, mistress?"

She made the throaty noise again. "They are keeping it on display at the Guggenheim Museum, a place which exists to parade works of art before the peasantry. Art! They think it is nothing but a bauble."

"Ah, yes," he replied, "the Guggenheim. It's a famous museum, actually. Upper East Side in Manhattan."

"Go," Moswen commanded, "and get it for me. Very soon. You must move before they take it to some other place, probably deeper into America. Then you would be forced to chase after it like a dog trailing a donkey cart."

She still hadn't fully adjusted to the Post-Industrial Age, but the image and its meaning were clear enough. New York City was already providing more than enough America for Alex's tastes.

All he said, though, was, "Yes, mistress. I obey."

"I must have that idol," she rasped, her voice stronger and harsher now. "I have not yet regained my full power, Alex. But that must change. And it will because you will not fail me."

The vampire hung up and the heavy click again seemed to echo through the receiver.

He breathed quickly in and out and scrolled inane words and images through his mind to crowd out anything that might sound disloyal as he placed his receiver on the hook. His brain tried to refocus as he sat for a few minutes and simply stared into space.

"So," he whispered to himself. "Break into the Guggenheim and relieve them of some priceless Egyptian artifact. No problem. I got this."

He lay on his bed and hoped the music connoisseurs next door were close to passing out by now.

"At least she doesn't want me to kill the president," he observed and tried not to let his voice crack and trail off into a moan. "Always look on the bright side, I say."

Bushwick, Brooklyn, New York

Remy laced his fingers together and flexed his hands outward to crack his knuckles. He might have to do more than his usual amount of typing and clicking, after all.

"So," he began, "let's see exactly who this mysterious Gilmore chick is. It ought to be a good test run for our kick-ass new computers."

As of today, Riley was back on duty. He'd picked her up first thing in the morning, handed over the requisite honey to her excited colony-mates, and they'd spent much of the day on boring legal and financial paperwork or jockeying the schedules of Taylor's nighttime clients. Volz and Bobby carried out their own duties in the main reception area. Now, at last, with daylight waning, he could move on to his personal responsibility in the investigation.

He started with the basics and simply plugged the agent's name into a search engine along with "FBI." A friend of his parents—a man named Hickenlooper—had contacts in law enforcement so he also sent a query to him.

The man hadn't, as far as he knew, joined the rest of the Remington family in refusing to speak to him.

Hickenlooper replied almost immediately but that was only because he'd never heard of a federal agent named Gilmore. He indicated, though, that he might be able to inquire about her and asked why it was that David wanted to know.

"Eh," he hemmed, "it might be better to wait before I respond to that one. I don't actually know that guy very well."

Riley had left a few minutes ago to talk to Volz, but due to Bobby's presence, he couldn't actually reply much. The fairy drifted back, opened the door to Remy's office magically, and left it ajar as she flew over to his shoulder.

"What are you doing, Remy?"

He waved a hand. "I'm trying to find some information. We have time before Taylor shows up and our shift ends, after all." By now, his tiny partner already knew about the fight in Times Square and he'd briefly filled her in on the mention of the FBI lady.

The name search proved more productive, but only slightly so. When he poked around a little, it seemed that there were seven different agents named Gilmore or Gilmour, but he had no idea how to narrow them down to the one who'd sought him out.

Riley put her hands on her hips as she stared at the monitor. "They have phone numbers," she pointed out. "You should call them all and ask which one is bad."

Remy bit his tongue as his eyes rolled spontaneously upward. "Thanks, Riley. I appreciate the suggestion.

However, in real, human life, these things usually aren't quite that simple."

"Aww." She pouted. "Why not?"

He had no inclination to even attempt to answer that age-old question. Instead, he tried to look for any mention of the agents' areas of operations or which field offices they were associated with. Any operating in New York would be the most obvious candidates. Of course, there was always the chance that his masked attacker had come all the way from San Antonio or something and that Agent Gilmore was therefore based in Texas.

Behind him, heavy footsteps plodded toward his office and came through the door, which was still stood open.

"Golden Boy," Volz said. "What are you doing there, if I may ask?"

Remy snorted. "If I'm Golden Boy, then by rights, you'd have to be Scruffy Short Ginger Guy. It's only fair."

"Hah!" the dwarf scoffed. "Fair. Hmm, an Internet search involving the human authorities, I see. It looks fun...albeit difficult..."

To look busy, he shuffled the mouse and clicked on a link to a news story he knew would be useless. "I'm surprised you didn't say 'difficult for a human.'" After a heavy sigh, he recapped the situation to the dwarf in the hope that he'd have some advice to offer.

Volz stroked his huge red mustache. "Hmm. Why not simply hack into the FBI's database and see which agent has an open case involving the Times Square incident?"

"Ha, ha." He chortled. "Good one, Volz. I'll get right on that."

The dwarf squinted at him and his mouth began to smirk. "Do you think I'm joking? Not at all. Cracking most mortal computer systems, frankly, is like taking candy from a somewhat tech-savvy baby. Humans lack the lifespan to learn things and aren't inclined to be good with systems, in general."

"Yes," Remy remarked. "What I really needed right now was a dwarven supremacist lecture. Is there any chance you could take over my seat for a second or two and get on with the candy-stealing?"

Volz grinned. "Of course. For a price, that is."

"I'm not shocked." He stood and turned the chair toward the dwarf. "Bill me later."

Chuckling with satisfaction, the tech squeezed himself into the chair and boosted its height up a few inches. He set to work and screens, windows, and strings of code and numbers appeared on the display at a dizzying pace while his fingers danced over the keys.

Remy puffed his lips out as he watched, impressed. "Damn. This is like one of those terrible hacking montages in movies or TV, where they make it look like this shit is really easy. I never even learned the basics of code. Do they simply hire dwarves for those scenes and film the results?"

"Sometimes," Volz quipped.

Riley also watched in awe. "I could make the computer do things," she observed, "but it would probably only burst into flames."

A few more moments passed before the dwarf leaned back in his chair and exhaled with satisfaction, a smug expression visible beneath his red brows and facial hair.

"There you have it, Golden Boy," he stated. "The official documents hidden within the private files of Senior

Special Agent Kendra Gilmore. And they won't even know we were here." He grunted and shuffled himself forward and out of the seat, which was a little narrow for his frame.

Remy peered at the screen. It definitely displayed a Docs folder—which contained mostly weird technical stuff —but also a sub-folder labeled *Reports*. That sounded promising.

He clapped a hand on Volz's broad shoulder. "Excellent work, Scruffy Short Ginger Guy. My people will be in touch with your people about the fee." He slid into his chair and lowered it to an appropriate level.

Volz shook his head. "Your cockiness is truly something. You'd almost make a good dwarf, you know, if you hadn't had the misfortune to be born human."

"Thanks." He flashed his tech specialist a brief smile before he turned his attention to his new discovery. Volz grunted again and stomped out of the room in time to field another inane question from Bobby. Remy ignored the discussion which, thankfully, was almost immediately silenced when the door closed.

Within Ms Gilmore's reports folder was an assortment of files. One, in particular, caught his attention—partially because it was the first and most recent item she'd added and partially because it was titled *Times Square*. Its date coincided with Remy's recent arrest.

"Huh," he remarked. "There isn't much in the way of shocking twists or ambiguity so far." He skimmed his eyes over the other files. None of their titles made much sense or rang any bells and he decided he would have a look at them later.

First, he opened the Times Square one. Unsurprisingly,

it seemed little more than a copy of the police report regarding his little fracas, along with some notes on how the media were reacting to it.

The NYPD merely classified it as an intoxicated disturbance of the peace between the ever-popular David Remington and an unknown second party. There was no indication, fortunately, that they planned to surprise him with any heftier, scarier charges like assault and battery or possession of narcotics. Although, if the latter were the case, they'd step on their own dicks anyway since he'd been on nothing but alcohol.

The file also mentioned that, of course, the press reported the matter as a brawl and made mention of his family connections. They seemed ignorant of the fact that he'd been barred from his inheritance until further notice.

Finally, and most interestingly, someone had added a few notes about eyewitness statements that one of the participants in the fight had seemingly demonstrated superhuman speed and strength. The cops and the press dismissed these comments as the ravings of persons equally as drunk as Remy had been, if not mentally ill.

Why, then, he wondered, had Gilmore drawn attention to them?

Riley, reading over his shoulder, snickered with what sounded like scorn. "Those imbeciles. They keep calling you David. Someone should tell them your real name is Remy." She broke into laughter at this and doubled over while her tiny body shook.

He shrugged. "Let's say I have two different real names, depending on the situation, shall we?"

The fairy calmed, returned to her normal posture, and

fluttered her wings to straighten them. "I guess that makes sense. Kind of."

"Of course it does." He closed the Times Square file and proceeded to examine the others.

In contrast to the relative banality of the NYPD report, the other documents were exceedingly bizarre. Some contained news articles but mostly, they were jumbles of notes, jargon, and code, interspersed with in-line photographs and charts.

"What the hell..." Remy murmured. "Look at this one. 'Two dead, entire herd slain in bizarre murder-suicide.' Some ranchers killed all their sheep and goats by slashing their throats and apparently gave themselves the same treatment."

She squirmed. "Eeww. I don't like blood. And I hate when animals are killed. Poor things."

As he continued to read the story as well as the comments attached by Gilmore or her aides, it became clear that the article was a translation and the weird incident had taken place in a rural area near Beersheba, Israel.

"Hmm." He stroked his chin. "I have a hunch..."

His instinct proved correct. He clicked and skimmed his way through all the other files and found that every one of them, save two—the Times Square file, and another from Ponta Delgada in the Azores—focused on events that had taken place in Israel.

"Hah!" He laughed and actually grinned as the pieces of the puzzle began to come together. "That big scary vampire Taylor says she's tracking is supposedly based over there. There's no way that's a coincidence. And given the nature of some of this shit, it would seem she and Agent Gilmore are working the same case."

Among the other stories were a wide variety of suspicious occurrences. Gruesome unsolved murders. Major burglaries of high-security facilities in which the perpetrators had stolen everything from money to food to weapons. And no fewer than three instances when local bystanders claimed to have seen someone leap to the tops of buildings or across entire streets and apparently literally fly to safety.

"Now that sounds familiar," Remy said a little darkly. His cuts and bruises still hurt.

Riley had trouble reading all the material as quickly as he could—at her size, it took more time and effort to scan all that massive text—but based on what she could see, she rubbed her arms and shoulders in discomfort.

"This is bad stuff," she remarked. "It's what usually happens in a place where vampires start running amok. I hope the people over there are okay."

He frowned. "It might be a little late for that. For the moment, I'm more concerned with people here. Especially myself, of course. Still, this info might be useful."

And although he did not say it aloud, it would be especially useful in helping him get one step ahead of Taylor.

With a smirk, he imagined the scenario in which she was forced to admit that he'd cracked the case on his own. It included a satisfying moment when she apologized for treating him merely as bait and for trying to keep him in a subordinate position by reminding him of the whole jail thing. It would be glorious.

Remy returned his attention to the screen. The folder

contained a sub-folder, within which was a single file. He double-clicked it open and read it.

This one dealt with an extremely old statuette of a black cat crafted in Egypt shortly before the Greek conquest. Apparently, it was about to make a display tour of the United States.

"That," he commented under his breath, "also sounds familiar."

Agent Gilmore's commentary went on to explain her view that "the target" was "extremely likely" to pursue the statuette, even positing that it might be the entire reason this shadowy individual had come to New York, to begin with.

Best of all, in his opinion, was the agent's recommendation that the FBI "take the object into custody" for the sake of setting up a sting.

He stared at the screen for a moment and adjusted his cufflinks. After a moment of thought, he turned his head and called, "Hey, Bobby! Come here for a second."

A chair scraped and heels clattered across the floor toward his office. The door opened. "Yes, Mr Remington?" she asked, smiling at having something to do.

He waved her over to his desk. "Show me that article from the Inquirer again, the one you pulled out when you were telling Volz about that museum exhibit. If you still have it, that is."

"Ooh, yeah, I do." She looked excited, probably because he had shown interest in her interests, even if it was purely professional.

She fished around in her voluminous purse, eventually produced the folded and rolled-up sheaf in question, and shook it into a viable shape as it dangled from her hand.

Remy took it before she could proffer it. "Thanks. Let's see here..."

Right there on the front page was a large photo of an ancient figurine fashioned in the likeness of a black cat. Above it screamed the headline *Occult artifacts of power come to the Guggenheim*.

With a satisfied nod, he used his index finger to trace his way through the article in search of the range of dates. "Oh, this is perfect," he gloated. "The display will still run for another four days. Thanks, Bobby." He handed the paper to her.

"Don't mention it." She almost looked like she might be blushing. "You can keep it if you want to read the rest. There are some really good articles about—"

"Nah," he interjected, "I gotta focus on work here. I only needed to know when that exhibit would end. If I need anything else from the Inquirer, though, fear not. I'll be sure to ask you about it."

She stuffed the rag into her purse. "Awesome. Do you... uh, need anything else? I'm basically caught up by now."

He waved a hand. "You are dismissed. Thanks."

The girl turned and walked out of the office, seemed to leave the door open a second or two longer than necessary, and as he stared again at his computer screen, he thought he felt a draft. Maybe Volz had left a window open or something.

Remy steepled his fingers. "Yes, Riley, now we're almost guaranteed to—"

"How interesting," a soft, elegant voice cut him off.

He almost bolted out of his chair when Taylor leaned over his shoulder and gazed at his PC. He managed to remain still, bit his tongue to keep from blurting out some stupid comment, and wondered how the hell she'd slipped in like this. She'd probably entered as Bobby left the office. That was the most logical answer.

"Yes," the vampire went on, "this idol may be of use to us. I'm glad you found out about it, Remington, especially if that FBI agent has taken an interest in it. I see you've hacked into her files. That's quite impressive."

Remy grinned sheepishly and adjusted his tie. "Oh…ha, it was mostly Volz. According to him, most humans suck at computer security, even the supposed experts. When did you get here, by the way? I…uh, never heard you come in."

She nodded to acknowledge his humble admissions, although she kept her gaze on the screen. "It was crafted during the twenty-ninth Dynasty, I see, so it's probably associated with the cult of either the cat-headed goddess Bastet, or perhaps Sekhmet, who had the head of a lioness…which is close enough."

He blinked. "Wait, did the file actually mention that? I basically only skimmed it and didn't have time to read the whole thing."

Taylor moved around his chair to stand more comfortably beside him while she continued to study Agent Gilmore's document.

"I know my mythology, Remington. And I know a thing or two about what the Guggenheim people refer to as 'occult objects.' Oh, and that's interesting… Gilmore says her target is after it." She leaned back and tapped a red nail to her lips.

"So," he asked, "what does all that mean? In your…uh, professional opinion." Inwardly, he felt like something was sinking, or even crashing and burning—his fantasy of getting ahead of Taylor suddenly seemed much less like a potential reality.

She gave him a sidelong look. "It means that we ought to acquire the statuette ourselves before either the FBI or our enemy can. With so many fearsome and determined people now in pursuit, it's effectively guaranteed to be taken out of the hands of the current owners, one way or another, and I would be a far better caretaker than the Feds, let alone our rival in Israel."

Remy watched her and actually studied her while she spoke. He knew her well enough to recognize when she was being entirely serious and had made her mind up about something, even if her demeanor remained calm. Right now, she seemed casual and almost flippant. It was a façade.

"I see," he commented. "Our friends at the Inquirer ran a story on this exhibit, you know—Bobby showed me—and I distinctly recall them mentioning that the piece was not for sale."

Taylor smiled ever so subtly. "Everything has a price, Remington."

Riley piped up. "That reminds me, Remy, you still need to donate another pound of honey to the colony tomorrow. I don't really mind spending time with you, but the rest of my family will throw a fit."

"Yes," he acknowledged and inclined his head toward the fairy. "That will be our first order of business tomorrow."

He turned back to Taylor. "Well, even if it does have a price, I can't help thinking that it's probably out of your range." He paused and suddenly thought of his own bank account. "Or mine. Definitely out of mine."

The vampire's smile broadened, and he could almost see her fangs. "No one said anything about buying it."

CHAPTER TWELVE

Solomon R. Guggenheim Museum, Manhattan, New York

Senior Special Agent Kendra Gilmore breathed in slowly through her nose and exhaled gently through her mouth. The cooler they all remained during this operation, the better, and it started with her. Anxiety was contagious and it flowed downhill, hierarchy-wise. She had an example to set.

"Ma'am," said Agent Mortensen, her usual second-in-command on field actions. "We're clear to go whenever you're ready." He sat beside her in the van and the other three were in the back.

She nodded. Now in early middle age—although most people told her she looked younger—she was a tall, athletic woman of mixed white and black heritage. She had retained freckles well into adulthood and covered them with makeup to make herself look more mature.

Not that it was necessary with people who knew her well personally or were familiar with her professional record. "Not yet. Only a little longer..."

A security guard patrolled the outdoor perimeter of the museum. Gilmore and her team knew that there were three more men inside. This was in addition to a laser alarm system and a veritable gauntlet of cameras.

They knew this because, yesterday, a third-party affiliate of hers had been in to run surveillance and had delivered all the pertinent information. He had even planted a few micro-cameras of his own.

They had to wait for exactly the right moment.

Mortensen kept his gaze on the mini-viewer displaying the feed from the tiny cams and reported what he saw.

"One guard is still at his desk. The other one on the ground floor is circling to the far side of the building. Number three is near the top and close to the atrium and might be able to see down, but it looks like he's moving on. The external guard passed the front entrance a second ago."

Very close, Kendra thought. *A matter of seconds, now, and we go in. We cannot screw this one up.*

She had not expected to actually be granted command of this kind of special task force—especially not for an unsanctioned, technically illegal black op. That they were there now was both a privilege and a stroke of luck.

And if they failed, she might not be so lucky again.

Their van was parked immediately across the street and a short way down. The location was close enough for them to quickly rush out and enter the museum but far enough away that it wouldn't look too obviously like they had targeted it.

They'd sneaked the vehicle in during the changing of the guard after normal business hours drew to a close and the place shut down. No one had really seen them arrive and no one seemed suspicious of their presence. So far.

And now, it was time.

Gilmore spoke softly into her headset. "On the count of three..."

She and the four other members of her primary force, including Agent Mortensen, would conduct the main strike into the building. Additionally, she had two other men in other locations.

Perched at the window of a nearby apartment complex was Agent Mgaywa, safely ensconced in gloom and shadows but well-positioned to keep an eye on things with high-powered infrared binoculars. He would be able to alert them, via headset, of any approach by backup private security forces, local law enforcement, or any other possible threat.

Hidden around the corner in an alley was Agent Gennaro. He was dressed in civilian clothes and was prepared to create a diversion as well as offer resistance by force is necessary. If the external security guard came too close to the main team once they'd entered the museum, he would stagger out, pretend to be some random drunk asshole, and engage the man in a low-level scuffle until the remainder of the team was in the clear.

"*One*," Gilmore said. Something like an electrical cloud seemed to rise from her teammates—the tightly coiled adrenaline seeking release.

On the viewer, no guards were in sight patrolling the ground floor. The guy at the desk could be pinned down by one of them while the others focused on the statuette.

"*Two*." The exterior guard passed out of sight to check

behind the museum.

Everyone fingered their weapons. They were loaded with rubber bullets, but things could still go wrong. There could be no mistakes.

"*Stop*," Agent Mgaywa hissed through their earbuds. "Someone's coming."

Gilmore froze and echoed her subordinate. "Stop —wait!"

The five members of the main team stilled as they looked around for whoever it was their teammate had seen. Mortensen checked his mini-viewer furiously and paid special attention to the micro-cam on the outside wall of the building with a view of the corner of Fifth Avenue and East 89th Street.

Their overwatch spoke again. "Someone all in black is moving really fast toward the front door."

Kendra glanced at her second-in-command, who licked his lips in his concentration and added his own commentary.

"Yeah. I see them. Holy shit, Mgaywa ain't kidding."

Now, they all caught a glimpse of the mysterious intruder. A lithe, petite black silhouette moved across the pavement. It instinctively avoided the pools and columns of light that fell on the streets from the plethora of city lamps overhead and it seemed logical that it made almost no noise either, although they had no sound to confirm it.

At first, Kendra almost thought it was an animal—an oversized cat or a coyote or something. The way it moved did not, in all honesty, look human.

However, it ran on two legs, albeit close to the ground. She drew in a sharp breath. Cold pinpricks ran down the back of her neck and all along her spine to trigger shockwaves of ice through her whole body.

She hesitated. They might be able to accomplish a last-minute change of plans—spring a trap on this infiltrator, wring information from them, and justify their own presence by saying they expected an attempted theft and were there to stop it.

It was a good strategy but there was no guarantee that this person was their real target. And even if they were, it would leave the Black Cat Idol still in the hands of its current owners. The bastards who wanted to steal it would simply try again—only next time, they'd be more careful.

"Stand down," she whispered into her microphone. "Watch and wait."

Kendra sensed a ripple of tension go through the men around her and some of them sighed faintly in frustration. They had been on the verge of action after a great deal of intense preparation to perpetrate this heist.

And a heist was exactly what it was. The Federal Bureau of Investigation could not exactly take credit for the extra-judicial theft of a precious object. Hence the operation being off the books.

Accordingly, their hands were tied if anything threatened to toss a monkey wrench into the proverbial gears.

The dark figure finished its indirect and evasive yet fleeting passage across the street. At one point, it moved past only about fifty feet from the van.

Gilmore could not be certain, but she suspected this

cat-burglar, or whatever they were, was a woman. There was something about the shape of the silhouette and the way it moved that suggested a female. It could, however, be a particularly small and nimble man but moved too rapidly for her to get a good look.

The entire team watched, alert and breathless, as the newcomer stopped momentarily at the museum's main entrance. A couple of gentle footsteps became audible as the exterior security guard appeared at the building's far corner.

She blinked in disbelief. The instant the guard had appeared, the dark figure had vaulted upward, seemingly without even a need to crouch or otherwise prepare for the motion.

She—it had to be a woman—simply became airborne. One moment, both feet were on the ground and in the next, she somersaulted through the shadows and somehow avoided the lights as she tumbled upwards. The security guard strolled forward without missing a step, none the wiser that she'd even been there, to begin with.

Mortensen gasped. "Did you see that? Who the hell is this character?"

Kendra had one or two ideas, but she only shook her head as if in total ignorance. Now, however, this began to make a modicum of sense. The rumors weren't total bull-shit, after all.

The shadowy figure landed—apparently soundlessly as the guard wasn't alerted—on the flat ledge that overhung the entrance area to place her level with the second-floor part of the atrium. Kendra stared, curious whether their guest would try to leap down once the guard passed and go through the front or use a more unconventional form of entry.

The black-clad figure remained on the ledge. Slowly, she crept over to the curved surface of the museum's cylindrical main body and hid in a narrow slat of darkness.

Down on the ground, the guard sauntered on, his attention on this area already waning as he navigated the corner to patrol the side and rear of the building.

One of the guys in the van exhaled sharply from his nose. "What is she doing?"

He received his answer almost immediately. The cat burglar's dark shape began to scuttle up the exterior of the atrium. She moved like a lizard and far too quickly for them to believe what they saw. It was almost surreal.

Kendra raised her pair of field binoculars to her eyes and briefly caught a glimpse of the figure during her ascent.

There was no climbing gear that she could see. Unless the party-crasher had some kind of specialized grip embedded within her gloves, she simply pulled herself along the vertical surface as though gravity meant nothing to her.

"Well," she said quietly, "it would appear she's going in through the goddamn skylight." She lowered the binoculars and shook her head.

Mortensen checked the cams again. "I have a camera on the top floor that has a partial view of the skylight. We should be able to see what she does if she goes that route. She might also go over the top and try to get in through the back, you know."

Kendra nodded. "That's possible…"

Someone in the back, whom she recognized as Agent Villareal, finished her thought for her. "Yeah, except this is already some Batman-type shit. I half-expect her to crash through the glass on a cable."

They huddled around Mortensen's viewer and watched as the slender black silhouette darkened part of the skylight and stopped there. She took a moment to do something to one of the panes of glass.

The interior guard patrolling the highest level of the atrium strolled past and suddenly, the infiltrator was gone.

"Shit," Mortensen said. "Did anyone actually see her move? It looks like she simply blinked right out of existence."

Gilmore did not like the almost superstitious vibe she now felt from her men. "I think I saw her jump. Listen, we may have some powerful steroids and prototype technology at work here, but she's not a ghost or a gremlin. Whoever she is, she's still a part of the normal world that we're trained to deal with."

That seemed to calm them a little.

On the screen, the guard continued his slow walk and the dark figure returned to work. She abruptly removed an entire pane from the skylight, crawled through the opening, and moved upside-down along the interior of the glass before she dropped silently to the floor.

Horror gnawed at Gilmore's gut as the intruder advanced behind the top-floor guard and seemed to move directly toward him.

Jesus. She's not going to kill that guy, is she? We can't let her—

The dark figure pounced and immediately caught the

man in a triangle choke. He struggled and flailed for a moment or two before he lost consciousness. His assailant dragged him behind a dividing wall as if he weighed about five pounds.

"Damn." Villareal snickered. "I'm almost starting to like this bitch. This is like, poetry in motion."

Another odd fact soon became apparent. The black-clad figure moved constantly in such a way that her face was never directly caught by any of the museum's security cameras.

She must not have known about micro-cams planted by Kendra's ally, though, since her face did pass directly in front of the one focused on the top and skylight. The intruder wore a black veil or balaclava of sorts. All they could see was a pair of smoldering black eyes.

The team stared, rapt, at the screen as the lady worked her way down to the ground floor. There, she neutralized the other patrolling guard the same way she'd disabled the first. The man seated at his desk up front was not even aware of her presence yet.

"Mortensen," Gilmore said. "Pull up and maximize the cam watching the area where the statuette is. That has to be what she's after."

Her right-hand man did as instructed. The viewer was filled by the feed in question, which looked out on the Peter B. Lewis Theater, current home of the Occult Objects display. The Black Cat itself rested on a stand at the far rear of the chamber.

Faintly, in the dim security lighting, they could see the latticework of lasers that protected the entire room from intrusion.

The agents held their breath as their rival slipped into the theater. She paused and examined the impossible net of luminous tripwires before her.

"All right," Kendra said, "if she crashes and burns here, which she probably will, we may have to go in ourselves in case she panics at the alarm and tries to kill the desk guard."

Instead, the stranger executed what looked partly like a gymnastics routine and partly like ballet.

"No way." Villareal gasped as the woman leapt and slipped and danced between the faint beams. "No fucking way."

Their gaze could barely follow the speed and grace of her movements before suddenly, she stood before the idol.

She plucked it calmly from its stand and slipped it into a small padded satchel at her waist. Nothing happened. The museum's security personnel must have assumed that the laser alarms were already sufficient as a last line of defense.

The thief pranced and wheeled through the beams once again and at times, her body appeared almost to float between them.

Mortensen shook his head. "My God. Ma'am, are we going to intercept her when she comes out?" He'd returned the viewer to split-screen. "It looks like she'll simply waltz out the normal way, at this point."

Kendra bit her lip. "No."

The mysterious figure emerged from the theater and, to their surprise, lobbed a small object back into the room she'd just left. It crossed one of the lasers and tripped the apparently silent alarm. Lights blazed on all throughout the building.

The last guard bolted up from his chair, his face slack with surprise, and he ran in the direction of the empty theater. Despite the lights, the thief had somehow located the one corner near the side of the atrium which still lay swathed in black shadows. She vanished into it and the guard ran past her.

When he'd moved on, she stepped out, moved at a trot, and walked out the front door.

Kendra shook her head in amazement. A perfect heist had been accomplished with inhuman precision.

Their guest had one more surprise for them. As the burglar emerged into the darkened street, she stopped, turned toward the van, and pulled her black facemask off. When she waved cheerfully at them, it looked like she was smiling.

She knew we were here all along, the agent raged. She brought up her field camera and made her hands work as quickly and efficiently as she could to snap a couple of photos in rapid succession.

The mysterious woman had stood in the beam of a streetlamp, so they'd likely be able to get good resolution on her features once the photos were processed.

What in God's name does she think she's doing? Kendra knew the others wondered the same thing. They'd somehow stumbled directly into a game whose rules turned out to be way more complex than they'd anticipated.

Villareal laughed and put his face in his hands. "Oh,

man. That was something else. What do you think, ma'am?"

Kendra folded her arms over her chest. "Right now, I don't know what to think. I'm impressed, I'll say that much. And I still intend to get that statuette."

She rolled her tongue around her teeth. "I do think, though, that we need to do our homework on the Black Cat's new owner."

Fifth Avenue, Manhattan, New York

Alexander Thomas crouched on a ledge, hidden in the deep nighttime shadows of Manhattan's tall, ziggurat-like buildings. Below him, the strange, circular mass of the Guggenheim brooded.

He'd arrived there too late and had seen everything.

With his senses heightened and his perceptions sharpened by the power which Moswen had imparted, he'd known instantly that the street corner was being watched by someone. He identified four or five people in a van opposite the museum, as well as a guy with binoculars in a nearby high window.

There was also some derelict-looking prick lounging in an alley out of sight. At first, he had assumed he was simply another street person, but when he'd heard the soft report of headsets, he realized the man was wearing an earbud. He, too, was one of them.

They were probably agents of the US government. Alex suspected he might be able to destroy them himself but it would be risky. All that needed to happen for him to fail was for one of them to scream and summon the cops.

Or, for that matter, to bring his comrades to the battle, toting automatic weapons and probably in a really shitty mood.

He had augmented strength and speed and perception but he was no more resilient to bodily trauma than any other human being.

Given that, he'd paused to gather his thoughts and re-plan his strategy, and simply waited. Then, Taylor herself had arrived. The Feds seemed as shocked as he was. They'd done nothing to stop her.

If Alex didn't try, no one would. And he didn't think he'd have another chance.

"Damn," he panted under his breath, almost mouthing the word rather than saying it. Nothing went right for him lately.

But he knew—he was certain—that all these setbacks combined would be insignificant compared to what would happen to him the next time Moswen called and he had to report that he'd failed her. Again.

There was, however, one thing that finally worked to his advantage. He recognized the single aspect of this debacle in which, finally, the universe gave him the small break he so richly deserved after all his hard work and needless suffering.

Taylor made her exit down Fifth Avenue. That placed her on a trajectory toward him.

Okay, his brain said as he forced himself to not speak out loud. She was a vampire, and her hearing might be able to pick up even the faintest of sounds. He tried to avoid even breathing. *We know she's killer-bad. But she also doesn't know I'm here. I'm as strong and fast as she is. And she has no fucking idea what a terrible week I've had.*

It was now or never. He could either get the statue and neutralize Moswen's most obvious rival in one fell swoop, or wait for the brand on his chest to finally cause his whole body to burst into flames and be done with it.

Taylor trotted down the sidewalk almost directly below him. A gargoyle-like griffin statue was mounted on the ledge at his side. Those two facts struck him as a good combination.

Do it.

The vampire paused for a fraction of a second and seemed to tilt her head up toward his position. By then, he'd already sprung his hasty ambush.

The stone griffin's base shattered beneath his fist and the bulk of it, along with other shards and fragments of material, hurtled down toward his target. In the same motion, he launched himself toward the pavement in front of her.

He was terrified. Wind hissed past his ears and the ground surged toward him. But his heart sang with gleeful joy when he realized that his feint had worked. She'd dashed forward reflexively to avoid the toppling statue and now, his feet would land on her head and shoulders.

Only about a meter of air separated them when her gaze flickered up and saw him. Then, somehow, she was already out of the way.

Fuck!

Alex pounded into the pavement a half-second after the shattered gargoyle did. The concrete collapsed inward in a spiderweb of cracks under the impact of his feet.

Taylor had barely avoided his first move, however, and he needed to make the most of the slight advantage. He used his landing as a launch to spin toward her, his arms out and teeth bared.

"Give me that—"

She lashed out and struck him in the face. While she hadn't had time to pull back far enough for a full-strength blow, it was still powerful enough to detonate thunder-claps of pain through his head and drive him back two steps, even empowered as he was by Moswen.

He stumbled and tried to turn the motion into a clumsy roundhouse kick directed at her knee. She merely caught his leg in her small, steel-hard hands and shoved. He catapulted into a lamppost and buckled the metal.

"So," a soft female voice said, "you must be the second party involved in the infamous Times Square Brawl."

Alex sprang to his feet and tried to mask the growing pain with rage and desperation but did not answer. He also tried to ignore the fact that the woman's voice betrayed no hint of fear whatsoever.

He pounced.

Moswen's loaned power enabled him to continue—for almost a minute—a fight that would have been over in seconds for an average human. His speed and power were the equal of his foe's. But, as he learned almost immediately, these gifts meant little when he barely knew how to use them.

If Taylor was taken aback by his raw physical power, she overcame it quickly enough. His lunging, undisciplined strikes failed to connect. She was ahead of his every move, anticipated all he did, and countered it with ease.

Blows battered him. The glancing strikes of her hands and feet and elbows and knees still carried enough force to drive him back, stun him, and leave him gasping in pain.

The minute she landed a good strike on his skull or caught hold of one of his limbs at the proper angle to break it, the duel would be over. He had almost no chance.

Goddammit. He punched wildly at the woman, only to encounter thin air before she reappeared behind him. *Goddamn everything.*

He rolled forward and barely dodged a lightning kick she'd aimed toward his neck.

"I only want the statue!" he cried. "Give it to me. She'll fucking kill me otherwise."

Taylor paused for the space of about a heartbeat, and Alex poised himself across from her, ready to fight again if he had to.

"You're not from around here," she stated. "You don't belong. And she will not even have the chance to kill you."

She advanced and he suddenly felt his bowels turn to liquid and his bladder to ice. He had to get the hell out of there, and now.

He jumped back without looking and relied on his enhanced strength to save him if anything was in the way. His only thought was to flee from the vampire.

A tiny part of his mind suggested that Taylor might have already ripped him in half if she was determined to end his life and that it was possible she was simply trying to intimidate him into surrendering.

The notion was easily dismissed. The cold, merciless determination she projected did not inspire him to take any further risks.

Alex dropped partially to one knee, pretended to be even more badly injured than he was, and slid his right hand out of sight as she glided toward him on the left. His fingers crunched concrete and gathered residual dust and gravel from the street.

"Fuck you!" he snarled and hurled the detritus at her face.

It worked—or, at least, as well as he needed it to. She hadn't expected such a cheap move and she stopped and almost fell back a step as she raised a hand to her eyes.

In the second it took her to recover, he had already bolted.

He sprinted, loped, scrambled, and stumbled. Concrete and asphalt blurred beneath him. He bowled through trash cans and lampposts, hurdled moving cars which honked or screeched their brakes, ricocheted off brick walls, and even crashed through the windows of vacant apartments. Quite simply, he did whatever it took to put as much of the city as he could between himself and his opponent.

At first, Taylor pursued him and he caught fleeting glimpses of her lithe form hopping from shadow to shadow or stopping to ascertain where he'd fled. But soon, she fell behind.

Once his desperate, brute-force retreat gained him a lead, he slowed enough to leave a less obvious trail.

Somehow, he didn't think she would prioritize him. If he kept moving, she would be content to return to her lair with her prize.

Alex worked his way south and soon reached the East River. He crossed it to stop on Roosevelt Island before he continued into Brooklyn and from there, to Queens.

Finally, he arrived at his shitty motel. It had never occurred to him that he'd be so grateful to see the place.

Now, I need to make sure I didn't sustain any terminal injuries in that shitshow and find a way to stop Moswen from killing me remotely in the meantime. And think up some final, insane ploy that will satisfy her will and save my arse. No problem.

CHAPTER THIRTEEN

Bushwick, Brooklyn, New York

Agent Kendra Gilmore paused on the curb and studied the façade of the Moonlight Detective Agency's relatively modest office building. The sun had set about an hour before. Somehow, she suspected the place might look even humbler during the day. In the gloom of evening, though, it commanded a modicum of respect.

"So," Agent Villareal queried, "what level of cooperation do we expect here, ma'am?"

She considered the question. "Uncertain. Open hostility is unlikely. They'll probably try to dodge giving us real answers, though. Keep an eye on things and let me do most of the talking."

While she had originally considered bringing her entire team, that would look too much like a paramilitary occupation of Ms Steele's office. Instead, she'd only selected Villareal, Mortensen, and Gennaro, and Mgaywa would wait in the car. Four federal agents seemed like enough to get the point across.

They pushed through the front doors, noted the security cameras, and found themselves in a small but brightly-lit, reasonably cozy reception lobby.

"Hi!" a woman greeted them. "Nice to see you guys. I hope you didn't have trouble finding the place. My name is Roberta Diaz, but you can call me Bobby. Everyone does."

Kendra smiled curtly. "Not at all. Finding the place, I mean."

Ms Diaz, she saw, wore a barely professional top that exposed at least half of her impressively large, round breasts. She also saw out of the corner of her eye that the gazes of her subordinates were drawn toward their hostess.

The woman had arrayed several trays of snacks and drinks on a long table against the wall. Crackers and cheese, deli meats, veggies and dip, and sliced fruit were placed within easy reach next to a bowl of bright red punch and a stack of plastic cups. A folding table and chairs were a little farther ahead on the open floor.

"Help yourselves." Bobby gestured toward the refreshments.

The three men glanced at Kendra. She nodded and they smiled and dug in before they almost immediately turned in the general direction of the young woman's chest.

Kendra looked, instead, at her face. "Thank you for the hospitality. May I ask if Ms Steele is ready to speak to me?"

"Sure." Bobby pointed down the hallway. "She's in her office, right over there. You can go and talk to her whenever you're ready."

"Good." She smiled faintly and scanned the floorspace around her. Another office opened toward the side of the building. It probably belonged to Steele's assistant, she assumed. A maintenance closet and a unisex restroom carried signs denoting their purpose. Security cameras monitored them from the corners of the ceiling.

She exchanged a quick glance with Mortensen, who had at least joined her in examining their surroundings before he allowed himself to become entranced by Bobby.

"So," Gennaro quipped to the receptionist, "how is it, working here? This neighborhood's better these days, isn't it?" His gaze appeared to have been stuck somewhere in her cleavage.

Nodding and hoping this wasn't all a trap, Kendra walked toward the big office in the back. She whispered, "I hope this doesn't take too long," into the microphone hidden in her lapel, which was a signal to Mgaywa that everything was fine so far.

She rapped on the door. "Hi, it's Agent Gilmore. Ms Steele?"

"Come in," a soft voice replied.

Kendra turned the knob and stepped inside. The office beyond was furnished in a tasteful, comfortable, and unremarkable style, with a jasmine plant and a decent print of some abstract modern art piece. The bizarre scene at the Guggenheim flashed again in the agent's mind.

A nice faux-leather chair faced the desk. She seated herself and looked across at Taylor.

The vampire kept her face on the pleasant side of neutral as she watched Agent Gilmore sit. She avoided turning her head since she wore an earbud, albeit a well-camouflaged one. Remington had wanted to participate in the interview, but she felt it better to keep it one-on-one.

She'd compromised, though, by allowing her partner to listen in on the conversation with an earbud of his own. Of course, if the other agents broke down the door of his office and discovered what he was doing, he'd be entirely on his own and she would claim she'd never have permitted such a thing.

Now, however, she focused her attention on her guest.

Gilmore was a tall, healthy-looking, mixed-race woman with curly light-brown hair tied back. Her face had a youthful appearance that made it difficult to judge her age. She could have been anywhere between twenty-nine and forty-nine in human years. Her demeanor suggested a subdued toughness and an intelligent, determined competence.

Being mortal, she was not in Taylor's league but she was probably someone to be respected.

The vampire smiled. "It's good to see you, Agent Gilmore. Bobby ought to keep your team entertained so we can speak for as long as you feel is necessary. And we intend to cooperate with your investigation to the best of our ability, so your man in the car can come in and have refreshments, too, if he wants."

Her visitor did not react in any obvious fashion. She had good control of herself. "Thank you, Ms Steele. I noted that you had an impressive system of cameras in place. That's always wise for any urban office, I feel. Especially since you handle cases for such wealthy clients. I heard some of them even pay in cash."

Taylor nodded. The agent had probably done her homework although, in part, her words were a bluff to see how she would react. She would quickly learn that she was not the only one with a poker face.

"Of course." She folded one red-nailed hand over the other on the desk. One of her nails was a little chipped from cutting through the glass of the Guggenheim's skylight.

Kendra was the first to continue the conversation.

"Now, then. As I briefly mentioned, I am investigating the individual who attacked your employee in Times Square. I might like to speak to him at some point. For now, though, I'd be content simply to know if you have any information that might be of use to us. We understand that your clients expect confidentiality and we're not interested in their affairs beyond any bearing they might have on our current cases."

"I see," she acknowledged. "Yes, my clients pay well to have their privacy respected since we often help them with highly personal matters. However, I certainly don't want anyone else attacked the way my assistant was. Perhaps, then, we can exchange enough information to be of mutual benefit."

A minor flicker of irritation passed over Gilmore's face, probably because she had implied that her small, private company had the right to demand quid pro quo from a federal agency.

Taylor was unsurprised, therefore, that the woman moved quickly to establish dominance by playing one of her bigger cards.

"Perhaps," the woman said. "We believe the Times

Square attacker may be connected to—or even the same person as—the individual who burglarized the Guggenheim Museum. Eyewitness reports of the perpetrator's methods and abilities seemed far too similar to be a coincidence."

The vampire adjusted her expression to look grave and concerned. Inwardly, she almost laughed. Both of them knew exactly who had perpetrated the Guggenheim heist. She was almost starting to like the agent now.

Remy whispered into her earbud. *"Crap. They're onto us. Does that mean they think you're the one who put on the ski mask and kicked my ass?"*

Ignoring his foolish commentary, she merely said, "You may be right. We still don't know who the Times Square attacker is or if they're connected to the cases we're working. May I ask why the FBI is taking an interest in these matters?"

Gilmore's face suggested, subtly, that she was almost starting to like Taylor, too.

"Well," the agent began, "I'll be frank with you. We believe that both these incidents may be connected with a dangerous overseas syndicate."

Taylor cocked an eyebrow. "Overseas, you say? I was under the impression that your bureau only dealt with domestic matters."

She nodded. "Our prime suspects, currently codenamed Ein Avdat after a canyon west of the Dead Sea, are based in Israel. However, their activities have fallen under FBI jurisdiction for two reasons."

"Do tell." Secretly, she was fairly confident she already

knew, but hearing Gilmore confirm her suspicions would be useful.

"One," the agent explained, "some of their activities have affected individuals with dual US-Israeli citizenship. We are allowed to investigate crimes committed against American citizens who happen to be living abroad."

Taylor made a show of widening her eyes as if this surprised her. "Interesting. Yes, I believe I heard something to that effect, come to think of it."

"And two," Gilmore went on, "as you might have guessed, certain suspicious activities connected to Ein Avdat have been traced here to New York City."

"I did guess," she quipped and allowed herself to smirk a bit. "Perhaps you're not allowed to tell, but I'll ask anyway. Do you have any idea who this Ein Avdat person, or group, or whatever they are, may be? And what their motive is?"

The agent tensed slightly. Most humans wouldn't have caught it, so again, Taylor had to admit that the woman was good at keeping control of her reactions. Still, between her vampiric senses and many, many years of experience, the telltale markers were apparent.

"I cannot," the agent stated, "divulge all the information, as I'm sure you can appreciate. Suffice it to say that they are very likely to be some element of organized crime. Israel has at least sixteen extant criminal families, some of which have ties to operations in other countries, not least the US."

This was mostly review for Taylor, but she wasn't up to date on all the details of human international mobs. Learning more about them might help point her in the appropriate direction to investigate what ties these groups might have with the preternatural.

Gilmore continued her spiel. "In the 1980s—slightly before my time, really, and probably before yours too—a New York affiliate of the Israeli Mafia perpetrated a massive jewelry heist in Manhattan. Following that, around the year 2000, the Abergil crime family was implicated in trafficking seven million dollars' worth of ecstasy pills into the US."

"That is disturbing," the vampire remarked. "Although international crime never seems to go away."

"Exactly. Many of the top criminals there have killed each other in feuds, by now, or been arrested by the Israeli police, but someone always comes along to fill the void. We believe that Ein Avdat may be the next big player on the scene, and we intend to stop them before they can gain a foothold in New York—or anywhere else in America."

She seemed to hesitate before she elaborated further. "Ein Avdat is suspected of involvement in several murders in Israel, and one of the victims was a dual US citizen. They've also drained the wealth of prominent families in both countries. It's possibly outright theft, but we think extortion is more likely. The evidence suggests that they're building up a power base to expand in New York City and beyond."

Taylor had not, while examining Gilmore, detected any clear signs of deception. The woman was telling the truth to the best of her ability. Of course, she was withholding all but the broadest information but she wasn't flat-out lying.

That meant the human authorities assumed this was a mundane criminal matter. Someone higher up the totem pole might suspect preternatural involvement, but the agents working the case thought they were dealing with regular mobsters.

She leaned back in her chair and affected a friendly and open attitude. "I admire your dedication, Agent Gilmore. We are in slightly different lines of work but have a shared commitment to uncovering certain dark secrets that may threaten innocent people."

Gilmore smiled with legitimate good humor. "'Dark secrets' sounds fairly melodramatic, but given the name of your agency, I suppose you have appearances to keep up. Seriously, though..." Her demeanor hardened. "How much do you know about what's been going on lately, if I may ask?"

This, the vampire realized, was an opportunity. By divulging her knowledge of some of the case's stranger and more esoteric aspects, she'd be able to gauge the woman's reaction and determine how much further she could confide in her.

There was also the possibility that Gilmore might decide to reveal more of her own information once she knew Taylor was aware that this was no ordinary investigation. Full confidentiality might be a moot point.

She opted to play hardball. "I know there are rumors going around of criminals with 'superhuman' abilities. The unidentified assailant in the Times Square brawl, so they say, had strength and speed beyond that of any normal person. Multiple eyewitnesses, with no connection to one another, all said the same thing. I even heard that similar rumors have been filtering out of Israel."

The agent tensed again and leaned forward. She decided to keep pushing.

"In fact," she went on, "some of what people have been saying is so strange and disturbing that my clients in the case even mentioned they wanted to avoid alerting the regular authorities if possible. Perhaps they're simply being paranoid, but it's the kind of thing that screams 'coverup.' According to them, anyway."

Taylor smiled and looked Gilmore straight in the eye.

Remy whispered into her earpiece, *"Are you sure you know what you're doing? Christ, I don't want to get arrested again, especially if you're in jail too."*

The agent, meanwhile, fidgeted in her seat. She must not have expected this. "I see you are well-informed, Ms Steele—at least when it comes to rumors on the street."

She laughed softly. "People do talk a lot, don't they? I only hope I haven't put my own life in danger by revealing all that to a federal agent. But you don't strike me as being here on a mission to silence anyone who knows too much or any of that other Men-in-Black, mindwipe kind of nonsense."

The other woman did not respond but waited for her to continue.

She did so without hesitation. "No, Agent Gilmore, I think you're truly out to catch the criminals. And based on that, I think it would be best if we openly exchanged information. Worked this case together, even, you might say."

The woman chewed a lip as she thought about it. "I will agree to that in a general way, although I may have conditions. I'll get back with you on those. Also, I can't promise that people above me in the hierarchy won't give you a certain amount of grief if you ruffle their feathers."

She paused and Taylor knew she was about to add something else of significance.

"I will say," she ventured, "that my team was keeping an eye on the Black Cat Idol at the Guggenheim prior to its theft because Ein Avdat seemed interested in it. We don't know why. Possibly for its monetary value or maybe for sentimental or even esoteric reasons. Criminals are often superstitious. In any event, we estimated it would make good bait. However..."

She stopped now to look the vampire directly in the eyes.

"We care far less about the Black Cat itself than we do about Ein Avdat. And at this point, I'd say the first step in unraveling their plot is to catch the individual who assaulted your man, Remington."

"Yes," Taylor conceded. She drummed her nails on the desk, aware that her visitor had now abandoned her notion that the Times Square attacker was none other than herself. "It's interesting that you mention superstition with all these strange rumors surrounding the incidents."

"True," Gilmore conceded. "Some of the aforementioned gossipers in the street believe we're dealing with... non-human entities. Supernatural creatures. I think it goes without saying that we don't even need to consider that."

Again, the woman was not lying, unless she was exceedingly good at it, and Taylor didn't think she was.

"No," the agent went on, "our theory is that Ein Avdat has obtained something like new, experimental steroids from the Israeli Defense Forces or Mossad. They've committed a couple of burglaries that the Israeli authorities have been suspiciously vague about, so it could be that they found a secret weapons stash. Worse, they might have compromised someone within the government or military. We're trying to work with the CIA and State Department on this, but it's tough going. In any event, we know there's a scientific explanation."

"Oh," she agreed with a smile, "of course."

A short pause followed as the agent moved her gaze strategically aside and pretended to casually examine the room before she spoke again.

"And, Ms Steele, I have done my homework on you and your agency." She brought her gaze to Taylor's face again. "It seems that some similar rumors have occasionally popped up in reference to your...abilities."

The vampire maintained her pleasant expression but allowed it to cool somewhat. "We pride ourselves on our competence."

"I did not," Gilmore continued, "put much faith in those mutterings. They seemed grossly exaggerated—the same type of superstitious drivel we try not to buy into. About things you've accomplished that were...impossible."

She shrugged. "My women's studies professor said people would exaggerate due to fear of strong women. Meanwhile, my physics professor said people would exaggerate out of imaginative boredom because reality isn't good enough for them. I don't claim to know why it's so difficult to get the truth out of people. But I do know that my own view of what is possible has been broadened by this case."

Remy's voice snorted in her ear. *"Am I the only one who actually believed you were a vampire?"*

Still looking at the agent, Taylor only nodded.

With a slight narrowing of the eyes, Gilmore said, "You may keep some of your secrets, Ms Steele. But, going forward, don't let them damage our working relationship."

"Agreed."

The agent breathed deep, looked around, and flexed her hands in a way that suggested she was about to end the interview. "Well..." She stood smoothly. "I'll take my leave. We'll remain in touch, though."

Taylor stood also and extended her hand. Gilmore shook it. Her gaze wandered to a framed picture of Taylor and Remy standing beside one another. His hand rested on her shoulder. She'd had Presley take that one mostly as PR for the agency.

The agent looked at her. "If I may ask, how long have you and Remington been a couple?"

Over her earpiece, Taylor immediately heard two voices exclaim, "What?"

"Not long," she explained. "A couple of months. It grew out of our professional relationship."

Riley's tiny voice raged in her ear. *"That's bullshit! Remy, you are not with her. Are you? I'll fly out there and levitate a desk unless you set the record straight."*

Taylor summoned all her powers of self-control to keep a straight face as her visitor nodded and turned toward the door. She accompanied her, opened it, and escorted her to the lobby.

Remington, meanwhile, attempted to keep the fairy under control and his voice came through her earbud in a hurried jumble of words. *"She only said that to fool the FBI chick, okay? Play along, Riley, and I promise I'll take you out on a date ASAP. Please? Be cool here. I swear—"*

The three male agents had formed a circle around Bobby, who prattled away about paleo foods and soaked up their rapt, almost hypnotic attention. The vampire decided Remy had been right to hire her.

"Hey," Gilmore snapped at them. "It's time to go. I hope you enjoyed your little audience with Ms Diaz, but we have work to do."

All their faces fell in disappointment.

Off to the side, a door opened and Taylor was suddenly worried that Riley was about to carry out her threat. She would have to go through the bothersome and risky process of mindwiping all four of the Feds if the fairy did perform a magic trick right now.

Fortunately, it was Remington.

"Oh, hi," he stammered as though he'd had no idea that Gilmore's team were even there. "You've probably heard of me. I'm the guy who was beaten up in Times Square. Are you only leaving now?"

He glanced at Taylor in an oddly emotional way which, she realized, would probably confirm Gilmore's suspicions that they were romantically involved.

The agent turned toward him. "David Remington, also known as Remington Davis. Nice to meet you. I'm Senior Special Agent Kendra Gilmore. Yes, we're about to leave. So far, we've gotten enough information from the police and various other eyewitnesses, but don't be alarmed if we do end up interviewing you at length in the near future."

Remy nodded dumbly.

The agent's demeanor warmed. "Don't worry, though. We'll catch the man who attacked you. This whole business will be resolved soon."

With that, she turned and left, practically dragging her men with her as they waved mournful goodbyes to Bobby.

Taylor glanced at the security monitors and watched the four agents pile into their car along with the man they'd left outside. They seemed to confer for a moment before driving away.

She looked at Remington.

He was stewing. Something Gilmore had said rankled with him. It might have been the presumption of romance between them, but she worried it was something else.

"David," she began, "you don't plan to do anything stupid and ill-advised, do you? Nothing of the kind I warned you not to do, such as pursuing that guy yourself?"

Remy smiled and adjusted his tie. "Not at all. The only stupid thing I'll do is take the fairy out on a date, as promised."

"Hey!" Riley protested from somewhere in the office.

CHAPTER FOURTEEN

New York Botanical Garden, The Bronx, New York

Outside the visitor center, Remy stood with his hands thrust deep into his pockets. His head moved to take in the sights between bouts of pacing along the paved walk.

"It never fails," he whispered and hoped the two girls who passed on his left wouldn't overhear him. "Almost literally every single date I've been on, she's been late. Regardless of who she is." Somehow, he had foolishly thought Riley might be different, but no. The fact that she was from a different species didn't seem to change the fundamental essence of her being a woman.

He sighed and checked the time. It was already 10:17 am. They wouldn't manage to start the case until almost lunchtime, he guessed.

Shaking his head, he turned and shuffled in the opposite direction with his hands now clasped behind his back.

"Hastily made promises…forgive us, O Lord, for we know not what we do."

Riley had refused to help him track the douchebag in

the ski mask until after they'd had a proper outing, thus fulfilling his vow. He had hoped he could persuade her to delay it until after this case was solved.

But as he knew by now—or ought to have known—fairies were capricious and temperamental little creatures. It was almost impossible to reason with them or bargain with them once they'd made their minds up about something important to them.

At least it was a nice day. Winter was well upon them now, but it was mostly sunny with poofy white clouds interspersed through the blue sky, and neither too cold nor damp.

As such, her insistence on having an actual picnic didn't seem quite as silly as it had first sounded.

"Hey!" a woman called.

Remington glanced over his shoulder and turned. It was easy to see who had spoken since they looked directly at him and bounced on their feet while they waved a greeting. What took a moment, though, was allowing his brain to process the information.

It was Riley and she was human-sized.

"Oh…I…" he stammered. "Ah, hi there! Yup…" He stared.

Once, shortly after they'd closed the file on Gabriel's ill-fated coup d'état, Taylor had persuaded the fairy to perform a simple magic trick and grow herself from five inches to around five-three.

He had tried not to think about that little incident since he'd spent these last few months gradually trying to cure himself of the worst of his vices—aside from moderate drinking. The last thing he needed was to be distracted on the job by helpless, drooling lust over a supernatural being whose anatomy he wasn't even certain of.

"You look..." he began and hesitated as he searched for the right words. "Um...attention-grabbing! Very vivid."

She wasn't naked, which was a relief, although he had explicitly instructed her to come fully clothed and to dress classy. He should have known, though, that the Fair Folk had a completely different notion of what classy meant than humans did.

Beaming with delight, she ran toward him, her bright pink plastic purse swaying, and leapt to throw her arms around his neck. "Aww! Thanks, Remy. I wanted to make sure you would be able to see me in a crowd."

She released him and lowered from her tiptoes. Nodding and scratching the back of his neck, he quipped, "Well, yes, you definitely succeeded at that. Your outfit is highly...vibrant."

The dress she'd selected—or made herself, perhaps?—looked like it had been made from a Pride Flag, except she'd rearranged the order of the colors so it bore less resemblance to a proper rainbow than it did to something sewn together from random strips of tie-dyed fabric.

"Good," she responded and calmed a little but still strutted and grinned, obviously pleased with herself. "And vibrant is a nice word. I don't understand why humans don't dress more colorfully. If you have to wear clothes, you might as well have fun with them."

Remy led the way toward the visitor center. "Well, fortunately or not, someone long ago decided that the less fun an outfit is, the more respectable the person wearing it is perceived. Especially for men. I have appearances to keep up, you see."

Inwardly, he cringed at his own hypocrisy, even if it was mostly a joke. He had only recently begun to rebuild what little respectability he still had, at least in the eyes of his family and most of the other society types.

By now, wearing a suit and tie was mostly force of habit.

"Oh," he snapped his fingers, "the food. I almost forgot this would be a picnic. It's a little chilly, but we'll manage."

Riley waited for him and her smile faded to mere satisfaction and happiness as he hurried to his car and retrieved the picnic basket. He had no idea what kind of food Riley might have brought, besides honey, so he'd taken that responsibility on himself.

He strode back toward her, the basket dangling from his arm. For a moment, he was able to appreciate the craftsmanship of her dress, now that the shock of its garish color arrangement had passed.

The top was designed to lay about her shoulders almost like a shawl, yet it was still noticeably low-cut in front. If Riley had designed it herself, she'd probably taken a cue from Roberta "Boobs" Diaz at the office.

The middle fit snugly about her waist, while the rest flowed in asymmetrical waves that were curiously elegant. A split ran up the side but stopped only a few inches above the knees, so nothing too risqué.

He had to admit that in its own strange way, the getup was damn classy, after all.

"Ooh," she said and caught his attention, "what did you bring to eat? Something sweet, I hope. I have trouble eating things that don't contain sugar or honey or NutraSweet or stevia."

"It must be nice to be a fairy," he said and immediately glanced around to make sure no one had heard. The nearest other visitors were a couple of hundred yards away, thank God. "To be able to subsist entirely on candy and never gain weight."

She squinted as he stepped beside her. "What exactly is gaining weight? I know some humans get fat, but it never made any sense to me."

"If we eat too much–especially sugar and grease and bread products—our bodies turn the extra food into fat. It's highly annoying, except during famines and Ice Ages."

"Oh, I see," she said and tapped her lips thoughtfully.

They approached the line forming at the entrance gates. It was longer than he would have liked, despite today being a weekday and in winter, no less. He supposed that New Yorkers were determined to enjoy what might be the last nice day of the year.

He glanced at his date when they came to a stop at the back of the line.

"You really do look nice," he told her. "I mean that."

She blushed, which only made his words truer. "Thank you, Remington. I tried really hard to look pretty for you."

Remy decided she had been successful.

While the more explicit details of her lovely body were tastefully obscured by the rainbow dress, there was still an infectious and gently erotic energy that seemed to emanate from her and her face was visible for all to see.

Up close, with her the size of a human woman, he could appreciate her features far better, not to mention the subtleties of what she'd done with her hair and makeup.

She had round cheeks but a fairly elongated facial structure, giving it a heart-shaped appearance that was highly appealing. Her lips were full and red, her nose perfectly symmetrical, and her eyelashes looked like they were close to an inch long. Her platinum hair was mostly pinned back, but she'd strategically allowed a few locks to fall over her face.

"Damn," he muttered.

"What?" she asked.

He cleared his throat. "The length of this line, is all. It'll take, like, twenty minutes to get in, probably. At least in this weather, the sandwiches won't spoil anytime soon."

"What kind of sandwiches? You never answered my question about what you have brought for brunch."

That was true. He'd been distracted. "I made an Italian cold-cut for myself—you probably wouldn't like it—and a peanut butter and jelly for you. The jelly has tons of sugar, so don't worry. I apologize if it's a little soggy, though."

"Oh." She tittered. "I don't care about sogginess."

By now, a few other people in line had noticed Riley's existence. Her brightly-colored reflection in the glass might have done the trick, or perhaps her cute, musical voice. A few were women who either scowled or simply gawked at her dress.

Most, however, were men.

Remy hooked his arm through hers. "In any event, dear, we'll be in before you know it." He leaned over and planted a quick kiss on her cheek, quite confident that most of the male onlookers saw.

The oversized fairy giggled and blushed again but swatted at him with her purse. "We're not dating yet. This is our first date, remember." She settled into a calm posture and smirked into space.

Most of the male onlookers probably overheard that, too.

Fuck. Remington adjusted his tie and cufflinks and wiped the palms of his hands on the edge of the picnic basket.

When they finally reached admissions, Remy paid twenty-three dollars for each of them. He could have saved a few bucks by pre-ordering a New York City Resident Grounds Pass, but that would require proof of residency and somehow, he didn't think the Gardens would recognize Fluttershire Fairy Colony as a legitimate address.

The notion that he even had to pay attention to such things made him mope a little. How had he ever allowed himself to become this poor?

Once I'm rich again, small expenditures like this will not be a problem because I won't waste two-thirds of my money on booze and drugs and parties anymore.

Heads continued to turn toward Riley and her bubbly behavior and goofy dress as they proceeded into the gardens. Mostly, she remained blithely unaware but in some cases, he realized, she noticed people's attention.

"This is so exciting!" she lilted. "I've never been on a real date before, like a hu—er, normal person." She tittered. "Can we go to a drive-in movie theater after this? Wait, do they still have those? I saw one of them in an old movie once when I snuck into someone's house."

Remy shrugged. "I think there are a few of them still

around. We don't really have time today, I'm afraid. Maybe some other time?"

They strolled out toward one of the pools. He was impressed with the verdancy of the plant life. The gardens obviously did a fine job of keeping the environment friendly to plant life even during the opening phase of winter. Of course, most of the flowers had gone dormant but the majority of the trees still had most of their leaves.

Some guy appeared out of the bushes. He was balding and sweaty, and his demeanor suggested that he had spent considerable time at nightclubs twenty or twenty-five years ago.

"Hey, hun," he said to Riley and completely ignored Remington's existence. "Don't go back there. There are still a few bees hovering around even this late in the season." He smirked, confident that his masculine offer of safety advice would impress the rainbow-clad maiden.

"Bees!" she responded brightly and her eyes lit up. "I love bees. I wonder how their honey production is going." She spun toward Remy. "I need to ask them. I'll be right back."

Before either of the two men could stop her or ask what the hell she was doing, she plunged into the bushes. Her soft, high-pitched voice wafted out of the foliage as she tried to engage the insects in conversation.

Remy stared at the man. "My date is the uninhibited type. That's part of why we're, you know, together. I like uninhibited women." He considered how that sounded. "Loyal, of course, but free-spirited."

The man chuckled innocently, stuffed his hands in his

pockets, and strolled off in the opposite direction, whistling.

Once he was gone, Remy poked his head tentatively into the plant labyrinth to make sure Riley hadn't gotten herself stung. For all he knew, she might be susceptible to bee sting allergies and crap like that while in human form.

She burst out as he stepped in.

"They wouldn't talk to me." She pouted. "Is it because of how big I am? That's the only thing I can think of."

"Maybe you can't hear their responses," he suggested.

As they resumed their amble toward the pool, a few other males began to hover around them.

What the hell is this? Remy tried to suppress his irritation. *Can't a girl dress like a circus performer and attempt to converse with yellowjackets without attracting a group of random dudes?*

He would have thought that New Yorkers, of all people, would be more tolerant of what might look like insanity. After all, when he talked to her while she was invisible to most people, the most he ever got was an occasional weird glance.

Watching the gathering horde, though, he had to amend his assumptions. The various guys made no attempt to police her bizarre behavior, nor were they simply curious what the deal was with her. Instead, seeing her, they responded according to nature.

Riley was hot. Really, really hot.

She deliberately bumped into him as she walked. "I think everyone likes my dress," she quipped. "That guy keeps looking at the slit I put up the leg. I wasn't sure if I got it right. I guess I did."

He glanced at the gentleman in question. "Yup."

The guy blushed, bowed out, and disappeared behind a tree. The others, however, watched him continually for any sign of inattention so they could make their move.

He became so busy watching them that he didn't notice, at first, when Riley saw the pool and bolted toward it.

"Riley—wait!" he called.

She was already at the edge of the water and jumped in to skip amidst the half-dead lily pads and scatter crystalline droplets into the crisp air.

A security guard appeared out of a nearby conservatory. "Hey—*hey!* Get out of the water, lady." He jogged toward the pool, his face distorted with aggravation, and probably contemplated a change of career. "Christ, it's too friggin' cold for this shit."

Remington, too, ran toward the water. To his annoyance, so did about half a dozen other men.

An old couple was already helping Riley out of the water. Or, rather, an old man was. He took her hand and pulled her out gently, while his wife watched with her hands on her hips.

"Young lady," the geezer commented, "I admire your spirit, but you don't want to get your skimpy dress all wet at this time of year."

Riley merely giggled. Her outfit had twisted in such a way that more of her legs were exposed and the damp fabric clung to her chest and suggested that she probably wasn't wearing a bra.

Before Remy could reach her, a big, beefy college kid muscled in.

"You need to get dry," he offered, removed his jacket, and draped it over her shoulders.

"Aww," she cooed, "thank you."

His teeth gritted, her date pushed through the throng, slipped an arm around her waist, and yanked her away from the beefcake to leave him holding his jacket over an empty patch of air.

They hurried toward what looked like the least-populated area of the gardens. The security guard watched him, probably to make sure he and the college boy didn't get into a fight.

For perhaps a full minute, they were alone together. Then, even more men began to drift over and insinuate themselves.

Remy gave up, for now. He selected a bench that would only hold two people, seated the two of them on it, and opened his picnic basket to distribute the sandwiches. In the end, he munched his cold cuts in silence while Riley chatted with four or five guys between mouthfuls of peanut butter and jelly.

It occurred to him that he might resolve the situation by announcing loudly that no motherfucker was to talk to his woman and any who dared defy his proclamation was welcome to challenge him. As tempting as the idea was, he refrained.

Moments passed before he realized why he didn't do that. It would advertise that he was jealous. He'd have to admit that he cared.

Fortunately, at least, the fairy did not have a phone number to give out, so when they made ready to leave, all she had was the experience of being the center of everyone's attention. It sure seemed like she'd enjoyed it.

Well, at least this suggests she won't be so desperate to flirt with me in the future. She's discovered that I'm not the only man in the world.

They walked arm-in-arm past the visitor center and toward his car.

"Remy," the fairy said, "thanks for the good time. The Botanical Gardens are really pretty. I might sneak in again sometime when I'm normal-sized. And I met so many nice people. They liked me too. Maybe I can meet up with them again."

"You're welcome," he replied. "Hey, let's go on another date sometime soon, shall we?"

She blinked at him. "Maybe." She seemed distracted.

He hated how much it stung—like a hot needle in the gut—to hear that.

CHAPTER FIFTEEN

Times Square, New York City

The fairy might be getting over her crush, but Remy concluded that she at least still cared about him. He couldn't come up with any other reason why she'd nag him like this.

"You know," she chided, "if you'd had me with you, this might never have happened. Your dumb friends wouldn't have even been able to see me, after all. Besides, I think it might have been interesting to see more of what humans do for fun."

It helped that she'd returned to her usual size, not to mention made herself imperceptible to most mortals again. She was once more his co-worker, his sidekick, and his bodyguard rather than his date.

As they strolled down the sidewalk, he waited for a relative lapse in human traffic combined with an increase in noise from the street before he responded to her.

"It wasn't actually all that much fun—intoxication, wandering around, spending money, saying stupid shit, and acting like an asshole, basically. I used to think things like that were the best possible way to spend my time. Well, that and snorting cocaine. Which is even worse."

"Hmph." She frowned and put her hands on her hips while she fluttered in midair. "If you have to snort it, I'm sure it can't be very good. That's simply weird."

They were now close to Ninth Avenue, which was approximately where the ski-masked prick had almost turned him into someone's oversized hood ornament. With the holiday season approaching, shoppers were everywhere.

"I agree," he said, "on that. No more nasally ingested substances for me, unless I suddenly develop allergies to something other than cats and need a prescription for those awful nose drops. More importantly, though, this is the place."

He gestured with his hand. The concrete and asphalt looked distressingly familiar.

"Okay," the fairy began, "but there isn't much I can do if you don't have anything from him."

Remy stood and stared at her. "Wait, what? What do you mean, from him?" Then he recalled, with a mental clap of thunder, that in the past, she had always had some kind of scented trace of her quarry.

"Like hair," she reminded him, "or something. Anything I can smell or taste. Or maybe a picture of him. But I guess you don't have one of those either, now that I think about it."

His jaw clenched as a few pedestrians grumbled and maneuvered their way around him. "Shit. I forgot about that. For some reason, I assumed you could maybe astrally recreate the scene by taking a snapshot of a past point in time…or something. One of these days, I'll have you type up a detailed list of exactly what your magic powers are."

A large, biker-esque man passed and gave him a skewed, skeptical look before he vanished into the crowd.

"I'm only talking to my trusty fairy," he muttered, mostly to himself. "Ugh, and in this day and age, someone will probably catch it on camera."

Riley floated up and around to examine the street from above, seeking clues.

Remington stood quietly, tried not to be too obstructive to foot traffic, and allowed his own words to echo in his mind. After a moment, his eyes bulged, and he brought his hand up to snap his fingers in front of him. "Aha! That's it. Riley! Get back down here. I have a solution. Kind of."

The fairy wafted to eye level. "Really? What?"

"Cameras." He smiled, overjoyed to be cocky again. The power of overconfidence surged through him and made his extremities tingle. "At least some of these businesses probably have security cams. They might have caught the bastard during the assault or perhaps later when he fled the scene."

Then, he frowned. "He wore a ski mask, granted, but now that I think back, it almost looked like he was starting to lift it up when he ran away. He must have had trouble breathing in the damn thing, superhuman stamina or no."

"Okay," she acknowledged, "how do we watch the camera footage? Don't we have to pay an admission fee?"

"Eh," he countered, "not quite. What we need to do is… be persuasive." He checked the inner pocket of his jacket. A couple of business cards for Moonlight Detective Agency were still there. That was a start.

He scrutinized the establishments on this side of the street in the direction in which the unknown assailant had bolted. The first was a Chinese restaurant.

"Hello," the hostess greeted him as he stepped into the eatery's pleasant shade and splendid décor. "Only one?"

"Actually," Remy began, "I'm an investigator." He whipped a business card out.

The woman frowned as she read the text.

"Don't worry." He chortled and put on his best public relations smile. "You're not in any trouble. I'm actually here to look into that Times Square brawl from a couple of days ago. Do you remember that? If you might be able to help me, we'll be able to keep this neighborhood safe from similar incidents in the future."

The woman became slightly standoffish once she realized that criminal matters were potentially involved, but he layered on the charm as thick as he could and mentioned that he'd heard good things about this restaurant and would love to spread the word.

He also strategically opened his jacket a little and made sure the lady caught sight of the large wad of cash he had in another pocket.

"So," he went on, "I'd be happy to help your establishment if you can help me. Let me speak to someone about reviewing the security camera footage from that morning. I saw you have a camera out front. It's a good idea, these days."

After he'd slipped her a couple of twenties and repeated his spiel to the manager—an elderly Chinese gentleman who seemed slightly more receptive to cooperating with an investigation—he finally found himself viewing a recording of the cam from the pertinent time period.

The device was positioned to give a better view of the storefront than of the sidewalk but nonetheless, after a moment, a figure in black streaked past. They caught a brief glimpse of his ski-masked head and that was all.

"Damn," Remy sighed. "Well, sir, this won't be of much use to us, but thanks anyway for your cooperation, and I promise to recommend this restaurant as soon as I can. Hell, I'd even stay for dinner myself if I had time."

He noticed that the old man glanced at a position over the investigator's shoulder—where Riley hovered. He said and did nothing, however. Still, it occurred to him that he might, later on, want to mention this to Taylor. The man was perhaps simply old-world Chinese enough to believe in the preternatural. At the very least, he seemed to sense that something was off.

"Well," Riley said as they exited, "I don't think he saw me. But that didn't work anyway, did it?"

Remy waved them farther down the street. "Let's keep trying."

Next up were a bar and grille, a souvenir shop, and a tourist agency offering guided bus excursions through the city. In each one, he repeated a slightly modified version of his pitch to the Chinese restaurant. And at each, until the last, they succeeded in looking at the security footage, only to fail to see anything substantive.

Now, watching the camera recording in a back room at the tourist agency, he saw the attacker dash by. In the next instant, he yanked his mask up and glanced around.

"There," he snapped, suddenly afire with excitement. "Go back to that and slow it down. If possible, I need a freeze-frame of this guy's face."

The manager, a constipated-looking little fellow who clearly hoped this would be over soon, grimaced and did as he asked. It took a couple of attempts, but they finally got a still frame of the assailant looking almost directly at the camera.

"Ha!" Remy laughed. "Bingo. Don't worry about making a copy. I'll take a picture of the monitor. That should suffice." He retrieved his camera and snapped a photo. There was no appreciable loss of detail.

It wasn't a great picture but it still provided a fairly good indication of what the man looked like. He was an almost nondescript white guy, blond and tanned, and probably in his late twenties or early thirties. The expression on his face, he realized, was mostly fear.

He could tell Riley wanted to say something but she remained silent as they thanked the manager and headed to the door.

They wandered out onto the street. It was the middle of the afternoon, now, and nightfall wouldn't be more than a couple of hours away.

Riley drew a long breath in, then let it out in a tiny puff. "Okay, with a graven image of him—or phone image, I suppose—I can cast the tracking spell and we can see where's he's been since the picture was taken." She hesitated. "It's only that...well..."

Remy turning to look at her and raised an eyebrow. "Only what? Is the picture quality too low? I might be able to run it through a high-res, image-crisping program or something, but I don't think we'll find any other photos or motion still of him better than this one."

The fairy glanced around and bit her lip. "No, it's not that. I'm worried."

"About what?" He had a hunch that he knew where this conversation was going but he resolved to hear her out and tried not to get annoyed in advance.

She looked at him with her tiny, bright eyes. "You. This is dangerous. That man almost killed you before, didn't he?"

He frowned. "Kind of. Okay, he tried, and I got banged up, but nothing serious. But I was drunk at the time and he got the drop on me from out of nowhere. This time, the tables will be turned. He won't know what hit him."

A smile grew as his thoughts turned inward to fantasies in which he kneed the prick in the face, hurled him through a plaster wall, and maybe ass-smacked him with a frying pan or a broom.

No, we'll be professional about this. I'll apprehend the guy, bring him back, and let Taylor question him. He'll cooperate if properly persuaded. There's no need to get messy. Think of how impressed she'll be.

Riley interrupted his reverie. "Remy, we don't even know what he is. I think he's a human, but everyone says he has some kind of…powers. We don't know how well he'll be able to fight back or protect himself. My magic usually works well, but not always. And I can't directly harm a human, remember?"

Remington glanced around to make sure no one was too close before he responded to her. "No one's asking you to kill the guy. That would be pointless. All you have to do is stop him from killing me until we can get him to surrender. We faced a whole group of mobsters and thugs at that warehouse and got through with a few scratches, but not many."

"They were regular humans," she pointed out. "Aside from the werewolf, that is. But at least we knew what he was. I think we should take this picture to the office and let Taylor and that Gilmore lady apprehend him."

The muscles around his jaw clenched and his teeth ground in frustration. He wasn't angry at the fairy, exactly. The rational part of his mind understood what she was saying and under other circumstances, he might even have conceded that she had a point.

But there was more to it than simple rationality. This was about his dignity and his competence. The vampire had tried to use him as bait, only for him to have his ass kicked, then arrested, then scolded and told to lie low because he couldn't handle one asshole with superhuman strength. She still treated him almost like a child.

"No," he proclaimed, "we're doing this. Don't worry. I'll be smart about it and have already made a few preparations, in fact. Besides, I have faith in your powers. With you by my side, we could probably even go all the way to Israel and capture whoever this master vampire is. This is probably only one of their little underlings."

It looked like she might protest again, so he cut her off. "I'm tired, Riley, of bait duty. Not to mention being left out of the decision-making process. And of people thinking I need protection even during very basic tasks. And the constant sting of rejection and condescension. It gets old, it really does."

Her lip trembled and her eyes were even shinier than usual. Afraid she might cry, he decided to reassure her but he would not give in.

"It's not you, honestly. You've been great, Riley. It's Taylor, mostly. Oh, and my family. And most of the rest of New York. Those cops looked at me and decided I was such a clown that they didn't even afford me the dignity of being treated like a potentially dangerous fuck-up, for God's sake. I'm sick of it all. It's time I won at something."

Now, the fairy merely squinted in confusion. "Remy, I don't understand why—"

"Cast the tracking spell," he ordered her. "This is the way it'll be. I'd rather have you do it but if you won't, I'll go back to Fluttershire with a new jug of honey and hire another fairy who will."

Her shoulders slumped and she hung her tiny head, defeated. After a moment, she nodded.

"Okay. But please…be careful."

Remy swallowed the acrid saliva that had pooled under his tongue. "Yeah." He woke his phone and held it up for the fairy to examine the photo.

Riley straightened and made a sweeping motion with her arm. A faint silver-blue glow appeared around the screen and faint, sparkling traces erupted from the sidewalk ahead, weaved into the nearest alley, and ran up a tall building near the end of the passage.

He inhaled and his nostrils flared. "Let's go," he said.

Tenor Extended Stay Hotel, Queens, New York

"Yes," Riley said, "this is where the trail ends. I'm sure of it." Her little face frowned. "I don't like the look of this place, though. Or the feel or smell of it."

Remy parked across the street—far enough away to be inconspicuous from the motel but close enough that he could keep an eye on his rather nice, expensive vehicle.

"Well," he remarked, "this is a crappy neighborhood. It's not supposed to look, feel, or smell good."

He looked around. Two of the streetlamps were broken. Most of the nearby businesses were vacant, and it sounded like a couple was having a colorful argument in the tenement down the road. Potholes pitted the street but no gang members loitered around, at least.

"You know," he added, "it's almost charming, really. That bus tour place ought to sell tickets to come through here. 'See New York the way it was back when they made *Death Wish 1.*' I bet they'd make a ton of money."

He rolled the passenger side window down. "Riley, do me a favor and fly out for a while. Scout the area, find out which room our friend is in, if there's any security we'll have to deal with, if there are any local pricks we'll have to deal with, that kind of thing."

"Okay," she replied. "I'm glad you're at least being—what's the word?—strategic about this."

He smiled coolly. "It's the best way to be about things when your goal is to kick some ass."

The fairy floated out and was quickly lost to sight.

While she did recon, Remy glanced into the back seat. A picnic basket was not the only thing he'd brought today. There was also a zipped duffel bag, mostly hidden under the passenger seat.

It contained a few items that he had borrowed from

Taylor. Things that would help persuade their friend in the motel room to come along quietly.

He reached back and, after a struggle, dragged the bag into the passenger seat. Once he'd unzipped it, he selected a Taser, a loaded .357 Magnum, and a police-style nightstick. Superhuman speed and strength or no, it was only one guy, after all, and the idea was to apprehend him rather than kill him.

Unless absolutely necessary.

Remy shoved the Magnum down the waistband of his pants at his back. It was a smaller, snub-nosed model, so it fit although it was a little awkward. That weapon, being lethal, would be saved as a last resort or possibly for serious intimidation. If he struck the bastard with the Taser and held the club over him, that ought to do the trick without the need to resort to blowing his head off.

A tiny, iridescent form fluttered toward him, the dragonfly wings reflecting the lamplight in flashes of bright gold. When the fairy was almost upon him, he pressed one of the switches to open the window for her and closed it once she floated in.

"Okay," she said breathlessly. "I looked everywhere. No one else is around. Everything outside seems to be safe."

Remy nodded. "Good. I don't feel like dealing with a horde of appetizers before we get to the main course. Now, point out which room he's in."

Riley hesitated and bit her lip as she glanced to the side. "Remy…the aura coming off that room gives me a really bad feeling. I don't think this is a good idea."

He'd been about to open the car door and step out but

he stopped, mostly in annoyance that she now tried to have this conversation again.

"We've already been through all this, Riley." He sighed. "With the element of surprise, plus help from you, we—"

"There's powerful magic coming out of that room," she protested. "Dark, evil power. I've only smelled or felt anything like that twice before, and both times, I flew away. Maybe he isn't the source of the power, but much of it has rubbed off on him. Please, let's think about trying something else."

Remy scowled and a tremor of tension rippled through his body. He refused to back down now when his chance to redeem himself was right across the street.

And yet, part of him had to consider that the fairy knew what she was talking about. Something else went through him then—an old, time-honored response to stress, to uncertainty, and to any sort of negative emotion or personal setback whatsoever.

The desire to get high.

"*No*," he snapped. Riley probably thought he was speaking to her. In fact, he'd spoken to himself as well. "We will not run away. I'll go first and you follow and offer help if you think I need it. Really, this can't be that hard, can it?"

He opened the door and eased his legs out onto the pavement, the Taser in his right hand when he closed the car. The nightstick hung from his side and the Magnum remained secure in his rear waistband.

The fairy drifted upward and allowed him to pass beneath her as he walked briskly but without hurrying toward the motel.

The office appeared to be locked for the night. There

was a security light on but no one in sight and when he approached, he saw a *Closed* sign on the door. That was good. It meant no one would pester him as to what he was doing there with a collection of weapons.

Unless one of the other guests tried to intervene.

I have legitimate reasons. I'm a professional private investigator, after all. And since the preternatural is involved, well, Taylor can probably cover it up if anything gets out of hand.

Riley must have pointed toward the room he was looking for since a faint silvery glow emitted from one of the doors at the far end of the motel. He walked casually toward it and stopped when he was only a few feet from the edge of the window.

The occupant had pulled the curtains all the way shut, so he wouldn't see anyone pass. A faint glow behind them, though, confirmed that their target was indeed in his room. All that was left was the door.

The fairy fluttered ahead and now hovered above the entrance. Remy caught her eye and pantomimed turning a door handle. She nodded and made a motion with her hand. A few sparkles erupted from the latch as it silently unlocked itself.

Remington stepped in front of the door and took a deep breath. The memory of how easily he'd had his ass handed to him on the edge of Times Square returned, unbidden and unwanted, and he pushed it out of his mind.

The only decision now was whether to say, "Freeze," or make some other authoritative or even heroic kind of comment, or merely to fire the Taser immediately. Now that he thought about it, shooting first would be a smarter course of action.

He stretched his left hand out and thrust the door open.

About a second passed in which he took in the scene before he acted.

The room was essentially a studio apartment, small and dumpy, its main floor dominated by a bed that barely qualified as a double. On the far side of the room, almost directly across from the door and beside what was presumably the bathroom, was a creaky little desk, at which a man sat in a swivel chair.

He swung to face the intruder. "Hey!" he exclaimed. There was no time to get a good look at his face, but he was blond and average-sized, and his bright blue eyes looked familiar.

Remy aimed and shouted, "Don't move!" even as he began to squeeze the trigger.

The man launched upwards, as quickly and forcefully as if gravity had been canceled or as if he were made of metal and someone had turned on a giant magnet in the ceiling.

"Fuck!" the investigator exclaimed. Everything happened too fast. He eased his finger off the trigger, suddenly on the verge of panic.

This wasn't supposed to happen like this, goddammit! He cursed himself. *How am I already screwing it up?*

He swung the weapon upward. The man had already scuttled across the ceiling and now dropped directly on top of him, his average-looking face contorted in rage and cornered-animal fear and his hands outstretched like claws.

Remy stumbled to the side, half-fell and half-rolled along the wall, and realized a split second after he'd moved that he should have backed away and bolted from the room. Instead, he was now trapped within it.

The man thumped onto the floor, roared, and spun on his feet toward his uninvited guest. His jaw slack, Remy aimed his Taser and fired.

The twin darts rocketed out to strike the man in the chest. He was about three feet away and while the attack slowed him a little, it didn't stop his charge.

His hands pounded into the investigator's chest and shoved him into the opposite wall.

"Urgh!" Remington grunted and pain seared through him when he collided. The wall behind him shook and he was reasonably sure he'd cracked at least two ribs.

The blond man hunched over and clutched his own chest. His muscles vibrated and sparks erupted from his body. Veins stood out on his neck and temples and his teeth clenched and scraped against each other.

Remy took a step forward and tried to pull the nightstick from his side. A sharp pang of agony ran from his chest to his right shoulder and he froze in place.

His adversary yanked the two electrified barbs attached by their copper wire from his chest and threw them aside. He stood, his body heaving as he breathed. It was almost as though he had swallowed the electricity within him and digested it.

He glared at his opponent with blue, blazing hatred.

"Crap."

A small, silvery form flitted behind them both and now floated near the ceiling.

"Remy!" the fairy cried.

The man pounced. Remy flung himself to the side, onto

and over the bed, and he wasn't sure if it was Riley's intervention or merely some distortion of his consciousness, but it seemed that the blond guy moved in slow motion.

He barely evaded the charge. Even slowed as he was, his enemy's hands closed around air only inches from his legs as he toppled backward and rolled himself to the other side.

"Nice try!" the other man barked.

Remy spun off the bed. He wobbled and jerked clumsily, his ribs still jabbing at him, and tried to pivot toward his foe. One hand fumbled for the Magnum and relief almost overwhelmed him when he found it was still there and hadn't slipped out during his impromptu gymnastics.

Briefly, he saw Riley flail her arms as she tried to concoct a new spell to interfere with whatever the blue-eyed man's next move was. The force or entity that empowered him must have made him immune to magical sleep effects.

His hand closed around the revolver's hilt. In the next second, his adversary grinned savagely, grasped the bed, and flipped it up toward him.

He had no time to react and was in shock, besides. The bed's quilt-lined top suddenly careened into his face.

Again, he was hammered against a wall. This time, he screamed, but the bed thumped into him and muffled the sound. There were only darkness and stuffiness and blunt-force impact.

Riley's small voice called somewhere from the other side of the room and sounded faint and distant. "Leave him alone!" She seemed almost strangled with dismay and frustration.

As Remy fought to keep himself coherent, he struggled forward and pushed against the upended piece of furniture. The mattress slouched off it and began to weigh on his legs.

The other man took a couple of quick steps across the floor and delivered another powerful blow in Remy's gut.

With a yelp, he collapsed against the bed and realized his assailant had punched through it to strike him in the abdomen with the debris as well as his fist. He felt sick like he might spit blood.

I fucked up. His mind acknowledged the truth, on the verge of despair. *This might be the end.*

The bed tottered and fell toward the center of the room. As the space before him became visible again, Remy gaped. The blond man and the tiny fairy had become locked in some barely perceptible magical duel.

Silver flashes and sparks erupted from the air in front of Riley, and other flashes, like golden flames, blossomed before the strange man. Both stared, bug-eyed, and seemed to strain against some invisible element of the other's power.

The bed crashed to the floor and he stumbled around it and along the far wall, trying to settle his aim on his foe while also positioning himself near the room's door to flee if he had to.

He succeeded. The opened doorway and the free night air beyond were only a step or two to his right.

But with the man distracted, he had to try, one more time, to capture the bastard.

Remy drew his gun, knowing his movements were too slow after the ass-kicking he'd taken, and watched with horror as a yellowish flash seemed to engulf the whole room and Riley was driven back, squealing, through the door.

The man's eyes almost glowed when he turned to look at Remy.

He aimed the Magnum and prepared to cock the hammer. "Okay," he gasped, his cracked ribs and bludgeoned stomach making it hard to talk or breathe much, "hold it right there. You're coming with us, you prick. Come along quietly, and uh—"

Faster than he could comprehend, the man cleared the distance between them and battered the gun from his hand. It struck the wall so hard the cylinder popped out and some of the bullets clattered on the floor.

For a second, they stood, three feet apart, and stared into each other's faces.

Remy turned and ran. Or hobbled, at least. The room fell away behind him and he reached the parking lot. He staggered desperately to his car, trying not to even contemplate the odds that Mr Superhuman would catch him within the next second and snap him in two.

To his surprise, the man did not pursue him.

The seconds dragged while he got closer to the car. He collapsed against it and fumbled in his pocket for his keys as he looked over his shoulder.

Riley had again leaped to his defense and tried to stall the man with her magic once more. Sparks lit up the night.

Remy opened the car door and fell in, grunted with pain, and turned the keys. He wheeled the vehicle, opened the passenger side window, and yelled, "Riley! Get in!"

The small form darted through the window and he

stamped on the accelerator. Squealing tires added to the roar of the engine and the cheap motel dwindled in the rearview mirror.

Riley floated around him as he drove through Queens and tried to calm himself enough to avoid running a red light or something similarly stupid.

"Are you okay?" The fairy certainly still cared about him. Of that, he had no doubt.

He coughed and tasted the salt of blood on his lips before he answered her.

"No."

CHAPTER SIXTEEN

Tenor Extended Stay Hotel, Queens, New York

Alex hesitated in the open doorway, frozen in the mental chaos of indecision, and stared out into the city night. The Lincoln accelerated out of the parking lot and into the street.

Before he could make up his mind whether or not to pursue Remington and his minuscule companion, something else made the decision for him.

"Oh, God!" he cried as an incendiary bomb seemed to detonate in his chest.

Light pulsed from the brand. He wasn't more than half a second into the punishment session when he knew this was beyond anything Moswen had done to him before. The pain penetrated to his very core.

Shaking violently, he collapsed and his fingers clawed at the floor, his brain almost entirely deprived of the ability to think. The only thing it could muster was a hope—or perhaps merely a need—for it to be over soon.

If it didn't flare viciously until it killed him.

He had defied Moswen's will to the greatest extent possible. She wanted the opposition either on her side or dead, not running around, free and defiant. Which was exactly where both Taylor and Remington were right now.

Even with the fairy's interference, he could have killed the rich kid. He'd had half a dozen chances during their brief scuffle alone to end the bastard's life and be done with it. But he'd held back.

Now, as he writhed on the ground in torment, he paid for that inaction. Worse, he might be paying for the secret motivation behind it.

His only chance, he'd surmised, to be free of Moswen's enslavement was the slight chance that Taylor might still help him. It wasn't likely, especially after the ugly fight outside the museum, but there was still a sliver of hope.

If he'd killed her human pet, though, she would never listen to him. She'd regard him purely as a threat and would probably want revenge. And so, he'd stopped himself from slaying the prick outright and tried to either drive him off or capture him instead.

Now, he regretted that decision.

"Stop!" he pleaded and spittle trailed from his mouth. "Enough! I'm sorry…"

As rapidly as it had slithered into him from the depths of hell, the agony eased and finally, vanished altogether.

He hunched over, his breath coming in short, ragged gasps, and his mind flooded with relief as a single thought pushed out all the pain and fear:

I am alive. She stopped short of killing me.

No sooner had this truth articulated itself than he realized something was wrong. Or, at least, something was different from the other times the brand had flared up.

The room was silent. The phone didn't ring.

"What?" he murmured. "What the hell does that mean?"

If his mistress tried to read his mind right now, all she'd run into was fearful confusion. And if she had read it, she wasn't in any hurry to provide answers.

Perhaps she felt he'd gotten the point by now—that everything would be fine provided he didn't mess things up again. Maybe, just maybe, all he had to do was get that cat statue and all would be forgiven.

The chances of that seemed so slim as to be virtually invisible.

"Mistress," he said, using speech to help mask his deepest thoughts, "I only spared him because I needed him alive to set a trap for Taylor. You have to believe me! I'm so close. Trap or no trap, I'll get that idol. I won't fail you again."

The mark on his chest did not burn him again but the phone didn't ring, either.

Moswen's patience was wearing thin. Somehow, he knew that. He did not dwell on the idea lest she pick up on it. There wasn't much need to try to deceive her right now, though. His dread was genuine enough and it might serve to remind her of his servitude.

His time was running out. He didn't know how much he had left, but it wasn't exactly a lot. Already, he'd had too many chances. Taylor still lived and the Black Cat Idol was still in her possession.

How many times could he disappoint his mistress—and how many times could he cryptically attempt to defy her—

before she grew tired enough of the whole game that she simply came to New York to deal with things herself?

Alex looked around his room at the destroyed bed and cracked walls. He hadn't heard much noise over the last day or two, so it was possible that he was the only person currently in the motel. But if there were any neighbors, they would have heard the fight. The police might already be on their way.

He gathered his things and stuffed them into his backpack. It was time to move on. This place was no longer viable.

There might still be a chance to buy himself more time to protect himself. He needed a win. Something he could hold up to prove he hadn't crashed and burned.

In his mind, he repeated the same pleas and questions he'd already directed at Moswen, allowing them to dominate his surface-level mental activity to distract her while on another level, his brain quietly had other ideas.

If he could steal the Black Cat Idol out from under Taylor's nose without antagonizing her too much more, he might be able to trade it back to her in exchange for her aid. That is if Moswen's fiery brand didn't kill him first.

Packing up the last of his meager possessions, he tried not to choke on his own rising sense of desperation.

Just my luck. He hoped he managed to keep his thoughts buried enough to escape his mistress' attention by adding a few signs of his loyalty. *I only wanted to make a name for myself with a spectacular dig and now, all this crap has gotten in the way. Of course, I couldn't have found a nicer vampire to end up working for. Or a weaker vampire to be assigned to destroy.*

It occurred to him, also, that even if his plan worked, he

might end up similarly enslaved to Taylor. Still, it was his best chance to survive.

None of this is my fault. But sooner or later, someone will pay for it.

North Queens, New York City

Remy pulled the car into a vacant lot next to an old, closed-down auto parts shop. His head almost fell against the horn.

"Riley," he moaned, "I…need to rest. Can you enchant the car so no one can break through a window?"

The fairy sounded like she, too, was out of breath. "Yes. I think I need to rest too. It's been a long day. And that man…he channeled power from someone—or something—really powerful. I don't have much more left in me."

He glanced around. A trio of teenagers passed on the other side of the street but ignored him.

"Do your best." He groaned. "I…uh, might need…medical attention. I'm not sure I can drive. Give me a minute to, uh…think it over…"

The words he tried to say seemed to spiral into the darkness as he passed out.

It seemed like only a few minutes had passed when Riley yelled in his ear. "Remy! Wake up. We need to get you some help. *Remy!*"

He'd been having a dream in which he'd laid in a hospital bed while his parents and cousins and grandparents, aunts and uncles and family friends, all filed past and reprimanded him for ending up like this. Now, it faded as he came to, stiff and in considerable pain.

"Uhhh…what?" He blinked. "How long were we—wait, never mind."

It was still dark but the light had begun to peek between the buildings of the city. They'd been unconscious all night.

The fairy moved in front of his face. Her own was etched with fear and concern. "I'm sorry, I fell asleep too. I was so tired after that battle."

Remy nodded. "That's quite understandable."

He tried to shift in his seat and pain stabbed at him from multiple directions. "Goddammit. I definitely lost that fight, didn't I? Shit, I can't drive. It looks like we'll have to call Mom again."

The notion was not encouraging. Still, passing out again in the middle of a busy intersection would be even worse.

His hand shook from the sharp burn that ran down his arm, but he managed to retrieve his phone from his pocket. Two missed calls from Taylor's cell caught his attention immediately. He dialed her house number instead. It was barely dawn, so she might still be up. And by calling the house, at least he'd get Presley if she was already coffin-bound.

On the other end of the line, there were two and a half rings before someone picked up.

"Yes?" an elderly male voice said.

"Presley," Remy gasped, knowing he sounded like shit. "Old boy. I had another encounter with our man in the ski mask. In Queens. I'm beat to hell and I don't think I can drive."

He stopped to catch his breath and the butler waited for

him to say more. "Riley is with me, but she's exhausted too. We need…uh, you know, extraction. And probably a doctor. Is there any chance you can come to the rescue?"

"Oh, dear," the old man lamented. "It's probably for the best that Ms Steele has retired. Yes, tell me where you are and I'll be right along. I also know a private doctor who can be prevailed upon to make house calls. And I'll see about getting your car towed."

Remington was so relieved to hear the butler's words that he almost cried. He'd half-expected to be told, once and for all, that he'd screwed up for the last time and was now on his own.

He sighed into the phone. "Jeeves, you're the best. Presley, sorry. Shitty habits die hard. And yeah, I know I'll have to face the music with Taylor later."

"That you will." At least he didn't try to sugarcoat it.

He gave the old man his exact location within the labyrinthine backstreets of northern Queens. Once he'd thanked the butler again, he ended the call and slumped in his seat.

Riley was now perched on the dashboard. "They're coming, right?" He'd never seen her look so nervous.

"Yes." With slow, shaky hands, he adjusted his tie. "Since you're not exactly operating in top form, either, Riley, I suggest that after Presley shows up, you head back to your colony and recuperate for a night or two. Get some rest and gossip with the other fairies about who can't hold his pizza. Don't worry, I'll want you back soon. But you'll be more helpful when you're not wiped out."

"Okay," she agreed. "Let me know how you're doing. You don't look good, Remy."

"Nonsense," he retorted. "I always look good." He raised a hand to his mouth and felt some of the salty crust of the blood he'd coughed up. "Always."

Presley arrived within half an hour. Remy was impressed since that was about the bare-minimum time he would have estimated to get there from Harrison. Preternaturals obviously had more than enough time to hone their driving skills. He was also pleasantly surprised that neither the locals nor the NYPD had bothered him yet.

A black Tesla pulled into the empty lot and the old man got out. He stepped over to the Lincoln and peered into the window as Remy rolled it down.

His eyes widened. "Oh dear. With all due respect, sir, you should have called nine-one-one instead of me. Then again, that could have led to complications. Can you get out of your seat?"

He explained the gist of the fight and the nature of the pain he'd had to deal with since.

"Well," the butler said, "you probably did break several ribs, yes. And you might have a hernia or some similar internal injury. Are you still coughing up blood?"

Remy attempted to smile. "Not anymore."

With a small amount of help from Riley's depleted magic, they managed to get him to his feet despite his body's agonized protests, moved him into a prone position in the back seat, and strapped him in tightly.

The fairy waved. "Okay, I'm going home now. Remember to come back and get me soon."

He waved in response. "Take care of yourself, old girl."

She elevated quickly. "Good luck with Taylor!"

Both men nodded at that but didn't bother to reply out loud.

Harrison, Westchester County, New York

Remy phased in and out of consciousness during the drive and after they returned to Taylor's mansion.

He was only dimly aware of Presley calling a tow truck, of himself being wheeled out of the Tesla on a stretcher, of a man he didn't know—the doctor?—poking him and talking to the butler before he injected him with painkillers and other meds. At some point, everything went black again.

Thanks to all the substances the physician had put into his system, he didn't dream much. There was one brief nightmare, though, of the blond guy from the motel chasing him through Fort Washington Park, hurling him aside, and burrowing into the Fluttershire Colony after Riley.

In the dream, he lay there helplessly and blubbered at the fairies to evacuate when someone seized him and shook him awake.

His eyes opened and immediately, gasping and tense from the nightmare, he stared into two intense black pools.

"Shit," he mumbled.

"Why," Taylor almost snarled, "should I even have to ask what the hell you were thinking, Remington? Why, again? Why don't you learn from your mistakes like a normal, sane person? You almost got yourself killed!"

Remy braced his arms against the bed and shifted himself slowly into a seated position. He shook with the effort. The painkillers had numbed the worst of the agony pangs but he still felt awful and his mind was heavy and foggy, besides.

He looked to both sides and realized he was in the guest room on the house's second floor, where he'd spent the night before. The curtains were drawn but no light seeped in from the windows. He estimated it was about thirty minutes after nightfall.

The vampire wasn't the type to wait long to chew someone out, even if he was still in bed and she'd barely woken up herself.

With an inward sigh, he returned his focus to her. She stood ramrod-straight at his bedside, her arms folded over her chest, and the red nails of her right hand drummed on her left arm.

He took a deep breath. "Well—"

"Don't." She cut him off. "Don't even think about answering yet. That was a rhetorical question. You can attempt to explain after I've had my say."

Uh-oh, he thought, although he tried to keep his face neutral and relaxed as though these proceedings were already boring him.

Taylor unfolded her arms to point one finger at him. "You should know better. I cannot fucking believe, David, that you would do something this reckless again. You'll be on the mend for weeks. You probably won't be able to do anything outside of office work, and you're lucky that you're not already headed for the goddamn morgue."

He grimaced at that. It was true. The mysterious man had almost punched a hole through him as well as the bed, and if he hadn't hesitated, he might well have torn his head off while he was at it.

"I'm glad you're not dead," she went on, "but with this level of stupidity, you essentially deserved to get beaten within two inches of your life. Do you suppose our suspect is still waiting in that same motel room as we speak?"

Remy almost asked if this was another rhetorical question but stopped himself at the last instant and waited for her to continue.

She did and with a significant degree of scorn. "Of course he isn't. Agent Gilmore and four of her men went there earlier today to investigate. They found the room badly trashed and, to the shock of no one, empty. The man fled and he's probably not stupid enough to ever come back."

The vampire leaned forward. Her temper had cooled a little, but this only meant her anger had grown icy instead of hot.

"You chased off our best lead, Remington." She folded her arms again. "Tracking him down will be extremely difficult, if not impossible. He'll take measures to cover his tracks. He might even leave New York or the United States altogether. We're reasonably sure he's Australian, after all."

Remy slowly and carefully wiped his palms on the lower part of the nightgown they'd put him into. "You know, it sounded like he had a slight accent. There are so many foreigners in New York all the time, though, that it barely registered."

Taylor waved a hand sharply. "And not only is he gone, but you left evidence of your own presence. The .357 you stole from me was still lying in the corner of that room and had been all night."

Crap. He chided himself for forgetting that.

"And as it so happens," she ranted, her voice louder again, "the NYPD arrived on the scene before Gilmore did. We are incredibly lucky that she guessed it belonged to us, pulled rank, and talked the police detective into turning it over to her—although they will still note all of that in their reports, of course. And if Gilmore hadn't stepped in, the city cops might be examining your fingerprints even now, cursing themselves for ever letting you out of jail."

Then, it struck him. The magnitude of what he'd done last night—on top of everything else that had happened lately, not to mention everything that had happened in the last decade or so—welled up, charged, and attacked the center of his soul.

Suddenly, he almost wanted to die.

Not quickly and cleanly via actual suicide, though. No, he'd rather resume the gradual process of killing himself that he'd tried to halt months before.

He wanted to throw in the towel, announce to everyone that he was a failure, a loser, and a complete asshole, and tell someone to hold his calls. If anyone really needed him, he'd be off snorting coke, injecting heroin, popping pills, maybe trying meth merely for fun, and washing it all down with about a bottle of liquor per day.

His remaining finances might hold out long enough to keep him continuously high and drunk until he finally passed out in an alley, or perhaps on his own couch, and simply never woke up again.

For some reason, that struck him as almost humorous.

He imagined a pretentious film student making a docudrama about his life as a kind of warning to other dumb rich kids. The ending of such a movie would be as depressing as hell, but at least prior to that, there would be a string of really, really funny parts.

Although the film probably wouldn't include the fact that he'd allowed some ruthless overseas vampire to take over New York.

Remy looked at Taylor and forced a thin smile while he summoned what little remained of his usual bravado.

"The cops always curse themselves when they have to let me out of jail," he remarked. "How often do they get to deal with someone who's such an excellent conversationalist?"

She stared at him and shook her head slowly. "You've gotten the point, then. I know abject self-hatred when I see it—and the fact that you tried to look cocksure means that at least you have some spirit left."

When she sighed, his gut tightened as a confused mess of emotions fought within him for dominance.

"I suppose," the vampire went on, "that you cannot be blamed for the fact that your family assumed good behavior was hereditary and you're only now, in your early thirties, learning how to be a responsible human being. And you've made some strides. I'm sure it isn't easy."

That was the truth.

"However"—her voice sharpened again—"you are still accountable for your own actions, regardless of what might lurk in your past. I'll need all the help I can get against this new enemy of ours, and that includes you. But I don't know how many more fuckups I can deal with. If you truly want to help me—and all of New York—I need you to wise up and act like an adult."

Remy hesitated for a moment. He breathed in through his nose and out through his mouth and considered a smartass remark. Instead, he simply said, "I understand, ma'am. Thank you."

She nodded and almost smiled. "Good. Now, then. Agent Gilmore is on her way here to discuss our next move. You ought to be able to at least walk and talk and I'd rather have you in the loop, so I suggest you get yourself cleaned up if you want to join the meeting."

This time, his grin, although subdued, was genuine. "I think I'll do that."

Taylor helped him from the bed and allowed him to work his way slowly toward the bathroom. She explained that he'd broken two ribs, one each in front and back, and had had some internal bleeding in his abdomen. Luckily, it had stopped on its own before surgical intervention was required.

"The doctor will check on you in another week," she told him. "Until then, and probably for weeks hereafter, no running, no heavy lifting, and no fighting. And, of course, no alcohol."

Once in the bathroom, his skin crawled at the sight of his ashen, sickly face. Almost his whole torso was bandaged. He freshened himself as best he could without taking an actual shower and changed into one of Presley's suits. The two men were, thankfully, about the same size.

Gilmore arrived about a minute after he dragged himself downstairs to the sitting room. She was dressed in snappy civilian clothes and eyed him with a mixture of sympathy and disapproval. No doubt, she knew everything he'd done.

The two women sat facing each other in comfortable chairs and he reclined on a sofa off to the side. Presley stood near the entrance, ready to wait on their guest's needs but also a part of the discussion.

On the table between the two women stood the Black Cat Idol.

So, Remy surmised, *FBI lady knows Taylor took it and doesn't care. At least that means we can trust her for now.*

The vampire was first to speak. "Agent Gilmore, thank you for coming all this way. I can assure you that we have privacy and security here."

They exchanged a couple of other pleasantries, including asking Remy how he was recovering, and moved on to business.

"So," Gilmore began, "our man's name, we're almost sure, is Alexander Thomas. That's the identity he checked into the motel with and it doesn't seem to be a fake. He's an Australian national, as you suspected. Unfortunately, we have no idea where he is and no good leads, either."

Taylor frowned and folded one hand over the other on her lap. "Yes, finding him will not be easy. We have tracking methods of our own but will not be able to deploy them until tomorrow, and they may cease working, anyway, now that Mr Thomas is aware of us."

The agent nodded. "I won't ask what your methods are, but I can't promise that other parties won't take an interest in such things later. For now, though, our concern is finding this guy and his boss. That reminds me—"

"Oh?" Taylor asked.

Remy leaned forward as well.

She looked from one to the other and continued. "Our contacts in Israel intercepted a few communications from persons of interest, mentioning someone named Moswen. A woman, seemingly. We suspect she may be a high-ranking member of Ein Avdat or even its leader."

The vampire closed her eyes and seemed to scan through the many files in her brain. Finally, she spoke. "Yes…I strongly suspect that is exactly who we're looking for. Don't ask me how I know. Let's simply say a very good hunch."

He felt a chill at the back of his neck. Somehow, he imagined her as a young vampire back in England, hearing campfire stories of some ancient and powerful princess of the undead sealed away in the Middle East.

Gilmore shrugged. "We're looking into it and need more evidence before we jump to conclusions."

Taylor frowned. "What I don't understand is, if the Black Cat is so important to Moswen or whoever Ein Avdat really is, why isn't she here herself? Sending only one guy after it seems almost careless."

Both women examined the statuette, turned it over, and speculated as to its value. He struggled to his feet and hobbled over to the table to peer at the idol while they turned it in their hands.

Remy blinked and suddenly felt as though he'd been slapped in the face. "Wait—hold it!" he exclaimed.

The women looked sharply at him.

"It's a forgery," he stated.

"What?" Gilmore responded in disbelief. "How can that

be? It was displayed at the museum—" She glared at Taylor. "You didn't switch it for—"

"No," the vampire responded coolly. "This is the piece I took."

He almost grinned. "Ha, oh, this is rich. Do you see that little tiny mark on the underside of the tail? That's a signature. Some asshole who calls himself Osman, whatever that means, and who makes a living by faking rare pieces like this. It's definitely his mark. It almost looks like a natural flaw in the material, but it isn't."

Taylor looked slightly amused. "And how would you know?"

"Because," he replied, "I was scammed by him at least twice back when I purchased swanky *objets d'art* to furnish my penthouse. I planned to hire a PI to track the guy and kick his ass, but I got drunk or something and forgot about it. This makes me feel better, though, since it means he even fooled the Guggenheim."

Gilmore's nostrils flared as she considered what he'd said. "Well, this changes things. Does this mean that Moswen was duped as well? Or is something else going on?"

The vampire drummed her nails on the table. "No, somehow I don't think our adversary would be so careless. I can tell, Agent Gilmore, that you don't think she'd make that kind of a mistake either. And yet, her henchman still pulled out all the stops to come after it."

"He doesn't have all the information," the agent concluded. "He's a patsy, an expendable pawn. But what is her goal, then?"

The other woman's gaze went distant. "Bait," she said.

"Moswen is trying to lure me out. Our interests lie at cross purposes. And she succeeded, to some extent. But if Mr Thomas doesn't know it's a forgery, he'll continue his attempts to steal it."

Remy recalled the ugly mixture of fear, rage, and desperation that had emanated from the man and he knew, instantly, that she was right. He would never give up.

"So," Gilmore ventured, "you think he'll target you?"

"No," she replied. "He'll try to steal the statuette again, but not when I'm around. Our last altercation went rather badly for him, and I crudely threatened him to make sure he got the point. He won't want to fight me again. And it would be unwise for him to take Presley on, either. Don't let his age fool you, Agent." She smirked.

The butler merely said, "Thank you, madam."

The FBI agent nodded. "So, we use the Black Cat to trap a thief. But this time, both of us will be ready for him."

"Exactly." Taylor steepled her fingers. She looked aside at Remy. "A new strategy is forming. And, Remington, you'll even get to help. Unfortunately, it will involve you playing a role you seem to greatly dislike."

He turned his eyes heavenward. "Bait." He sighed.

CHAPTER SEVENTEEN

Moonlight Detective Agency Office, Bushwick, Brooklyn, New York

Remy sat in silence and waited for Taylor to speak. Once again, she was the one with the answers, and she'd probably be the one to have the final word on their course of action.

"All right then," she began, "here is the plan as it now stands."

Everyone was present. In addition to the two of them, Bobby, Volz, and Riley hovered around the edge of the office lobby. Nearer the center and near Taylor, Agent Gilmore stood with her right-hand man, Agent Mortensen.

Remy glanced at Riley, partially for moral support and in part because he wanted to make sure she paid attention.

He'd brought her from her colony under the George Washington Bridge this morning after the usual obligatory haranguing and nonsense from the other fairies. Taking the night off and resting seemed to have done her good. She was chipper and spry again.

However, she also seemed somehow distracted once again. As though she were thinking of all those men at the Botanical Gardens who crowded around her and made her feel special.

Getting that much attention must have been...addictive, he thought. That was the perfect word. The cocktail of itchy boredom and pathetic longing that emanated from her reminded him far too much of any given druggie who tried not to relapse—such as himself, for example.

Still, she was overjoyed to see that he was fit enough to at least walk and excited to help bring this whole mess, at last, to a decisive end.

Taylor set the Black Cat Idol on a desk before she continued her spiel.

Bobby gasped. "I forgot my talisman! I really wish you'd warn me before you brought occult objects in here."

"It's a fake," he pointed out. "Trust me on this. The museum was duped."

"Oh." She relaxed. "Well, good. My horoscope was fortuitous this morning, after all."

Volz coughed, and Taylor continued.

"We brought the statuette in this morning, and we were loud and obvious about it. If our friend Mr Thomas or some ally of his has had this office under surveillance, he'd have seen or heard everything. The NYPD is cooperating. We've convinced them that Gilmore had to remove the statuette from the museum for its own safety."

Remy wondered, with a certain amusement, if the folks at the Guggenheim had become more accommodating once they'd learned it was a forgery.

"And"—she raised a finger—"if any man on the street

asks, the local cops have instructions to mention, offhandedly, that the Black Cat is being kept at 'some agency.'"

That sounded almost too obvious to him but Alex was likely desperate enough to pounce at any opportunity he could get.

"Meanwhile," Taylor explained, "I will, once the sun sets, pursue a so-called lead upstate. I won't be too far—only far enough to convince Mr Thomas that I'm not around. We believe he'll therefore conclude that it's safe for him to strike."

She turned to Remy and fixed him with her dark gaze. "That will leave Remington as the sole guardian of the idol. Bobby, Volz, you two will go home after you help us make a few preparations. For your own safety, of course."

But not mine, he lamented while the receptionist and the tech specialist nodded their heads.

Gilmore turned to face the rest of the group. "However, it's a trap. My team and I will wait in the abandoned store down the street. If I may say so, our response time is excellent and we're well-trained to deal with highly dangerous individuals like this. At the first indication that Thomas has made his move, all seven of us will be on him like flies on shit, if you'll pardon the expression."

Volz chuckled. "Consider yourself pardoned. I've heard worse."

The agent turned toward him and arched an eyebrow. "I'll bet you have. You're not a One-Percenter, are you? Staying out of trouble?"

"Why," the dwarf sighed, "do law enforcement officers always ask me that? I don't even own a motorcycle. Although it might be fun to tinker with one."

Taylor raised a hand. "Save the banter for later. For now, we need to focus on the task at hand." She produced three small black devices, each with a single discreet button, and laid them on the desk before her.

"These," she explained, "will trigger a silent alarm in the form of a low-intensity flashing light on Agent Gilmore's equipment. We'll set up all three of them at various strategic locations within the office. Remy, all you need to do is press one of them the instant Mr Thomas makes his move. We'll have you positioned at the one in the center of the office and if need be, you can flee toward one of the others to either side."

Remy was about to ask what good that would be if Alex was able to sneak in and snap his neck before he even noticed him, but she cut him off.

"Of course, we're taking precautions to ensure that whatever his first move is, it's something you will notice—and before he attacks you, to boot. He might try for stealth, but he also knows you're no match for him in close combat, which ought to make him reckless and overconfident." She paused. "And we brought a couple of portable stretchers, just in case."

His mouth twisted into a sour expression. "We can only hope. I can walk, but I'm not up to much fleeing if I do have to reach one of the other two buzzers. Let alone trying to fight the bastard."

Gilmore put a hand gently on his arm. "Don't worry. My people will handle the fighting. As soon as we show up, you get out of the way and we'll take care of things. We've apprehended guys on PCP before who could have wrecked three or four tough-ass bouncers at once."

"That's good to know," he acknowledged, "but whatever this guy is on, it seems to be even worse than PCP." He wondered how much the agent truly knew about what was going on—if she still held to her mundane, scientific explanations for all the recent phenomena.

The woman exchanged a glance with Mortensen. "We're aware of that," she mentioned. "Based on everything you've told us, we have a good idea of what to expect."

The two agents conferred with Taylor one last time, left a plan behind for how to set up obstacles for their target, and nodded to the others before they took their leave. They all felt certain that Alexander Thomas would not show up until after dark, so it seemed prudent for the Feds to depart before then.

Taylor then set the rest of the crew to make a few alterations and rearrangements to the office, the better to welcome Mr Thomas when he arrived and ensure he wouldn't want to leave too quickly.

In the rear of the building, Volz unspooled barbed wire while Bobby held the wheel in place and stared at it with slight distaste and discomfort.

"He might be able to snap through it," the dwarf declared, "but I imagine it will slow him down."

"Ick," Bobby said. "Okay, I know he's an enforcer for a drug lord or whatever, but I don't like the idea of anyone stumbling into barbed wire. What if it gets tangled around his—"

"More likely"—the dwarf cut her off hastily—"it will slow him down in that he'll need to stop and think of how to climb over it."

Riley, of whose existence Bobby was still unaware, fluttered near the ceiling and occasionally helped with small bursts of magic. She still acted a little odd, although she now seemed pouty rather than distracted.

Meanwhile, Taylor ensured that Remy was armed.

"Now," she inquired as she set a heavy crate of weapons on a desk, "you did say the Taser you stole stunned him for a moment, right?"

He nodded. "He got over it a lot faster than I would have liked, but it still took him a second. It probably saved me from getting killed."

"Good." She reached into the crate. "Take two, then. And don't hesitate to use them." Her hands emerged and each held one of the black, pistol-like electroshock weapons. "Try to save the first to slow him before you press the alarm button. And the second to keep him off you until Gilmore's team arrives."

Remy accepted the weapons but left them on the desk for now. He intended to help the others with their preparations and would holster them later.

Something in her eyes changed and she turned to face everyone at once. "All right," she announced, "the sun has set."

It struck him that she had risked pain and injury, not to mention the possibility of clueing Gilmore into her vampiric nature, in order to be at the office during daylight hours to make their preparations.

She glanced at the nearest clock. "Mr Thomas will probably wait a short while after he knows I've left to be safe. Therefore, I'll stick around as we finish our preparations. We must not wait too long, though, or he might change his mind and come back tomorrow night, instead.

Let's hurry."

They set to work.

According to Gilmore's instructions and with Taylor's added guidance, they rapidly advanced beyond the laying of barbed wire and transformed their cozy corporate office into a dangerous obstacle course. The idea was to make the whole area difficult to traverse for someone who moved at highly advanced speed.

Of course, there were also booby traps.

"Ugh," Remy apologized with a little embarrassment, "I'm sorry I'm not more help. I can't lift very much right now. Doctor's orders."

"Ha!" Volz scoffed. "You couldn't lift much even before you were busted up, either. Look at that frame! It's like someone stretched you out with a giant vacuum cleaner."

"Nonsense," he countered, "it merely looks that way because someone dropped a six-foot-wide anvil on your head as a child."

The dwarf laughed. He was in the process of securing a levered bar to the ceiling. Remy held the tripwire as he worked.

The nature of the trap was that anyone who touched the tripwire would cause the bar to swing down toward their chest, its end bristling with needles on which a powerful sedative had been smeared.

Once Bobby was out of sight, engaged with the extremely simple task of smearing grease on certain parts of the floor, Riley also joined their efforts. Being able to fly, she could secure wires to different parts of the walls and ceiling that were difficult for the non-winged to reach.

She also lent an invisible, telekinetic hand to Remy as

he struggled to push a few desks and chairs into inconvenient locations.

"Are you okay?" he asked her.

She didn't look at him. "I'm fine."

He cursed inwardly. As all men knew, that statement meant she wasn't fine.

Taylor examined their handiwork one last time and noted the locations of the various traps. "All right, we've done what we can. It's time for me to leave." She looked at her co-workers and nodded.

Remy hobbled to her side. "Hold on a second."

She hesitated and seemed about to brush him off but instead, she stopped and locked gazed with him. "Yes, Remington?"

He swallowed and tried not to clench his jaw as he spoke. "Was I…I mean, was I being bait really the only thing I was ever good at? You at least owe me honesty on this, Taylor. I've tried to do more than simply stumble around and attract trouble to myself. Is that my only real skill? Do I have any other function?"

A smile, slight and wan but faintly warm, spread across the woman's pale, beautiful face. She rested a hand on his shoulder.

"Perhaps," she said tentatively, "at first, I thought it was thus—that you might possess some basic competence at the tasks I assigned but that mostly, you were simply for drawing out my enemies. I apologize."

He blinked and stared at her. *She really means it. She's actually apologizing!*

"You have proven surprising in many ways," Taylor went on. She retracted her hand. "Both in the positive and negative sense, granted. I've already discussed the negative matters, so we needn't dwell on those. But you also have a certain...business acumen. Maybe that's not what you would prefer to hear, but it's true, and it's something you can take pride in. I would not have allowed mere bait to rent an office in my name, after all."

"Well," he returned, "thank you. Business acumen, yes. That sounds accurate."

"It is," she assured him. "Now, get ready. In this situation, being bait is perhaps the most heroic thing you could do. Which is to say, it's dangerous. Take care."

She turned and left, a slim, dark, graceful form vanishing out the doors with nary a wasted sound.

Moments later, Volz and Bobby finished their tasks.

The dwarf took Remy's hand in his powerful grip. "Good luck, my friend. You can handle this. But please, don't mess up my computers. I worked hard on those, as you well recall."

Remy smiled. "I'll see what I can do."

Bobby approached and gave him a quick hug. Her breasts smashed against his chest and he tried not to yelp at the pressure on his broken rib. "Be careful, Mr Remington. Try to trust those Feds. Think about it. They're probably the ones who invented whatever drug this guy is on."

"Could be." He gasped when she released him. "I'll see you tomorrow, fear not."

The two took their leave. Now, only he and the fairy remained in the office.

He took a deep breath and glanced to the top of the file cabinet where she sat and kicked her legs idly, her jaw set in subdued aggravation. "Riley...what's wrong? And don't pretend like something isn't wrong. Even human males can figure some of these things out, you know."

She looked at him, her eyes huge in her tiny face, and she sighed. "It's only… Well…"

He waited.

She wavered between gushing emotionality and stand-offishness for a moment before she continued. "I haven't been able to stop thinking about how, back in Times Square, you threatened to replace me. That was really mean. I know you were angry about what Alex did to you and how Taylor didn't respect you, but you shouldn't have said that."

He frowned, although more in sympathy than exasperation. She was right.

"And," she pressed on, "you ignored me when I told you it was dangerous to go after that man and you ended up getting badly hurt. I was afraid…that you might die. And without even getting the chance to apologize."

Once again, he felt almost like a dark wave had crashed over his head—the inescapable sense that he was a schmuck.

This time, however, he fought it off. As best he could, given his injuries, he straightened his spine and threw his shoulders back.

"Riley, I'm sorry," he said and meant it. "That was a foolish thing to say even if I was pissed off. Not only because I shouldn't have hurt your feelings, but because it was based on a totally incorrect assumption."

She leaned forward and tilted her head, waiting for him to explain what this meant.

He smiled. "You can't be replaced. As my friend, ally,

helper, protector, and one-time date, you are irreplaceable."

Suddenly, she beamed. Her wings flapped and she rocketed toward him to plant a minuscule kiss on his cheek. "Aww, thanks!" she exclaimed. "I don't think you'd be replaceable either. Which means I don't want anything to happen to you."

After a hasty glance at the Black Cat Idol, he picked one of the Tasers up and slid it into his waistband. He took the other in hand, for now. "Don't worry too much about me, now or in the future," he assured her. "I'm too awesome to die."

An Abandoned Building, Bushwick, Brooklyn, New York

Alexander Thomas had begun to feel good about himself and his situation once more. It had certainly been long enough since that had been the case. After everything he'd been through, he was fairly certain he deserved it.

The FBI agents considered themselves so fucking clever. They had holed up in a disused shop a short distance down the street and watched the Midnight Detective Agency's headquarters—waiting, presumably, until they had some signal from their mates to leap into action.

He had surveilled the neighborhood before he'd made even the slightest move, determined not to fail again. No matter how desperately he wanted the idol, he wouldn't charge in recklessly this time. He would be smart about this—hell, he had a doctorate.

One of the agents stood guard outside a large, glassless

window to the right of the door. Alex was only about a hundred feet away and the man hadn't noticed him yet.

This might even turn out to be easy, he gloated. *Americans are always complaining about how stupid their government employees are, after all.*

He waited, hidden behind a dumpster. While he'd planned, he'd also practiced some of the more esoteric moves that Moswen's borrowed power had granted him.

One was the ability to leap in such a way that he practically floated through the air. He learned to descend with such grace that, when he landed, he barely made a sound. The ability to climb walls and ceilings was one he'd used before, but his form needed work.

He'd spent almost the entire time since his flight from the motel getting himself in peak operating condition. Now, it was showtime.

After some moments, the guard traipsed away a few steps, either to investigate a noise—Alex heard it too, probably a rat scurrying through a sewer grate—or simply to patrol other parts of the building.

The window practically welcomed him in.

He threw himself upward, discerned and used the currents of the night's wind, and soared in a perfect line toward the opening. The guard's footsteps returned as the sides of the window flashed beside him.

Still airborne, he focused all his strength on slowing and softening his impact. A wall rose up to meet him and he realized that the hall beyond the window was narrow.

Sweat poured from his forehead but he succeeded. He slowed to a hover and touched down gently on the floor, only a few centimeters from the wall. After a deep breath, he turned his augmented senses to everything around him.

There were seven agents total, he determined. Four in a main room around the corner, two at the wings of the building, and the guard out front.

Two of them in the main chamber were talking.

"No sign so far," a man's voice said.

"Be patient," a woman replied. "He'll come. Tonight's his best chance."

Aww. Alex smirked. *They set all this up especially for me. How flattering.*

The female voice continued. "They left Rem with three buttons. Even if the asshole chases him to a different part of the office, he'll be able to press one of them. As soon as the light blinks, we move."

He nodded in the shadows. *That's good to know, FBI lady. Thanks.*

With no discernible sound at all, he crawled up the wall and hid in the gloomy corner it made where it met the ceiling. Then, slowly and quietly, he crept into the main room.

Below him, the four agents huddled around a small console. It was dark and lifeless-looking, probably programmed to only light up when the signal was activated so as to not reveal their position with even the slightest glow.

While he would have assumed the device had battery capacity, the agents nevertheless had two cords running from it. He backed out of the room and followed the cords to the rear of the building.

There, he saw they were attached to two devices. One was some kind of transponder or something, which would receive the signal. The other appeared to be a small generator, which they had mostly wrapped in padded insulation to muffle the low grinding sound it made. This building looked like it had been abandoned too long before to still be hooked up to the local power grid.

There were no guards nearby. Alex dropped and again slowed himself so he landed with all the noise of a cotton ball. He yanked the cords loose from both the generator and the transponder and picked up the latter device.

On impulse, he took it with him as he crawled out the window and scurried to the roof when the outside guard turned his back.

With his enhanced perception, he heard the agents below him and within the shop continue their terse conversation.

"He punched through a bed, didn't he?" some guy quipped. "I think I did that when I was drunk once. Does this mean that Bushmills is the Israeli Mafia's secret weapon now?"

Someone chuckled but the woman said, "He did that and much more. Don't underestimate this guy."

Alex grinned as he crouched atop the old building. Confidence surged through him. He would absolutely and undoubtedly win.

Moswen will be so pleased, she'll probably get distracted and won't even notice when—

He cut the thought off. If she knew about his secret plan to barter with Taylor for his freedom, she hadn't shown it yet. And now was no time to clue her in.

A single, silent bound took him from the roof of the shop to another building, a Thai restaurant. He crawled down the far side of it, out of sight of the Feds, and dropped the transponder through a sewer grate. It plopped very satisfyingly into the befouled water below.

Satisfied, he turned toward the agency's office.

And after what I did to him last time, that Remington spacker will barely be able to raise a finger to stop me.

CHAPTER EIGHTEEN

Moonlight Detective Agency Office, Bushwick, Brooklyn, New York

Remy sat in the pale glow of the fluorescent security lights and reviewed Agent Gilmore's diagram of the booby traps they'd laid. He went down the list, double-checked them with his own eyes, and planned his route through the office if pursued, as well as how he'd reach for a weapon or activate one of the alarm buttons.

He could not move anywhere even close to as fast as he'd like to. It made him wonder if maybe this had been a bad idea and they should have cajoled one of the Feds into undertaking this particular duty instead.

Or even paid Volz extra and thrust it into his lap. He'd do practically anything for decent money.

Or bought a homeless guy a couple of fifths of vodka and told him everything would be all right once he pressed the button.

Anyone, really. As long as they weren't half-crippled by recent bodily trauma.

Riley had stayed with him, of course. They weren't sure how much effect her magic would have since she'd struggled to do much against this Thomas guy during their last encounter, but she might at least be able to levitate him out of the way of an attack or something if all else failed.

The fairy floated next to his ear.

"I heard something," she whispered.

He covered his mouth and responded to her in the softest voice he could manage. "Go check it out. Be back in...uh, two minutes, we'll say."

"Okay," she agreed. She whisked off into the space above him and vanished into an air duct, probably headed to the roof of the building.

It wasn't until after she was gone that the thought popped into Remy's head—he should have told her to create some kind of loud noise like a magical alarm if she saw anything suspicious.

"Damn," he cursed. He'd have to run it by her when she returned.

He wondered if Alex would really come tonight or if the Aussie prick would hesitate and instead, try to steal the Black Cat Idol another day while it was in transit somewhere. There was no way to be certain.

And which way will he come in if he does show up? He considered the options. *Probably not through the front door. He might burst through the back. Or do what Riley did in reverse —crawl down from the roof into the ducts and try to drop on my head.*

It wasn't an encouraging prospect. He checked the clock. One minute had passed.

At that moment, the front door exploded off its hinges and careened across the lobby.

"Jesus!" Remy yelled, stumbled back a step, and winced when his fractured back rib stabbed him.

He could actually see a foot shod in a heavy work shoe protrude beyond the point where the door used to be. It retracted across the threshold.

His heart thudding wildly, he scrambled into position next to the idol. Both Tasers were still secured in the back of his pants.

Okay, he took the direct approach. That means he'll blunder into the grease we put on the floor. Then...uh, I press the button and pretend to try to keep the statuette away from him long enough to stall for time.

A humanoid form literally flew through the door, skipped the lubricated floor altogether, and attached itself to the wall. The man began to clamber toward the ceiling.

Remy's heart sank. "Whoops," he said.

Button first. Button now.

His head jerked and his hand whipped out to retrieve the small device on the desk next to him. He located it and jammed the button down with his index finger. It clicked, but nothing else happened.

They said it was a silent alarm. It worked. They've seen the flashing little light and headed out to kick some ass. Right?

By now, Alex was halfway across the ceiling to where he stood and he'd noticed him.

"I cannot believe," the man remarked, his Australian accent somehow more obvious than it had previously been, "that they left you in charge of guarding that thing. Taylor must have a lot of faith in those FBI agents. I bet she gave them all a reach-around, including the sheila."

Remy grabbed the statuette with his left hand and hugged it close to his body. He backed away a step and, with his right hand, drew the first Taser.

"Back off, dickhead," he retorted and aimed the electroshock gun. "I seem to recall that these things kinda slightly hurt you. Also, her name is Kendra, not Sheila."

"For fuck's sake." The intruder sighed. He dropped from the ceiling, landed on a desk, and reduced it to a pile of fragments, some of which scattered and ricocheted off the walls. "You people never take the time to learn anyone else's slang, do you?"

He pointed the Taser at the man's face. "We have Hollywood and the Pentagon. Your argument is invalid."

More importantly, Mr Thomas was only about a step and a half away from the tripwire that would spring the tranquilizer-coated punji-trap.

"I skipped debate class," the man admitted. "But enough of this. I'll ask you to give me the idol now so I don't have to take it." His blue eyes almost glowed with crazed, strung-out fury.

Unfortunately, he didn't move.

Remy decided a little provocation should do the trick. He pulled the trigger.

Alex saw the attack as it happened and his superhuman reflexes kicked in. He launched himself upward but even he wasn't quite fast enough. The dual barbs caught him in the right leg below the knee while he was airborne.

"Goddammit!" He snarled.

The investigator hobbled back another couple of steps

and his foe fell sideways and again, clung to the wall. His teeth gnashed as the electricity caused his muscles to seize up.

In virtually the next breath, it was already over. The intruder stretched a hand and ripped the darts from his shin before he punched a hole through the wall to deposit them in the dusty gap beyond.

He pounced, easily cleared the tripwire below, and landed about two feet in front of Remington.

Shit, shit, shit. Remy slowly raised his hand holding the gun as if getting ready to surrender it to the police. *Where's Riley? Where's Gilmore?*

Alex stared at him. "Last chance." It sounded like a hiss, rather than a statement—the kind that preceded a snake about to strike.

He dropped the gun and instead, held the statuette over his own head with both hands, the way a second-grader would play keep-away with a kindergartner's toy. "I know you don't want to kill me if you don't have to, Alexander Thomas," he pointed out. "But you'll have to take it from me, anyw—"

A blur of color and mass rushed over and past him. He toppled back, aware of two simultaneous facts. One, his entire torso would become a volcanic eruption of pain when he struck the floor and two, the idol was no longer in his hands.

He heard Alex laugh as he landed.

"Fuck!" he gasped. Courtesy of his back rib, it felt like he'd fallen onto a knife blade. The kinetic impact jostled the front one, too, and his mini-hernia also tried to convince him that he'd burst into flames. "Oh, God…"

But he'd pressed the alarm button already. Gilmore and her merry men would be along any second now to lasso the bastard before he could escape with the fake statuette.

It seemed like it had already been an awfully long few seconds.

So much for excellent response time. He dragged himself painfully from the floor by holding onto a desk.

The blur swept past him again, this time in the opposite direction.

Remy stretched frantically and yanked a cord along the wall.

A loose section of scaffolding, seemingly attached to the ceiling, dropped in front of Alex's mad dash. The piping burst apart but the Australian also reeled and tumbled under the impact.

The Black Cat Idol rolled a few feet ahead of him. He crawled forward, thrust aside pieces of debris, and snatched it back.

This gave the other man enough time to heave himself into a standing position and draw his second Taser. He advanced on the prone form, the weapon aimed and ready.

"Riley!" he shouted. "*Riley!*"

Sweat oozed from his brow and his thoughts raced. *Where the hell is she? Did she get stuck in a spiderweb or something?*

His adversary rolled and his eyes widened. "You're seriously begging your fairy for help?" He pushed to his feet and steadied himself before he made ready to lunge toward the door.

Remy noted his position. He kicked the tripwire that Alex had jumped over when he entered.

The needle-tipped beam swung from the ceiling and two of the spikes embedded themselves in the man's left arm. "What the fuck!" he raged and stumbled as blood poured from his bicep. He tore his arm free and staggered forward.

Riley suddenly burst from the air duct overhead and flew to the side of Remy's face. "Sorry!" she apologized. She saw Alex. "Oh no, he's getting away."

The man's movements were slow and clumsy. Between the blow to the head he'd taken from the first trap and the dose of tranquilizer the second had delivered into his bloodstream, they might have a chance to stop him.

Remy gestured wildly at the retreating figure. "Knock him off his feet."

"How?" she protested. "My magic doesn't affect him. I already tried to stop him out there before he broke in."

A heavy chair stood only a few feet in front of them. Remington nodded his head at it. "Throw that at him."

"Oh!" she exclaimed. "I didn't think of that."

Sparkling with silver light, the chair levitated halfway to the ceiling before it hurtled toward Alex as if flung from a trebuchet. Remy cringed—the trajectory looked too low—but the chair struck the floor between the man's legs.

"Ha!" He laughed and limped forward when the intruder stumbled into the grease trap at the entrance. Cursing and sobbing, the man wobbled before his feet slid out from under him. He landed with a resounding thud and his head struck the baseboard of the wall.

Gilmore still hadn't arrived. Something had to be wrong. Remy remembered in that moment that Alex had mentioned the FBI team. He knew about them and might have tampered with their equipment somehow. Or even killed them all.

"Riley!" Remington ordered. "Fly out and make a…a big loud colorful explosion or something. Right now!" He wanted to kick himself for not thinking of that sooner, but everything had happened almost too fast for his brain to keep up.

The fairy swooped out of sight.

His adversary didn't seem to have heard since he had only now begun to recover from the battering he'd taken over the course of the last minute or two. He groaned and held his head in his hands when he managed to sit, his movements groggy.

Remy eased past an overturned desk to a position he felt was a safe distance from the man and aimed the Taser at his face.

"Remington," Alex all but snarled as his eyes refocused, "get out of my way or I will kill you. I've let you live as a favor to Taylor. But you will not get between me and my goal."

A strange, high-pitched, almost musical sound echoed from somewhere above the building. The Australian, in his semi-dazed state, didn't seem to pay it much heed.

Unfortunately, it looked like the sedative was already wearing off.

Remy bit his lip. Firing the Taser might buy a few more seconds, but that was it. And somehow, he didn't think Alex's death threat was an idle bluff.

Well, I guess it's time for a different approach.

"Alex," he said calmly, "you look like an intelligent guy. Someone even said you're a scientist or something. And you've been one step ahead of us this whole time. I almost can't accept that someone of your abilities would end up working for a monster like this Moswen bitch."

The man struggled to his feet, his lip curled. "All you need to know is that she's employed me because of my abilities. Most people wouldn't have been able to easily disable those Feds' communications equipment. Not to mention going toe-to-toe with Taylor herself and living to talk about it."

"Yeah," he agreed hastily, "clearly you have something on the ball there. Okay, you're a dick but you really thought of everything, didn't you? We might have been friends if you'd been born an American. I've heard…uh, that Australia has a really good educational system, right? Is that how you figured out what we had planned?"

At that moment, Alex could have shoved Remy aside and bolted out the door but he didn't. He couldn't resist stalling for another moment or two. Why leave when Remy had handed him the opportunity to look cool and smart?

"Ha!" he scoffed. "The University of Melbourne is one of the top educational institutions in the world. And Melbourne has consistently scored highly on globally recognized quality-of-life rankings. Higher than New York, to which we're sometimes compared. Your city might be bigger, but I always felt that quality was more important than quantity."

He took a deep breath to stop himself from simply charging in and decking the guy in the face.

Both men heard it at once—heavy footsteps approaching fast. Alex's head whipped toward the sound.

Remy pulled the trigger. The Taser's twin darts sank into the man's upper shoulder and drove him back as he jerked around, drawing sparks from his clothes and flesh.

"Well," he shouted, louder than was necessary for the calm statement he was making, "I think it was Stalin who said that quantity has a quality all its own. Like in the case of seven versus one."

Figures in black paramilitary gear leapt through the shattered front door, nimbly dodged the grease section of floor, and surrounded the Australian as he started to overcome the effects of the Taser.

"Don't move!" one of the agents bellowed.

He moved and pandemonium erupted.

Remy shuffled back, intending to get the hell out of the way as Alex, crazed and desperate and still operating with preternatural strength, tried to fight his way free of the well-trained, highly organized team. The Black Cat Idol rolled away from the melee and came to rest in the corner near his office.

The fairy reappeared at some point and took her position above his shoulder as they gaped at the confrontation.

Alex threw two of the agents off at once, only for four others to descend and hammer him with batons, Tasers of their own, and some kind of crusty foam. The entire group thrashed and whirled as they progressed deeper into the office.

"Shit," Remy gasped and glanced at Riley. "We might… ah, get cornered here."

The desperate intruder let loose with a powerful kick and one of the agents collapsed and screamed, along with an unpleasant crunching sound. The others continued to corral him and wear him down.

Moving and struggling as a unit, they all collided into a desk in the corner where half the office's computers had been piled. Remy winced as the devices toppled onto the floor and most of them cracked on impact.

"Damn," he muttered, "Volz will definitely have some overtime."

Riley watched the battle with concern. "Remy, do you think you should help?"

He bit his lip. "No." It looked like the Feds, slowly but surely, were winning. "I'm half-crippled at the moment and they're obviously using tactics that I don't have training in. I'd only get in their way. I think—hopefully—that we can let the professionals do their job..."

The next thirty or forty seconds proved him right.

Alex, his avenues of movement and attack cut off and exhausted by the lengthy struggle, finally landed on his back. Suddenly, Agent Gilmore's knee was on his chest and her pistol aimed at his head.

Another agent had also drawn his gun, and three more had pinned the Australian's limbs. The wild, cornered-animal-like urge to fight was dying off now, replaced by cold dismay.

"Okay," he gasped, "point taken. I surrender. Ha, yeah. Just..." He gulped. "Don't shoot me."

"Stay calm," Gilmore instructed, her tone hard and icy. "Don't do anything unless we say so."

Her other subordinates were already unspooling heavy cords to tie the man up. Remy hoped against hope that they'd put tape over his mouth while they were at it.

Alex attempted to grin but only looked grotesque. "Understood. I'm sure we…ah, can work something out, right?"

Remy cupped his hands around his mouth and shouted toward the man. "For starters, if you stop acting like a jackass, I'll buy you one of those 'I Heart New York' shirts."

CHAPTER NINETEEN

Bushwick, Brooklyn, New York

Taylor had spent the early evening mostly driving around Brooklyn. She enjoyed driving. By and large, it relaxed her while being—at times—challenging enough to put her into a "flow" state.

With her sharp senses and preternatural reflexes, the city's treacherous freeways and congested avenues were fun rather than stressful as they seemed to be for humans.

Furthermore, cruising around allowed her to identify anything suspicious that might be going on in the borough. By New York standards, anyway, it was a rather quiet night. Dull, even.

She'd set her phone in one of the cupholders in such a way that she could easily see any notification that might flash across its screen. At that moment, it lit up to display a text message.

Your package has been shipped! The sender was listed as *Unknown Number.*

The vampire smiled. Shipped, but not yet delivered.

The action had only started. If she could get back to the office fast enough, she might even be able to participate.

Hardly anyone was on the road, at least within a quarter-mile. Taylor pressed the accelerator at the same moment that she spun the wheel to the left and deliberately fish-tailed her way into a nearly perfect U-turn. She raced in the opposite direction toward Bushwick and their HQ.

She sensed more than saw a cop up ahead and slowed quickly to about two miles per hour over the speed limit and coasted nonchalantly past the police cruiser. Once it was safely out of sight, she accelerated again.

It took a few more minutes to arrive at her destination, weaving through back streets as needed and passing other cars with fluid ease.

Taylor spun into the agency's lot and came to a complete stop with the vehicle parallel to and about six feet from the front door. Within the building, she could hear a slight commotion, although it was dying down. They must have finished without her.

She stepped out of the Tesla and through the door and nimbly avoided the grease trap. The other devices all appeared to have already been sprung during the battle.

In the center of a cleared-out area near her office, surrounded by the debris of smashed desks and electronics, Alexander Thomas knelt on the floor, handcuffed and bound with powerful fiberglass cords. Two agents aimed guns at his head and chest.

Agent Gilmore stood four or five feet in front of him, also holding a pistol, although she kept it aimed at the floor for now.

"Hello," Taylor greeted them.

Everyone's heads turned to look. They must not have heard her arrive.

Remy leaned against the wall to the side and gasped in pain and exhaustion, although the almost goofy exaltation on his face meant he must have done a fine job. Riley hovered a couple of feet over his head, invisible to the agents.

Two of the Feds, she saw, had been wounded and were sprawled on the floor while another team member with medical training tended to them.

"Ms Steele," Gilmore said without moving her gaze from Alex, "mission accomplished. The bastard injured two of my men but they'll be okay with treatment. An ambulance is on the way."

"That's good to hear." She took a few steps closer and negotiated between the sprung traps and general chaos. "I'll take over from here."

The agent smiled grimly. "Of course you will."

"Thank you, by the way," she continued, "for agreeing to leave him in my care, rather than spiriting him off to some awful government black-site prison from whence he'll never be heard from again. I can assure you that my methods will be more productive."

She nodded. "Remember that you gave me your word. Any information you glean from your interrogation of the suspect is to be shared with us. I feel I can trust you, but on the off chance that you renege, we have ways to make things difficult until we get our end of the bargain."

"Don't worry," Taylor assured her, "I will tell you everything you need to know. Thanks again for your help thus far."

So as to not have civilian personnel around the scene, Gilmore loaded her two injured men onto the portable stretchers they'd left in the office and had the others wheel them out. She was the last to leave.

"Also," the agent stated, "I won't be around to witness the interrogation. Let's say that I understand the reality we live in but also that we're still Americans here and there are certain levels of ugliness we do not stoop to." She gave the vampire a hard look.

Taylor smiled. "I find that verbal and psychological persuasion is more effective than certain cruder methods."

Gilmore nodded. "Get to work then, ma'am. I'll be in touch. Oh, one last thing. Our communications equipment failed, and Remington managed to alert us with some pyrotechnic I've never seen before. A big silver-blue flash, accompanied by what almost sounded like weird, high-pitched music. May I ask what that might have been?"

"Oh," Remy cut in without missing a beat, "it's a little something I learned in chemistry class."

The agent glowered at him, her face skeptical. "Don't get too creative when it comes to chemistry. Or too greedy."

"Fear not," he countered, "I skipped out to the bar on the day they taught all the other students how to make crystal meth."

Taylor sighed. "Remington's family is rich enough that he never had to learn how to speak properly to law-enforcement personnel. In any event, thank you again, Agent Gilmore, and we'll take it from here."

The other woman nodded and walked out, shutting the door behind her. Mr Thomas, for his part, did not move or speak and kept his gaze fixed on the floor.

Remy took a step forward. "Soooo," he drawled, "does that last part mean that I'm not allowed to punch him in the face? Not even once?"

"Correct," she replied. "Until further notice, anyway."

She knelt, extended a finger, and placed it gently under Alex's chin to urge his face upward.

"Look at me," she said, her voice soft but infused with a little of her power of command.

The man looked up.

"Alex," she cooed, "we know why you're here. We know who you're working for. And we know what she is— can feel the stink of her power on you. And, of course, you know what I am. There's no point in arguing about any of that. We can move on to discussing the details and I want to hear all of them. Really, we already know the most important stuff. Your only real value is in helping us fill in a few of the minor gaps in our knowledge."

His face drooped in resignation. He sighed and opened his mouth.

"I'm willing to cooperate," he grumbled in his Australian accent, "but I can't guarantee that she won't—"

He jerked back, his jaw clamped shut and face contorted, and his words trailed to grunts and yelps of agony.

Taylor stood quickly. Beside her, Remy exclaimed, "What the hell? Is he having a delayed reaction to getting his ass kicked all of a sudden, or—"

Alex's eyes closed, then bulged open. "Brand..." He gasped. "On my chest!"

The vampire cursed inwardly. She should have expected this. With one hand and one motion, she seized him by the shirt, hauled him up, and laid him flat on his back on the nearest desk before she ripped the shirt off.

The other man stumbled against the wall. "Holy shit!"

Directly over the man's heart, a strange marking glowed with an amber-golden light. The illumination grew in intensity as it pulsed and flashed, and Alex's thrashing and screams grew louder and more forceful.

"Dammit," she cursed, "the Feds can probably hear this and they'll think that I'm the one doing it." She considered her options.

Remy stammered. "Well, uh, if you're not the one doing it, who is? Moswen?"

"Yes." She stared at the pathetic man in his throes of pain and knew that the brand's main use was to torment him into compliance with his mistress's will. Unfortunately, it would kill him within a few minutes if not deactivated. It would simply surge his heart into overdrive until it stopped beating.

Alex bucked in place. "Please," he cried. "God, *it burns!*"

Pity mingled with anger. "Alex," Taylor proclaimed, "brands like that can only be applied with the consent of the subject. You willingly agreed to serve her."

"She was going to kill me!" He choked and spittle flew from his lips.

Remy stepped in, his face pale with disgust. "Can't you do anything? We can't let him be tortured to death, for fucks' sake, even if he is an asshole. Do you really think he had much choice?"

The vampire's nostrils flared. "He could have chosen to die quickly, right then and there, instead of saving his own skin by coming into my city and murdering those dwarves on her orders. And trying to set me up."

Alex's shaking hand extended toward her. "I'll do anything! Serve you—help—anything."

"He means it," Remy said quickly.

Taylor leaned over the writhing form. "Yes, I believe he does. He's clearly a coward, after all. Fine, Remington, we will attempt the merciful option. I don't want to have to mindwipe anyone who asks why and how he died in our custody, anyway."

There was, however, no guarantee that she could remove or reverse the brand and the powerful curse behind it. The sight and smell of the golden inferno on the man's chest suggested a level of magic power that might be beyond even her capabilities.

She extended her small, slim hands, and used both to cover the glowing mark. Most of its light faded, aside from some residual illumination seeping out from the sides.

With gentle force, she pressed down. Alex froze momentarily and his body lowered itself flat against the desk's surface. His screams choked into a hollow gulping sound, and only his extremities trembled.

The light flared again and the man resumed his cries of agony.

"Shit," Taylor muttered. "This will not be easy."

Riley floated down. "Can I help?" She looked and sounded scared.

"Try dampening or reversing the power coming out of the mark under my hands," the vampire snapped, her words quick and sharp. She didn't have time to be polite. Alex would be dead within about a minute if this didn't work.

The fairy extended her own tiny limbs and sparkles of bluish-silver ether, essences of soothing and healing, began to hem in the violent yellowish fire.

Taylor calmed herself and held Moswen's power at bay as she delved deep into the core of her own being. She knew her eyes would start to glow right about now, and a faint blood-red glow appeared around the edges of her fingers.

Back through years and years, the memories of her powers stretched—through gallons upon gallons of blood and over the cold gray waters of the North Atlantic.

They touched her family, asleep in their moldering graves in England, and how she was all that was left of them.

Her victims slid before her—so many, in those early years, before she civilized herself and switched to drinking blood obtained through more ethical means. The life and the power that so much blood had granted her surged within.

The red light under her hands grew, its intensity drowning out the silver of the fairy and the gold of the other vampire.

Now, crimson and gold strained against each other directly, intertwining even as each tried to force the other to submit and retreat.

The memories of Taylor's own lengthy and unnatural

life were suddenly eclipsed by others which were not her own. Memories of dust and monumental earth, of a great river bringing life to a desert, of thousands of cowed and simpering slaves and peasants, all of them made prey. All were bled and cast aside at the slightest whim for sport or malice.

Centuries upon centuries of cruelty, wanton blood-gluttony, and vicious arrogance and entitlement lent urgency to a hunger that had never abated and still drove forward in time for endless, unlimited satisfaction.

Within the yellowish light, a face appeared, somehow dim amidst the glow like the shadow cast by the sun. A dark, bony face, subtly beautiful and regal but utterly, terribly evil stared at her.

"No!" she shouted. "*Back!* Return to the wasteland in which you were buried. *I reign here!*"

Red light surged from the man on the desk and engulfed the entire room as the golden light faded. Taylor pushed and sent streaks of crimson spiraling through the gold, weaving their way into its essence, and Moswen's power fled.

The red light flashed once more, then died, and the entire room went totally black.

Silence descended, broken only by the labored breathing of the humans, and the room's ambient illumination gradually returned. Everything was calm. Alex lay gasping, and only the faintest outline of the hieroglyph remained on his chest.

"Wow," Remy commented. "That...uh, that was a hell of a show. I didn't even know you could do that, Taylor. Whatever it was."

She leaned back, straightened, and flexed her hands. "If the truth be told, I wasn't certain I'd be able to. But now, Moswen knows that she'd best think of me as an equal."

Alex blinked repeatedly and glanced around with fast sharp movements like a bird or a lizard as though he expected something else to happen at any moment.

"Is it over?" he moaned. "Am I—"

"You are free," Taylor explained, "of Moswen's poisonous influence. She won't be able to read your thoughts, or hurt you, or kill you. At least, not by that method." She gestured to the Australian's bare chest.

He swung his legs over the edge, raised himself into a seated position on the desk, and rubbed his eyes.

"However," she added, "a small trace of the brand remains and it is now under my control. You will not be kept on so cruelly tight a leash as you were under her but if you try to flee the city, I will know and I will stop you. And don't even think about trying to harm me or anyone under my protection."

The man nodded and moved his hands away from his eyes and through his shaggy, straw-colored hair.

She leaned closer to him. "Now, tell me all about your mistress. Do not attempt to lie."

Alex breathed deeply and ignored the plump beads of sweat that rolled over his brow and nose into his eyes and mouth. "Her name is Moswen Neith. And yes, she's a fucking vampire. We accidentally freed her during a dig in Israel."

Remy cocked an eyebrow. "A Jewish vampire. The bad jokes about kosher slaughter practically write themselves."

"No, you idiot!" the other man snapped. "She's Egyptian."

"Okay." He shrugged. "Halal slaughter."

The Australian ignored him. "She never said exactly how old she is, but, well..." His eyes glazed over. "She mentioned something about how Caliph al-Mahdi—you know, the bloke who assumed power over the Abbasid Caliphate in CE 775—had her driven out of Egypt and into Sinai. They also prevented her from heading toward Baghdad, so she spent most of the next thousand years in the Negev and Syrian Deserts. She slept most of the time, woke up to feed every decade or two, and waited for the right opportunity to retake her birthright, as she called it."

Remy looked uncomfortable at that, Taylor saw. She'd noticed a similar look in his eyes when she'd spoken of her own distant past. Something about the vast abyss of time in which the undead existed tended to creep mortals out.

"Go on," she said.

Alex swallowed. "So, finally, when the Bedouin began to expand into southern Israel, they formed a posse and cornered her in an ancient Nabataean temple and trapped her in the deepest crypt under a mess of Islamic holy symbols. And some good masonry, of course."

His shoulders slumped. "We let her out. That dig...it was the opportunity of a lifetime. Of course, it was an accident, and it would be ridiculous to suggest that all this is somehow our fault."

"Oh," Remy snorted, "of course."

He shook his head. "I'd recently earned my doctorate. I had to go. Eitan Feldman was running things. He was one of my heroes. Then, she split his face open and tore everyone else apart…"

Taylor nodded. "I've heard of Feldman. I am sorry to hear that he's been lost to the world. You're an archaeologist, then. Interesting. You might actually prove useful to us in more ways than one."

Remy began to feel bad for the schmuck again, knowing that his mentor and friends had all been massacred by a pissed-off vampire, but something occurred to him and he simply couldn't help himself.

"So," he remarked, "you're a pro, but you never realized that the Black Cat statue was a fake, did you?"

Alex's head snapped up. "What? Bullshit!"

He smiled innocently and looked toward the ceiling. "Yeppers. That little flaw under the tail? That's the mark of Osman the Fake-Ass Scammer. He's probably made a fortune by now ripping people off, including the previous owners and even the Guggenheim."

Taylor held a hand toward Remy, palm outward. "That's enough, Remington. You forgot to mention that he also fooled you twice."

He made a pouty face but shut up.

She glanced at Alex again. "It's true, though, the idol is a fake. Moswen and I both used it as bait to try to entrap the other. She managed to draw me out enough to be detected, and I'm sure you told her all about me, but she has failed in the long run."

The man's eyes locked warily on hers. "Right. So, what now? How can I…ah, be of service?"

Taylor half-smiled. "We'll talk about it. The most important thing you can do, though, is nothing. I didn't entirely remove the brand she put on your chest. I reversed it. Now, it will act as a beacon on her location."

He looked confused. "What...what does that mean?"

"She can no longer use it to track you," the vampire explained, "but I can track her. However, she almost certainly has a general idea of what I've done. Which is to say that she knows you have been fashioned into a tool that will hurt her, rather than help her."

The man's face slowly fell. She placed a hand over his heart and closed her eyes.

"For example," she said softly, "Yes...yes, she's on the move already. Heading northwest. I imagine she'll have preparations to make, but I'd guess she'll hide in Beersheba for a while, then make her way to the nearest airport. I would be surprised if she didn't come to New York. Soon."

Alex's features, tanned by exposure to the sun in both Australia and Israel, suddenly turned the color of skim milk.

She removed her hand. "We'll protect you. But don't convince us that you're more trouble than you're worth, my friend."

Remy patted the man on the shoulder. "Well, then. It looks like you're the bait now."

CHAPTER TWENTY

Moonlight Detective Agency Office, Bushwick, Brooklyn, New York

"Hey!" Remy called.

One of the workmen, mounted on a ladder, looked petulantly at him. A lollipop stick dangled from his mouth. "Whaddya want?"

He moved his fingers in a ring around the interior of each of his cufflinks. "I'm curious as to when this section of the hallway will be done. It's been, what, a month or something now since we brought you guys on?"

The man deliberately looked away from him at the plaster. "Soon," he grunted. "The cops and that speed freak did a helluva number on this place. And we're backed up with work orders. We kinda want to be done with 'em all by Christmas."

With a brisk nod, Remington walked past the semi-friendly gentleman and his unspeaking partner. He was right, of course. The place had been fairly badly damaged. And it was almost Christmas.

Still, the back hall near the bathroom seemed to be the last place that needed significant work. Soon, the entire office would be better than new.

Remy turned the corner. Andrew Volz was there, installing shiny rounded stainless-steel panels to cover the wires he'd had to replace. He motioned with a thick hand and he came over to hear his pitch.

"Well, boss," he rumbled, "as you can see, this is coming along quite nicely. The next so-called speed freak who breaks in will have a much harder time damaging our network, ha. Not to mention that I've installed backups to the backups. I won't bore you with the details, but your computer system will soon be barely shy of invincible. Unless they launch a tactical nuke into the office."

Remy shrugged. "Who knows what the morrow will bring? Even some of the people who dislike us probably won't be that brazen, though. Good work, Volz. Keep earning that pay. One day, perhaps you'll even be able to afford to buy another inch of height."

"Hrmph!" He snorted and put his fists on his hips. "I have all I need and more. Plus, I'm a genius. You wouldn't want me to take my services elsewhere, now would you?"

He flashed his best PR smile. "Of course not. Therefore, I take back what I said. I bet that if you really wanted height-extension surgery, you could already afford it."

For a moment, it looked like the dwarf was about to argue—probably as a way to haggle for higher pay or more bonuses—but the man walked on to avoid giving him an opening.

Shortly after the fight with Alex, he'd prevailed upon Taylor to hire Volz as a full-time employee. "Every successful business needs a designated tech guy," he'd said, and she had begrudgingly agreed.

Now, thanks to his access to significant sums of Taylor's money, their office was operating at—or even beyond—the cutting edge of modern information technology. Seeing all the quasi-futuristic gadgets around made a weird contrast with the somewhat dated architectural style of the building itself.

Plus, it was always nice to have someone on hand who could hack through the FBI's security systems like a hatchet through drywall. Taylor seemed confident that Gilmore wasn't planning to screw them over, but there was always the chance that someone above her in the hierarchy might have other ideas.

They'd also returned the Black Cat Idol to its original owners with a tearful "*We regret to inform you that...*" letter explaining that it was a forgery.

Beyond Volz and his wires and plates, he entered the lobby.

Bobby waved from behind the desk. "Hi, Mr Remington." She was reading The New England Inquirer again, although he couldn't be bothered to examine the headlines.

He waved back and admired his surroundings.

The receptionist had a certain flair for interior decorating. She'd arranged the area to make it look like a cross between a hip college café and the parlor at someone's grandmother's house—cozy and welcoming but without being quaint.

Paintings lined the walls. Or cheap prints, rather, and nothing an art collector would be too impressed with.

They looked nice, anyway, and she'd organized them in a pleasing fashion that drew the eye to them in sequence.

She also had a seemingly endless supply of potted plants, which she rotated on a weekly basis. Currently, it was mostly pines and holly, what with the Holidays looming on the horizon.

Remy swaggered to her deskside. "Do we have any new customers?"

She smiled at him, conveniently putting her face in line with her cleavage, relative to where his eyes were at the moment. "Nope. Things were picking up, but I think they'll settle over Christmas. We'll probably be inundated on the second of January."

He nodded. "Yes, that ought to be enough time for everyone to sober up."

Footsteps approached. It was Alex, now dressed in slacks and a white button-up shirt like any other office worker. A pen peeked out of his chest pocket, and he held a manila folder under one arm.

"So," he announced, "I'm done putting all the completed case files in alphabetical order. And I swept the bathroom floors. Am I done for the day yet?"

"Hmm." Remy stroked his chin. He looked at the receptionist. "Bobby, the intern does not currently have anything to do. Would you like him to fetch you a cup of coffee?"

"Sure," she replied, her demeanor suddenly a little brusque.

Alex sighed. "Yeah, all right, I'll get right on that. You know, I have a PhD. This is a waste of my talents. You could at least have me do archaeological research on your clients' interests instead of all this menial labor like some bogan who's only been through secondary school."

He played dumb. "What's a bogan?"

The Australian ignored the question and gestured toward Bobby. "She's merely sitting there getting some very important reading done, while I could be investigating—"

Taylor appeared behind him. "That Nabataean temple?" she suggested.

The man spun, startled.

She smiled. "It would be helpful to know more about our enemy's origins. If you're unhappy with the work you're doing here, we could always send you to Israel. If you don't mind the risks, of course."

"I'll pass, thanks," he mumbled while he cringed and shuddered before he trudged toward the coffee machine.

The receptionist pretended not to notice that this exchange had even occurred. It was telling that she disliked Alex. Normally, she liked almost everyone. But when their new intern was around, she stiffened and grew terse and businesslike.

Remy supposed that the newcomer would be more successful in repairing his reputation if he didn't constantly try to fly under the radar with all the smartass sniper-comments. It was as if he tested to see if he had a reaction and assumed that when no one responded to his petty insults, it was because they were too stupid to understand what he was doing.

They all knew. But, mostly, they simply ignored him.

Otherwise, he'd behaved himself, though. There had been no aggravated assaults, larceny, or attempted murders directed at his co-workers, encouragingly enough. Nor had he tried to flee. It helped that he was still alive and aware of his good luck in no longer having an ancient Egyptian bloodsucker twisting a magical cattle prod around in his heart.

There'd been some friction with INS, however. Taylor currently stalled them while she tried to get Alex approved for Legal Resident status. It seemed obvious to Remy that the man would rather go home, but he was at least smart enough to know that the only place he'd be safe from Moswen's wrath was under the boss' wing.

Taylor glanced at Bobby as well—and at the paper in her hands.

"Oh," she marveled, "that's rich. *Remington scion's Times Square brawl found to involve Illuminati assassin*. By Jenny Ocren."

The girl looked up and pouted slightly. "I have to admit," she remarked, "that they don't seem to have all their facts straight this time. Normally, I expect a higher standard of journalism from them. But this Ocren chick never even called us. Hell, even I could have told her that the Times Square brawl involved some drugged-up guy from the Israeli Mafia."

She lowered the paper and glowered while she chewed on a finger. "Unless the Illuminati themselves paid them to carry out the hit—"

"I doubt it," the vampire quipped. "In any event, Ms Ocren is doing us a service by killing normal people's interest in the event."

Taylor turned to Remy. "I'll take over our operations for

the night once I've settled in. You may go unless you have anything else you want to discuss."

He thrust his hands into his pockets. "Not really."

Before he could return to his office, the front door opened to admit a stunningly beautiful young woman, about five foot three, with pinned-up, platinum-colored hair. She carried a shiny plastic purse—very un-corporate—but was dressed more or less professionally in a proper dress, albeit a bright red one.

"Hi," she said and waved by holding her hand horizontally while she flipped the fingers up and down. She locked gazes briefly with Remington. "I'll just…um, go right in." She walked past the three of them, past Volz, and let herself into his office.

"Hey!" Bobby called and brandished the sign-in sheet guests usually had to fill out. She glanced at her two bosses. "When did we hire her? I don't think I've ever seen her before."

Remy gestured dismissively. "Oh, don't worry. She's not a full-timer, only a kind of freelance contractor I discovered. She comes in for odd jobs."

He chuckled inwardly. *Like bodyguard work, for example. Or virtually infallible tracking of dangerous suspects. Or heavy lifting. All the usual stuff you'd expect from someone who looks like she stepped out of a hipster fashion ad in a music magazine.*

Still with a broad smile, he strolled after her, opened his office door, and stepped in to gather his things.

Riley sprang at him at once and wound her arms around his neck. Her hair smelled like lilacs.

"Are you happy to see me?" she asked.

"Of course," he assured her and planted a quick, semi-platonic kiss on her cheek to emphasize the point. "Admittedly, I am forced by my biology to be even happier when you're roughly the same size as I am. Also, that suit looks good on you. The color is a little loud, but you're a woman so you ought to be able to get away with it. Men are restricted to black, grey, brown, and navy-blue."

He sighed. For some reason, he'd always wanted to wear a green suit. Or maybe purple, even if it meant that Jenny Ocren would report that he'd become a seventies retro pimp to pay his debts off. Maybe one day, he'd get drunk enough to attempt it.

No. One drink per day, tops. Maybe two or three on special occasions. That's the new rule.

Remy released the fairy and picked his gym bag up.

She squinted at it. "What is that? I've seen you carry it before, but it looks like clothes. Have you had mud splashed on you in the street lately?"

"You're mostly right." He didn't bother to hide his amusement. "It's for my martial arts classes. I enrolled at an MMA gym two weeks ago. I go twice a week now but might increase it to three times later. Granted, it will be another couple of weeks before I'm healed enough to actually start any sparring or anything—you'd think ribs would mend themselves faster – but they at least have me learning some of the basics and doing preliminary exercise to get myself in proper shape. Which I've been working hard at, if I may say so."

Riley nodded. "Ooh, I see. You kinda are looking more…fit? If that's the word." Her mischievous smirk turned to vague confusion. "Why, though?"

He reflected on his first two encounters with Alex and

how easily he'd had his ass kicked. Magically empowered adversary or not, it had been humiliating and had very nearly cost him his life and the agency its credibility.

"I cannot," he explained, "ever be caught unprepared for the possibility of hand-to-hand combat again. I seem to have a natural talent with guns, I guess, but you can't always rely on firearms. Next time I have to take some asshole on *mano a mano,* I want to have some ability to handle myself."

"That makes sense," the fairy conceded. "I'm sorry my magic didn't work so well."

He shook his head and kept his expression apologetic. "It wasn't your fault. Moswen must have backdoor-hacked your spells after the first time you used them on Alex. In any event, she won't be able to try the same shit again."

As for himself, though, watching Gilmore and her agents subdue Mr Thomas had inspired him, in a way. They had no preternatural abilities, yet they'd managed to overcome someone who was almost as powerful as an actual vampire. That was the power of training, toughness, and know-how.

He stroked her cheek briefly. "All right, I have to go. Work hard and do what Taylor tells you to. Also, Bobby still isn't in on what's really going around here, so please, humor her and try not to say anything too...obvious."

"Okay. Bye." They hugged again and he took his leave.

Taylor was still standing in the lobby as he moved to the front door.

"David," she said.

He stopped at once. She hadn't used her command

power on him but he knew her well enough by now to recognize that she had something important to say.

"Yes?" He turned toward her.

In her cool, subtle way, she smiled. "You've done a good job lately."

Remy smiled in his own fashion—big and flashy. "Of course I have. That's, like, the normal state of affairs, isn't it? Any time I don't do something out of an old epic tragedy—or maybe a farce—I do well."

She folded her arms. "That is mostly true. Let us be serious, though. Moswen is still out there. She is profoundly dangerous and has considerable reason to hate us. At any moment, she might finally arrive at Port Authority or JFK International, eager to conclude her vendetta. She'll strike at me any way she can—including through those I care about."

This time, he merely nodded and opted to not respond with wisecracks. "I understand. Try not to worry too much about me since…well, let's say that the last month or so has been very educational."

That was as close as he'd ever come to openly admitting what he'd learned—that wise people frowned upon rash actions for a reason. If he'd continued to attempt to challenge Alex head-on even after losing to him previously, he'd likely spend Christmas with only six feet of cold earth for company.

And somehow, she knew what he'd stopped short of saying aloud. Like the invisible bond that drew magnets of positive and negative charge together, something passed between them.

For now, at least, the lingering tension and subtle

distrust were gone. At this moment, they were equals. They stood for a moment and looked at one another without the need for words.

The vampire broke the silence first. “Don’t be late tomorrow. We still have work to do before we break for the holiday.”

“Noted,” he quipped. He gave her an offhand thumbs-up and strode out the door and into the evening.

EPILOGUE

John F. Kennedy International Airport, New York City

The plane landed shortly after 3:00 am.

Two large men stood, stony-faced and unspeaking, and waited for the passengers to disembark. One man was black and one was white, but both were around six foot four and looked like they weighed close to three hundred pounds, most of it muscle. They were dressed in crisp, expensive black suits.

Even at this hour, there were enough people milling around that congestion formed to the sides of the two bruisers since no one seemed keen to get too close to them.

Soon, the plane opened its door and the passengers descended the rolling staircase. The men squinted to make sure and nodded their heads. The person they expected was the very first individual off the plane.

She'd come from first class and was dressed accordingly in a long, finely tailored coat of rich brown leather with tactful hints of gold trimming. A thin golden chain encircled her neck, although the pendant it suspended was somewhere beneath her blouse. She carried two massive, heavy-looking suitcases with no apparent difficulty.

The duo took a few steps forward. No one crossed in front of them while the tall lady approached.

The black man spoke first. "Miss Tarif?"

The elegantly dressed woman smiled thinly and approached them. "Yes," she stated in a low, husky voice. She had black hair square-cut slightly above her shoulders and she wore sunglasses, even though dawn was still quite a way off.

"Let me take your bags." The white man extended a massive hand.

She handed them over without breaking stride. The two men took them with their left hands—keeping their right free in case they needed them—and fell silently into step behind the lady as she sauntered into the terminal.

They proceeded through security, through the moderate crowds and the general light and noise and spectacle of one of America's biggest airports without incident. En route out of the facility, the woman stopped to examine the board of arrivals and departures and seemed fascinated as she read the bevy of place names.

Her escorts stopped about two paces behind her and waited.

"Interesting," she remarked. "So many people come and go. This New York City truly is the center of civilization in the present age. Yes?"

The men had been briefed on approximately what to expect when they met the woman who went by Miss Tarif, but something about her accent puzzled them. It was vaguely Middle Eastern as they'd anticipated, but neither of them could quite identify it beyond that.

The black guy cleared his throat. "That's right, ma'am. This is probably the richest and most influential city in the world."

His colleague sniffled. "They even call Times Square the 'center of the universe.'"

In front of them, she lifted her sunglasses for a moment but since she faced away from them, they didn't see her eyes. "The one who controls this place," she said slowly, "would be able to control much of the world."

Both men nodded.

They moved on and soon emerged from the terminal building. A sleek black car, expensive but not too conspicuous, awaited them. The driver emerged to help load the suitcases and the three men saw to it that the woman was safely in the back seat before they got in themselves.

As the car pulled out, Moswen Neith leaned back and took in the sights. Some deep, primitive part of her almost loathed the omnipresent artificial light here and yet, it was a sign of these peoples' wealth and power. It was something she intended to possess.

She reached into the astral void and felt for the brand she had placed on her human slave. It was faint—very faint now since the local upstart had interfered—but it was still there.

If they were to activate the brand now, she knew, Alex would know at once that she was in New York. That was the first of many problems she'd need to solve.

To keep herself entertained, she thought of all the myriad ways she might kill her traitorous pawn once she caught him. Her mouth smiled but even if she hadn't worn the sunglasses, it wouldn't have been seen to reach her eyes.

The three men escorting her did not look at her face as they drove her deeper into the city. Had they done so, the malice in her expression might have given them second thoughts about this gig.

AUTHOR NOTES FROM ISOBELLA CROWLEY (AKA ELL LEIGH CLARKE) AND MICHAEL ANDERLE (AKA YODA)

WRITTEN SEPTEMBER 30TH AND OCTOBER 1ST, 2019

Thank yous

As always, I'd like to thank MA for working with me on this series <<Same back at ya!>>. As always, it's been fun to come up with the concepts and bounce ideas around. I'm excited about the direction we're taking this. Thanks for playing, MA!

Many people go into making a series like this happen. I'd like to say a massive thank you to the team of suppliers who made this book possible: Brittany, Chiara, Nathan, Philip, Moonchild, and MA's editing team.

Thank you, guys. Your hard work, care, and attention make all this possible.

<< I'll save my comments until the end, just know I'm here in spirit for all of these thank yous. You all mean so much!>>

JITers

Massive thanks must also go to our beta readers, led by Brittany, for letting us know we're on track with the story and characters. It's a huge relief – and delight – to hear that the stories are being well received before we go through the process of editing them.

Thanks also to MA's JIT team led by their high commander, Zen Steve <<Zen Master Walking™>>. Thank you for all your hard work in making sure the words are published double-proofed, read and re-read. You're the best!

Reviewers

I'd like to offer my heart-felt mega thanks to our Amazon reviewers. It's because of you that we get to do this full time. Without your five-star reviews and thoughtful words on Amazon we simply wouldn't have enough folks reading these space shenanigans to be able to write full time.

I'm so grateful to you for reading and reviewing.

Truly, thank you…

(Also – see the Facebook page for the individual thank yous we post. If you leave a review under a name/ screen name, we give you a shout out over there!)

Readers and FB page supporters

I'd like to also thank *YOU* for reading this book. Your enthusiasm for the worlds and characters we come up with is heart-warming. Thank you for being here, for the giggles and interaction, and for always reading.

You rock, and without you, there really would be no reason to write these stories. <<Seconding this!>>

Firemen and Missed Connections

If you saw the latest Patreon episode of Author Shenanigans, you would have seen MA and I talking about a recent fire check in my building.

I had been feeling bad because the inspection had happened while I was busy on a call with a client, and I wasn't able to break from the call. These inspections kind of happen regardless of what else you might have going on. The maintenance guy basically just comes around with his key and opens up one apartment after another and the fire inspectors move from one to the next.

In this way, I kinda feel like there wasn't much I could do. I don't even have the option as to whether I open the door or not.

So anyway, this happened and I just stayed on my video call. The client was talking intently, stressed out with arguing against what I was recommending. I couldn't get a word in edgewise, but to anyone in the room I would have just appeared like I was sitting there with my headphones on, on the laptop.

The fireman came in, and I waved him on, and he started moving around the apartment, checking in the bedrooms. I guess they need to check each other the sprinklers. Anyway, while he was in the living room he asked something like "how's your day going?" I vaguely heard through my noise cancelling headphones.

But of course I can't engage him in conversation at this point. I just have to continue listening to the client.

I felt bad. <<She did – she told me the whole story on video and I'm SURE I was totally supportive to her plight.>>

He checked the other room, and then he left, saying

something. I tried to signal I was on a call, but I don't think he caught it.

And then he was gone.

I learned recently that this social conscientiousness is actually a female instinctual need to please – and it's heavily related to estrogen, and a lack of testosterone – which would otherwise provide us with a ton of protection from social cuts and bruises.

I was explaining this to MA and he thought it was hilarious. I may also have mentioned that the guy was kinda hot – so it was a missed opportunity.

<<You have to see the video; the whole setup was just handed to me. That's like giving a monkey a banana and telling him "Don't eat that." The monkey is GOING to look at the banana HANDED TO HIM and then back at the human…

Banana…

Human…

Banana…

MUNCH! I rest my case.>>

After some crude suggestions about learning how to pounce MA suggested I contact someone at the office and maybe get his name from one of the staff. That wasn't really an option, but it occurred to me that there is perhaps a way to reach out to him.

You may remember Svend from ages ago. Coffee shop Svend. I think I mentioned him back in the author notes of the Ascension Myth series. He had told me about how people kept coming in and mentioning to him about a post that a woman had written on the "Missed Connections" section of Craigslist. At this point he had to explain to me what Craigslist was, and what the point of missed connections was. I was fascinated. Not fascinated enough to go and look it up, but enough to remember it.

I mentioned this to MA, and in true form, he made me <<Ellie is a grown-assed adult. No one makes her do anything. This guy was HOW HOT??!?!?!>> commit to posting on Missed Connections, on this podcast recording, and that I was to report back.

So here I am reporting back. <<I'm typing in my comments as I read along, I don't know what is coming next and I'm on the edge of my bar seat (I'm at the Aria's Five50 Pizza place working.)>>

Note that the estrogen was still in play at this point, and so I hadn't reached the point of running a cost benefit analysis around the energy this was requiring. <<Spoken like a character from The Big Bang Theory... Oh yes, you who watch the show know who I'm talking about ;-) >>

The next day I got to it and posted.

Here's what I wrote:

++

hot FIREMAN, must have thought I was rude...

(google map)

I was on a video call with a client who was giving me a hard time. You came around to my apartment with one of the property maintenance guys yesterday to do the annual safety checks.

I couldn't talk to explain, I just waved you in. I think you tried to talk to me while I had my back to you at the counter, listening to my client.

I was torn!

You left and all I could do was wave.

You were super cute. Sorry for looking like I was ignoring you. Hope you hear about this post! ;-)

++

I feel like the geek in the posts. For the most part they are pretty raunchy… talking about how sexy someone was, and how much they regret not getting a number etc.

But since it was anonymous – until I copied it here! - I figured 'what the hey'. I mean, it's not like it's going to be seen by loads of people.

Within an hour I had half a dozen responses. A week later I've had about a dozen. This was waaay more than I expected. <<BWAHAHAHAHAHA…>>

One was just obscene. I flagged it. <<As you should have.>>

Three were people just getting in touch on the off chance I was someone they could hit on. (Note that there are no details or photos in this posts!) <<25% - There is probably a statistical factor at play here.>>

One was suggesting he was a fireman, but then admitted it was just a costume he dressed up in. He did send me a picture though. He looked about twelve. Ok maybe twenty… but still.

And three were actual firemen. <<Another 25% - Interesting…>>

Two thought they might have been the ones who came to my apartment, but after a little back and forth it turned out that they probably weren't. Neither seemed interested in helping put me in touch with the guy on the team who had actually been there. <<Apparently no helping a fellow brother out here. What's up with the Austin Firemen? C'mon Texas!>>

And one of those two was just looking for a FWB. I figured this meant "friend with benefits'. HA!

So all in all, an interesting, but ultimately pointless, exercise. <<Not exactly pointless...Look above at all of those interesting statistics that you can probably polynomial all to bits and extrapolate the answer to string theory – WOOT!>>

When MA reads this, he'll be getting this report for the first time. I'll be interested to see what he says...

<<I'll leave you a copy of this as I hand it to Steve. So Much FUN! Well, at least for me. I have to admit, I didn't think you would do it!>>

Austin Bergstrom

As I'm writing these notes I'm sitting in the Austin airport. Even though it's been a while since I travelled anyway, it feels like I'm never away from this place.

Apparently I'm here more often than I realize. I've noticed I have a favorite spot... Down by gates 33 and 34 there is an Italian café concession outlet. It had tables which are great for sitting and working, and though their coffee is ironically variable <<The cynical side of me believes it is because of the captive audience – don't have to try harder>>, they do have good tea. So this is where I plant myself.

I have a three-hour layover at Fort Lauderdale. I plan to get lots of work done. <<How in the hell did you have to fly through Fort Lauderdale to get to St. Petersburg?>>

This of course is contingent on the usual things like power supply, laptop space and quiet. None of these are a given, and I've also had an email from the airline saying that FTL is actually under construction. I don't like my odds, but I'm remaining optimistic.

UPDATE: I managed to find somewhere to plug in my laptop and phone and am perched with my laptop on my lap. <<I can imagine with aforementioned headphones on ears ignoring the hot firemen walking around. It's almost Halloween… Wait, is Halloween and dressing up even a thing in England? It's not, is it? It is?>>

5am Productivity

Fasting. In an attempt to overcome the low cortisol and testosterone.

One of the greatest things that has been happening to me recently, likely as a result of the adrenal recovery, and possibly affected by fasting, has been that I've been waking up at 5am.

Yep. You read that right.

Ellie, the girl who her whole life made a concerted effort to not get up before midday unless she had to, is spontaneously waking up uber early.

Go figure.

The reason I'm so psyched about this though is because I am incredibly productive at this time. Between 5 and 9am I can get half a weeks' worth of tasks done, effortlessly.

I love it soooo much.

I'm going to see if I can maintain this. It's not a case of just routine or will power yet: anyone suffering adrenal fatigue knows the first goal is to get as much sleep as you can, and conserve energy… But there is a possibility in sight! Weeeee….

<<I asked her all about Keto and if she was dipping into

Ketosis (which is something I was doing many years ago. I woke up WAY early and for a few weeks, it caused me all sorts of issues... Like wondering what do you do when it's still dark out in the morning and my mind was saying 'stay in bed'.) From a perspective of energy, ketosis is the bomb. Getting into Ketosis made me feel like I'd swallowed bombs.>>

Speaking of Adrenal Fatigue...

A few weeks ago I started wondering why I would just have slumps in energy. My acupuncturist has been checking my pulse and I've had jumps in improvement, and yet he might register an improvement, the same week I'd been laid out.

<<I asked her about this, yes – some of those sadistic pins come out with blood – Sorry – There is N.F.W. I'm going to purposefully ask someone to stab me. It's one thing to look for alternative medicine (I'm a fan) but I have to scratch my chin when it looks like a modern version of using leeches back in the old country. Which reminds me of a hilarious scene in the comedy series 'Black Adder'.>>

I started wondering what else could be going on. This, combined with my recent revelations about hormones and brain chemistry led me to wonder if there might be something going on with my cortisol and/ or testosterone levels. Yep, mostly known as a male hormone, us women need it too, even if it is in much smaller quantities.

So we had them tested – and both came back super low.

The doc changed up my tinctures <<For those (like me) who didn't know - A tincture is a concentrated liquid herbal extract. It is typically made by soaking herbs and

other plant parts in alcohol for weeks to extract the active constituents. >> and I'm seeing some improvement in my energy levels now.

But health stuff aside, what I found most interesting was the changes I've noticed in my thinking, especially in the stretch of months prior to the diagnosis.

I'd noticed my thinking had changed. I've always been philosophically bent. I joke that I've been having an existential crisis since the age of about eight <<BWAHAHAHAHa – I can just see this>> ... but, over this last year I've noticed drastic changes in the way I think. Not just the thoughts, but the way I process information. It's become less focused, less driven by necessity and goals.

More driven by curiosity.

Just want to read everything! <<blink...blink blink.>>

But at the same time, I've only had a few hours of productive time each day, and some days none at all, due to the adrenal fatigue. However, when excess energy occasionally bubbles up, so do all of these other motivations to read and study.

I also want to examine concepts and find new ideas about the bigger, more abstract questions – and ultimately what are some of the meanings we can ascribe to life.

I realized that the question we normally ask is "what is the point?" As in "what is the purpose?"

Which is a mine field of interesting ideas.

I think we all inherently know that it IS meaningful... but as to why is a conundrum. <<Would/Could it go back to if life isn't meaningful, then neither are we? Or, to phrase it the other way, Life is meaningful because we can make it so?>>

Unless you fall back on a set of beliefs, like a religion, or spirituality. <<No, I not suggesting that. I'm ascribing the act of making something 'good' (which, granted, usually comes from a system of belief on what is good.)>>

The other reason that gets invoked is the "kids" or "loved ones" argument... which is somewhat routed in societal expectations and evolutionary drives. It doesn't hold the same value to people who don't have families or close friends.

I've noticed that those who are more disconnected and intellectually inclined will argue that the *work* one leaves behind as a legacy is the meaning that they ascribe to their existence.

Of course, all of these are valid meanings or reasons.

But meaning is deeply personal, and these don't register with me on a deep level... so I'm continuing my exploration of the subject.

The other thing I've noticed in the past several months I've been actively pursuing this question is that most discourses on the meaning of life center around the male point of view. There's nothing wrong with that... other than it doesn't help me as a female. Those that do mention anything about the female perspective tend to point to children and significant others as the thing that gives female meaning... but when you've rejected the social spell that your only purpose is to produce and raise children, this also doesn't fly.

Apart from anything, the male and female brain are going to produce different ways of looking at things, as a function of different brain structure and different chemistry. The very discussion of the question is altered depending on the brain chemistry of the body we're in!

Having read about four books on the differences in male and female neurology and just completed two courses on the topic, I'm interested in what my female brain might come up with.

Something that isn't goal orientated or centered only around survival.

Viktor Frankel in "Man's Search for Meaning" talks a lot about meaningfulness being generated by the desire to survive: to just get through the bad things, and to get to a better time down the line. To me this is the product of a naturally goal-orientated organism, and having experienced very low levels of testosterone during my recovery, I've come to the conclusion that a lot of these ways of seeing the world as a series of goals as a function of testosterone.

I've found **one** book written by women on this subject.

It's called "The Power of Meaning: Crafting a Life That Matters", by Emily Esfahani Smith. It's right at the top of my *to read* list.

I'll report back. ;)

There's also a dude who is pretty big in literary criticism, Terry Eagleton. He'll have some interesting thoughts no doubt, so when I'm done reading his book on humor I'll take a look at what he has to say on "The Meaning of Life."

Plus Feynman, one of the coolest physicists who has ever existed, has written something on "The Meaning of it All". I think I'll appreciate his take on it, and chances are he might say something more on the subject than the 80% of what I've already read.

So far, and this will be interesting to track this exploration continues, the point I keep coming back to is that life is already ascribed the meaning of whatever we think it means. Ideas and concepts that have been layered into our minds by parents, and teachers, society at a whole, traumatic experiences along the way... and we're rarely prompted to re-evaluate these concepts.

But it's interesting to note that we can reassign the meaning, at any point. We can choose what meaning we give it. <<Or none, right? For example – and I'm going to modify my first response to not trigger anyone – could a person decide that life has no meaning ergo, they can decide for others what their existence will be. Since it has no meaning – doing something ugly is irrelevant.>>

I've often decided what meaning to assign to life based on the outcome I wanted to create! Yes, the irony of this doesn't escape me. I am not surprised that in a time of low-T I'm 'coincidentally' reconsidering how I construct meaning! I have toyed with the idea that while having such fluidity in my mental structures is an advantage in a lot of instances, there are times when it can leave one (me!) quite adrift. It has occurred to me to just pick a meaning again, and then use it... but since it's not hurting me to explore the possibilities and the intellectual pursuit of a new frontier, I'm going to hold off on that right now.

<<Ok, let's take this further. Since one theory is you are traveling through these concepts with different potential pre-determined mental leanings based on the high amount or lack of estrogen and testosterone, couldn't a person figure out their present amounts and record their feelings?

Then, take the medicines necessary to adjust the E/T (estrogen/testosterone) levels for a couple of days, and then try again? (Or weeks—I've no idea how this would work.) Further, wouldn't the premise then suggest that for a particular role to be a good fit for a person, the E/T of a person would be a good test? There are plenty of ladies with high testosterone and plenty of guys with lower testosterone. I'm thinking aggressive roles (military front line comes to mind) might require higher testosterone. It wouldn't matter (if the theory holds) what the sex is – you have to base it off of testosterone. Now, if a person needs to nurture (once again, gender is irrelevant), wouldn't it help to be higher in estrogen? I'm thinking (I know, I know, shocking!) that the discussion becomes one with no gender association at all. If, for example, I'm having problems connecting with my children, then I might WANT to take an estrogen enhancement? Is that sound thought at all? (No, I have NO idea the relevant secondary and tertiary issues with what I'm proposing. I'm merely off on a tangent like any good story creator goes through.)

I actually had to look up how estrogen is used in the male body since I've never had a conversation like this. Here is the answer (via Google) from a government site:

Traditionally, testosterone and **estrogen have** been considered to be male and female sex hormones, respectively. However, **estradiol**, the predominant form of **estrogen**, also plays a critical role in male sexual function. **Estradiol** in **men** is essential for modulating libido, erectile function, and spermatogenesis.>>

BACK TO ELLIE

Having read about the existentialists recently though, it seems this concept ties in with their thinking in the early years of Sartre and Beauvoir. They believed firmly that we get choose what we want it to mean. We get to choose the maxim by which we live – and this gave them unprecedented amounts of freedom – particularly from "society", or what I've been calling social "spells".

It's more work, because you have to question everything, and you need to examine your real motivations for pursuing any course of action... but I like it. It avoids laziness, and helps to countermand habit and thinking imposed from others.

Granted this kind of pursuit is only really possible when one's thoughts aren't preoccupied with thoughts of survival, or pursuing what other people deem important (read: money, status, fame etc), but I feel like it is a worthwhile pursuit, nonetheless.

Even if it does drive my friends nuts. <<Thinking through these concepts is NOT easy and it takes a certain personality who enjoys the effort and derives energy from the practice. Similar to an introvert and extrovert I apply no value on either direction a person leans. Merely it 'is'.>>

Okay, I'm nearly up to the word limit for this, so I'll sign off.

Thank you again for reading, and I'll see you on the next episode!

E x
&
Michael

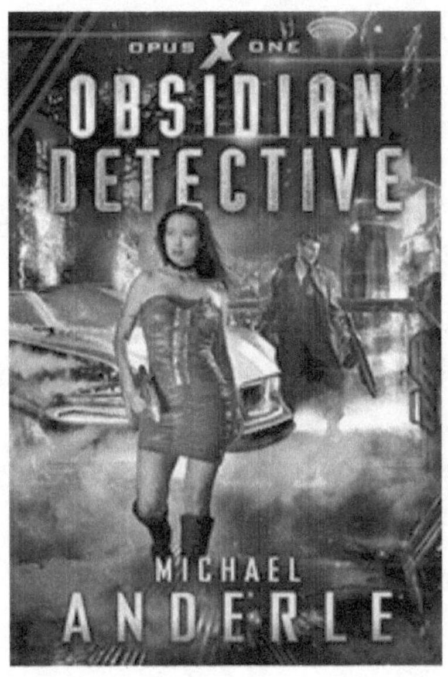

Pre-order now to have the book arrive on your Kindle November 1st.

Two Rebels whose Worlds Collide on a Planetary Level.

On the fringes of human space, a murder will light a fuse and send two different people colliding together.

She lives on Earth, where peace among the population is a given. He is on the fringe of society where authority is how much firepower you wield.

She is from the powerful, the elite. He is with the military.

Both want the truth – but is revealing the truth good for society?

Two years ago, a small moon in a far off system was set to be the location of the first intergalactic war between humans and an alien race.

It never happened. However, something was found many are willing to kill to keep a secret.

Now, they have killed the wrong people.

How many will need to die to keep the truth hidden?

As many as is needed.

He will have vengeance no matter the cost. *She will dig for the truth. No matter how risky the truth is to reveal.*

BOOKS WRITTEN BY ELL LEIGH CLARKE

The Ascension Myth

*** With Michael Anderle ***

Awakened (01)

Activated (02)

Called (03)

Sanctioned (04)

Rebirth (05)

Retribution (06)

Cloaked (07)

Bourne (08)

Committed (09)

Subversion (10)

Invasion (11)

Ascension (12)

Confessions of a Space Anthropologist

*** With Michael Anderle ***

Giles Kurns: Rogue Operator (1)

Giles Kurns: Rogue Instigator (2)

The Second Dark Ages

with Michael Anderle

Darkest Before The Dawn (3)

Dawn Arrives (4)

Interplanetary Spy For Hire

with Michael Anderle

Expelled

Deuces Wild

with Michael Anderle

Beyond The Frontiers (1)

Rampage (2)

Labyrinth (3)

Birthright (4)

The Sword-Mage Chronicles

Awakening

Taken

Heist

Resistance

Legba

Storm

BOOKS BY MICHAEL ANDERLE

For a complete list of books by Michael Anderle, please visit:

www.lmbpn.com/ma-books/

All LMBPN Audiobooks are Available at Audible.com and iTunes

To see all LMBPN audiobooks, including those written by Michael Anderle please visit:

www.lmbpn.com/audible

CONNECT WITH MICHAEL ANDERLE

Michael Anderle Social

Website:

http://www.lmbpn.com

Email List:

http://lmbpn.com/email/

Facebook Here:

www.facebook.com/TheKurtherianGambitBooks/

www.ingramcontent.com/pod-product-compliance
Lightning Source LLC
Chambersburg PA
CBHW031608100726
47898CB00006B/1705

* 9 7 8 1 6 4 2 0 2 4 8 8 3 *